THE INDIGO SKY

Also by Alison Booth

Stillwater Creek

To dear Tony and Judith,
With best wishes,
Alison Booth

Alison Booth
THE INDIGO SKY

BANTAM

SYDNEY AUCKLAND TORONTO NEW YORK LONDON

Permission to reproduce words from the Judith Wright poem, 'At Cooloolah' from *A Human Pattern: Selected Poems*, published in 2009, courtesy of ETT Imprint.

Permission to reproduce words from Bertrand Russell, *Education and the Social Order*, published in 2009, Routledge Classics, p. 32, courtesy of The Bertrand Russell Peace Foundation Ltd and Taylor & Francis.

A Bantam book
Published by Random House Australia Pty Ltd
Level 3, 100 Pacific Highway, North Sydney NSW 2060
www.randomhouse.com.au

First published by Bantam in 2011

Addresses for companies within the Random House Group can be found at www.randomhouse.com.au/offices

National Library of Australia
Cataloguing-in-Publication Entry

Booth, Alison L.
The indigo sky
ISBN 978 1 74166 932 9 (pbk)
Sequel to: Stillwater creek
A823.4

Cover photography by Corbis
Cover design by Natalie Winter
Internal design and typesetting by Midland Typesetters, Australia
Printed and bound by The SOS Print + Media Group

10 9 8 7 6 5

I found one day in school a boy of medium size ill-treating a smaller boy. I expostulated, but he replied: 'The bigs hit me, so I hit the babies; that's fair.' In these words he epitomized the history of the human race.

BERTRAND RUSSELL, *Education and the Social Order*

To my family

PROLOGUE

No bulb in the light fitting. No water, no food. The room hot and airless, the only furniture a battered iron bedstead with a thin mattress and stained cover. The palms of her hands felt sticky. Moisture trickled down between her shoulderblades and into the band of her knickers. Her shift was damp and clung to her skin. There were no windows, apart from a small roof light. Through this she saw the occasional lonely cloud drifting across the pale blue.

Although without a watch, she knew by the whitening of the sky that it was almost evening. The others would be at dinner and she wouldn't be there to look after them. This would be the second meal she'd missed today. After running her tongue over dry, cracked lips, she took a few deep breaths to stem her rising panic. She couldn't bear the thought of being enclosed in this small space once it was dark. Already the walls seemed to be pressing in on her, as if they had a life of their own; a living breathing organism that would crush her once night fell. She could die in here and no one would know.

The fading light began to turn greenish, as if filtered through leaves that she could not see. She inspected the roof light. Nothing more than a vertical glazed panel where part of the ceiling slanted up at an acute angle. Again she tried the door. Still locked of course, and bolted too. She'd heard the click-click of the two barrel bolts being pulled across after she was pushed inside all those hours ago. She rattled the door and put her shoulder against it; a futile gesture as the door opened inward.

Once more she looked around the room, and up at the ceiling. Closely she inspected the roof light. Maybe that glass panel wasn't so fixed after all; it looked as if there might be a handle halfway up the sash. She'd never be able to reach this though, in spite of her height, in spite of standing on her tiptoes. Again the walls seemed to be pushing towards her, and her heartbeat was becoming frantic. Slowly, deeply, she inhaled and exhaled until the panic started to abate.

Of course there was the bedstead, she thought. Although it was heavy, she was easily able to push it underneath the roof light. Standing on it, she tried to reach the handle, but it was still too far away. Doubling the mattress over would give her an extra few inches. Quickly she rolled the mattress up, struggling with the lumpy old kapok. Soon she was climbing up onto it. Just as she was balancing there, she heard footsteps approaching along the corridor outside. She had to get down fast. The bed had to be back in its proper place against the wall. No evidence; that would only mean more punishment.

Clip-clop, clip-clop. The footsteps passed by the door without a pause. *Clip-clop, clip-clop.* Straight down the hallway to the far end, where they stopped. A door was opened. After a few moments she heard it shutting again, and the footsteps returning.

'Let me out,' she shouted, banging on the door. 'Let me out!'

There was no response, apart from the clicking of metal-tipped heels, straight past the room in which she was imprisoned, and down the corridor. Then there was only silence. And with it she felt the return of her claustrophobia. Heart pounding, palms clammy, mouth so dry it was hard to swallow.

She wouldn't give in though.

She pushed the bed back under the roof light and again rolled up the mattress. After climbing on top of it, she balanced precariously, arms stretched out to each side until she felt stable enough to raise her hands above her head and slowly stretch towards the roof light handle.

Now it was within reach. She turned it and felt it move. A slight push, and cool air washed in. She gave the sash a harder shove. Hinged at the top, it opened outwards. After placing one hand on each side of the opening, she hauled herself up. *Lucky I've got arms like an ape*, she thought. That's what they'd said about her when she'd been brought here first, after they'd stripped her and washed her in carbolic soap and scrubbed her all over until her skin hurt.

As she pulled herself up and over the sill, she heard the plop of the mattress as it unrolled onto the wire bed-base. For a moment she sprawled on the metal roofing. The corrugated iron was still hot, although the sun had now set. Above her, a crescent moon hung low in the washed-out sky and the first few stars began to appear.

This was the furthest she could escape to, she knew that already. From the top of the three-storey building, with its steep roof dropping away on all sides, there was no way out. Although there were some trees nearby, they were too far from the building. She would never be able to reach their branches. For a moment she wondered if she would only break a leg if she were to jump over the edge of the roof. Probably not. She'd break her spine or her neck too, or be dead on impact. The choice was always hers to try. Not tonight though; not yet.

In the meantime she sat on the roof, her stomach rumbling with lack of food. The minutes passed, the hours passed. The sky was now swathed with stars. Big mob stars. Years ago, her mother had told her the story of how they'd formed. Once the sky had been dark, darker than anything she could imagine. Darker even than her claustrophobia. Dark until two ancestors had sailed up the river and into the sky, and transformed themselves into stars to shine down on their people. And from that time the spirits of the earth mob after death went up into the sky, and made a river of shining stars.

Tears filled her eyes. She desperately wanted to see her mother again. It had been four years since the last time. Worse even than this was the manner of their parting, without a proper farewell. How she longed to see her, to feel her warm arms around her, to rest her head on her shoulder, to smell that scent of sunlight on clean cotton. And to feel loved. *I love you*, she whispered into the warm night air. *I love you, Mum.*

PART I

Jingera and Environs
South Coast of NSW
November, 1961

CHAPTER 1

An instant before the doors of the school bus clanged shut, Zidra Vincent hopped down the three steps and onto the pavement. She'd just caught sight of her parents' car parked near the hotel, which meant they must be here in Jingera. Ahead of her were the other Jingeroids, the girls and boys who, like her, travelled to and from Burford each day. Among them was her friend Sally Hargreaves, whose family had moved to Jingera last September. Though, at fifteen, Sally was a year older than Zidra, they'd struck up a friendship on the school bus.

'Want to come home for a while?' Sally asked. She had freckled skin, blue eyes and long dark hair, and a laugh that could make even the grumpiest of people smile.

'Thanks but I might miss my lift. Saw Dad's car there and thought I could avoid an extra ten minutes on the bus with the Bradley boys.' Once the Jingeroids alighted, the Bradley boys were the only other kids on the bus. Living on a property a few miles north of where Zidra lived, their idea of sport was baiting her until she could get off at the entrance gate to Ferndale.

Now she strolled across the square in Jingera, around the war memorial with its wreath of red paper poppies from Remembrance Day, and down towards the post office. For a moment she stood next to the car, a vintage Armstrong Siddeley, and looked around. The new pub that had opened three years ago was a hideous building, everyone agreed on that. Walls an ugly brick, as yellow as jaundice, and a speckled red-and-ochre-tiled roof that fortunately could be seen only from the headland. There was a new clientele too, the surfer boys who, a year or two back, had got the message that the surf at Jingera beach had a good curl to it.

The car was unlocked but her parents were nowhere to be seen. She scribbled a note on a scrap of paper from her school-case and left it on the dashboard, before placing the case on the floor in front of the passenger seat, where they could see it.

After strolling by the war memorial, she accelerated past the post office – hoping Mrs Blunkett wouldn't catch sight of her, otherwise half an hour would be lost in idle chatter – and turned into the unkerbed street leading down to the lagoon. Weatherboard cottages lined the road; some were semi-concealed by hedges and others had no gardens at all. Several hundred yards down the hill she stopped at a gate, on each side of which was a glossy-leafed hedge studded with sweet-scented white flowers. She used to live with her mother in this cottage. She still thought of it as theirs, even though they'd stayed there for less than a year. They'd moved out nearly four years ago, after her mother's marriage to Peter Vincent and the adoption that had made him her legal father. The house, what you could see of it behind the vines, seemed shabbier now. Someone from Melbourne had bought it as a holiday cottage but it wasn't much used. Its windows gazed blankly at her without even a glimmer of a welcoming reflection.

She opened the gate and walked up the brick path. It had been several months since she'd last visited the cottage, and the verandah floorboards seemed more weathered and splintered than ever. Yet she found it reassuring that they still squeaked in exactly the same places as when she'd lived there. Though she loved everything about Ferndale homestead, visiting the cottage felt like coming home. She sat on the verandah's edge. The only sounds she could hear were the surf thudding onto Jingera beach and seagulls wailing.

At this point, Zidra saw her father passing by the front gate, marching purposefully up the hill. He had a rolled-up towel under his arm and wet hair.

'You've been surfing. You could have taken me!' she called, leaping up from the verandah.

'You were at school,' he said, giving her a hug. 'Anyway, what are you doing hanging around this place? You've got a new home now, remember?'

She laughed.

'Your mother and I decided to come into Jingera on an impulse. So I thought I may as well have a swim after collecting the mail. There are two letters for you today; they're in the glove box of the car.'

'Good. Where's Mama?'

'Seeing Mrs Cadwallader.'

'Oh, that means she'll be ages yet.'

'She said she'd be back at the car by 4.30. I think one of your letters is from Jim Cadwallader, by the way.'

Zidra tried to conceal her delight, and to saunter to the car rather than rush at it as she really wanted to do. She took the letters from the glove box. She wouldn't open them yet. She would postpone that pleasure until after she'd thoroughly examined the envelopes.

The first letter had a Vaucluse postmark and *Zid Vincent, Ferndale nr Jingera* scrawled across it in Jim's spiky handwriting.

He'd started addressing her as Zid from the time of his first letter to her, after he'd gone off to Stambroke College in Sydney as a scholarship boy. She knew it was to make all his new friends think that Zid was a boy.

She looked at the second letter. Her name and address were written in block capitals sloping from left to right, in a hand that she didn't recognise. ZIDRA TALIVALDIS, LAGOON ROAD, JINGERA. The old address and her former surname, but Mrs Blunkett had known which postbox to put the letter in. The envelope was of poor quality paper and very thin. There couldn't be more than a page inside and there was nothing written on the back of the envelope. She squinted at the postmark that was faint and smudged, and tried to decipher what the letters said. Her heart lurched as she made out the word GUDGIEGALAH.

Lorna Hunter had written at last.

Or maybe it wasn't from Lorna at all. That backward sloping printing wasn't in Lorna's style. The message must be *about* Lorna, and a little worm of anxiety turned in her stomach. Glancing around her, she saw that her father was heading across the square and into Cadwallader's Quality Meats.

With shaking fingers, Zidra ripped open the envelope and pulled out the single sheet of lined paper that had been roughly torn from an exercise book. The pencilled message was sloping from left to right for only the first few lines and after that the writing changed. It was now unmistakably Lorna's hand, although still written in cramped capital letters. Lorna must have been in such a hurry that she'd given up the attempt at complete anonymity.

WE'RE GOING BY BUS TO JERVIS BAY FOR A HOLIDAY WEEKEND 16th–18th FEBRUARY. TELL MUM AND DAD TO GO THERE TOO. I'M <u>*BANKING*</u> *ON YOU. THEY*

CENSOR EVERYTHING HERE AND I'M NOT EVEN SURE IF I'M GOING TO GET THIS LETTER OUT. I'LL TRY TO POST IT TOMORROW. WE'RE ALLOWED OUT SOMETIMES TO THE SHOP TO BUY LOLLIES, BUT I'M GOING TO BUY A STAMPED ENVELOPE INSTEAD. THOUGHT IT SAFER TO WRITE TO YOU AND ANYWAY I DON'T EVEN KNOW IF THEY'RE STILL LIVING AT THE SAME PLACE.

I REALLY MISS YOU, DIZZY. IT'S LIKE A PRISON HERE. I'M ALWAYS GETTING INTO TROUBLE – THAT'S NOTHING NEW – AND THEN I GET LOCKED IN THE BOXROOM. THEY DON'T KNOW I CAN GET OUT THE ROOF LIGHT AND SIT ON THE ROOF. HA HA.

CAN'T WAIT TO SEE MUM AGAIN. <u>PLEASE TELL HER TO GET TO JERVIS BAY SOMEHOW</u>. I'VE HAD NO NEWS ABOUT THE FAMILY SINCE NANA CAME TO SEE ME A YEAR AGO AND DON'T KNOW HOW THEY ARE.

WITH LOVE

Lorna used to attend Jingera primary school with Zidra in the days before the Hunter family had been sent to the Reserve. Soon after that, Lorna had been taken to the Gudgiegalah Girls' Home. She was a half-caste, that's what they called her, and Tommy Hunter wasn't her real father.

Zidra read the letter again. There were no names to identify the writer, or the recipient either, apart from *Dizzy*, and who would realise that this was short for Zidra? Yet if the message had been intercepted at Gudgiegalah Girls' Home, anyone would have been able to guess who'd written it. Zidra wondered how many letters had already been written and never gone out. The girls there were banned from all contact with their past.

According to the postmark, this letter had been posted less than a week ago. It was several months until the bus trip to Jervis Bay. She'd have to figure out how to get the message to the Hunter family, though like Lorna she had no idea if they were still at the Wallaga Lake Reserve.

'What are you reading?'

Her mother's voice startled her. For a moment she'd forgotten where she was and now felt irritated at being distracted from her thoughts. Her mother opened the back door of the car and sat down on the seat next to Zidra. She made a face to herself, but not so that her mother would see. It was doubly annoying that there was no *Hello darling, have you had a nice day at school?*

'Hello, Mama,' she said, kissing her on the cheek and folding over the letter. 'Have you had a good day?' Mama's hair was pinned up in some sort of topknot and her even-featured face, without its usual frame of exuberant fair hair, appeared tired. Zidra would tell her about Lorna later. She needed to digest the contents of the letter herself first.

Her mother smiled, apparently oblivious of Zidra's veiled reproof. 'It was *bonzer*.'

Zidra winced. An expression like this sounded ludicrous when spoken in a thick Latvian accent. After nearly a decade in Australia, her mother had acquired the local slang but not the diction. You'd think her musical training might have made her more receptive to the rhythms of speech.

'I just had tea with Mrs Llewellyn and Eileen Cadwallader,' her mother continued. 'Where's Peter?'

'At the butcher's.'

'What for? He killed a sheep only two days ago.'

'Same reason as you went to see Mrs Cadwallader and Mrs Llewellyn,' Zidra said. 'To have a chat.'

Her mother's grin was reflected in the car's rear-vision mirror above the windscreen. The brown dress she was wearing was almost the same colour as her eyes.

At that moment, Peter opened the front passenger door and settled himself into the seat. Her mother climbed out of the back seat of the car and into the front. After she turned the ignition and preselected first gear, the car kangaroo-hopped several feet before stalling.

'Foot on the change gear pedal,' Peter said mildly.

You weren't allowed to call it a clutch. That was because the Armstrong Siddeley Whitley was so special that all its parts had different names to ordinary cars. Zidra knew this because Peter had also been teaching her to drive around the home paddock, and she reckoned she was already a better driver than her mother. But it would be two years at least before she could sit for her driving test.

Her mother muttered something in Latvian that was almost certainly indecent, and turned the ignition key again. She'd been driving for three months so you'd think she'd have got the hang of it by now. She insisted on practising, and Peter didn't seem to care. In fact it was almost as if he enjoyed it, in spite of all the jerking and stalling.

Zidra's mother began to drive so slowly along the Jingera to Ferndale road that soon there was a queue of cars behind them. When Zidra mentioned this, Peter suggested that she give her mother a break. When she's had more practice she'll get her speed up and on no account are you to pressure her to go any faster. Fat chance of that, Zidra thought. Even the bus with the Bradley boys might be better than this slow crawl north.

Once home at Ferndale, Zidra went to her room in the attic. It had originally been used as a boxroom until she'd persuaded her parents to have it painted and insulated and made into her bedroom. Three dormer windows illuminated the space, which was large with steeply raked ceilings. Each window was rather small, but together they shed sufficient light that the room never seemed gloomy, even on the most overcast of days. One dormer looked to the east and the ocean, the other to the north with Mount Dromedary rearing up in the distance, and the third to the west. That was her favourite view, of the folds of hills rising to the distant mountain range, all framed by the pine trees that had been planted when the house was built in the late nineteenth century.

After throwing her school-case onto the bed, Zidra stripped off the Burford Girls' High School uniform – the navy blue tunic and white shirt – and put on old trousers and a shirt. She glanced quickly at her reflection in the wardrobe mirror. Several months ago she'd decided that she might actually be quite good looking – she'd been lucky to inherit her mother's regular features and even that high forehead could be disguised by allowing her dark curls to fall forward. Curls that periodically her mother said were just like those of her real father, *poor Oleksii*, whom Zidra herself always thought of as *Our Papa Who Art in Heaven*.

With the two letters now in her pocket, she clattered down the stairs and out to the kitchen, where the family's outdoor boots were lined up, in regimental order, near the door to the back verandah. Her piercing whistle summoned the two dogs, Rusty and Spotless Spot, who knew without being told that she was off to the stone stairway leading down to the beach. Here she perched on the top step while the dogs bounded down to the strip of white sand below.

Carefully she unfolded Lorna's letter and read it again. She had no idea whether or not the Hunters were still at Wallaga

Lake. She certainly hadn't seen any of them in Jingera lately. Glancing around her at the vast dome of the sky and the ocean in front of her, she thought of how much Lorna must loathe being incarcerated at her school. Training Centre was how it was described. Mama had snorted when she'd learnt that. Training to be domestic slaves, she'd said.

Zidra put the letter away and slit open the fatter envelope from Jim. Three sheets of closely written paper, which she began to peruse with great eagerness. After reading a couple of paragraphs, however, she puffed out her cheeks in exasperation. It wasn't that liking cricket was evil as such, it was more that inflicting lengthy descriptions of it onto others was deeply inconsiderate, especially when he knew how boring she found team sports. She skimmed through the letter until she reached the final paragraph.

> *I was interested to read in your last letter that you want to be a journalist. That would suit you, Zid, with your love of writing and history. One of the teachers told me that newspapers offer cadetships, so you might want to check up on that. By the way, did I tell you that my good friend Eric Hall is coming to stay with us in Jingera for a week or so towards the end of the Christmas holidays? He comes from near Walgett and you might remember I visited his family's property last year. Flat as a pancake out there, so he'll think he's in paradise at Jingera.*
> *I'm really looking forward to coming home.*
>
> *Yours sincerely,*
> *Jim*

She laughed out loud at the *Yours sincerely*, wondering how long she would have to know Jim before he could write anything a bit more affectionate. She always made a point of signing her letters to him *With love from Zidra,* just as she did with all her friends. *With love from Zid* mightn't go down so well if people thought she was a boy, though.

Jim's abbreviation of her name was nice and no one else ever thought to use it, although it wasn't as nice as Lorna's name for her, *Dizzy.* Together the nicknames made a good combination, she thought: *Dizzy Zid.* There was something glamorous and light about the name Dizzy.

Now she found that thinking about Lorna was bringing back all those feelings she'd been keeping squashed down ever since reading her letter and, having forgotten a handkerchief, she sniffled into her hands.

Lorna had been taken from her family almost four years ago. Zidra remembered waking from a nightmare at that time, convinced that Lorna was telling her something. Telepathy was how her mother had described it. Of course Zidra hadn't known then that Lorna was being taken away, only that she was in trouble. After that, Zidra's own life had become difficult. It wasn't just the loneliness and fear that she felt after her best friend vanished, but also the vulnerability. It was only Jim's friendship that had kept her going.

And she hadn't spoken to Lorna about any of this. Although longing to, she hadn't seen or spoken to her for years.

CHAPTER 2

After shutting the living room door behind her, Ilona Vincent hesitated for a moment. Through the windows she could see the dark silhouettes of the pine trees against the paler moonlit sky, but there was no point in drawing the curtains. The evening was mild and there were no neighbours to peer in. She made her way across the room, stumbling on some newspapers Peter had left on the floor, and turned on the lamp by the piano. She wanted to play a particular prelude by Chopin that for some reason had been in her head all afternoon. Something must have triggered off an association, and this piece that she hadn't thought of for ages, let alone played, was now obsessing her.

When she'd finished the prelude, she rested her wrists on the edge of the keyboard and listened to the sounds of the house. A slight creaking from one corner of the ceiling suggested that Zidra was preparing for bed. The faint clattering of the typewriter, coming from the direction of the dining room, signified that Peter was dealing with some correspondence. Outside a wind had sprung up. It worried at a loose windowpane and rustled the needles of the pine trees. All of these sounds might have produced a feeling of peace were she not so disturbed by the letter that Zidra had shown her after dinner.

The content of Lorna's letter had been unsettling, with all that it implied about internment and censorship. Thinking about that reminded her of her own captivity in Europe during the war. Those years that she tried to forget, years that she never spoke about, even with Peter.

Something had to be done for Lorna, she decided. They had to find out where her parents were and somehow get them to Jervis Bay in February. Lorna's happiness depended on this and helping her was the least they could do.

Now she shut the music book but stayed sitting on the stool. On the top of the piano were a number of framed photographs: Ilona and Peter on their wedding day; Peter in a dark suit grinning at the camera while she wore a lavender crepe dress and matching hat. There was a lovely picture of Zidra on her horse, Star. Next to this was a rather blurred photo of Zidra and Lorna, which Ilona had taken with her now-defunct box brownie camera. The two girls, ghostlike with over-exposure, were standing side-by-side in the front garden of the Jingera cottage; Zidra with a toothy grin and Lorna, a good two inches taller, standing on one leg with the other tucked up behind her. Zidra was wearing her best dress, a rare occurrence, and it was for this reason Ilona had wanted to take a photograph. Now Ilona wished she'd taken it on another day, when Zidra was more casually dressed, for the contrast between her attire and what Lorna was wearing was great. Lorna's dress was too small for her, the hem was coming down on one side, and on her foot – the only one that could be seen in the photo – she was wearing a grubby sandshoe and no sock.

After replacing the photograph of the two girls, Ilona looked at the picture behind it. This was a studio shot of a young boy, Philip Chapman, her favourite pupil of all those she'd ever taught. Not only because of his talent but also because of his vulnerability. There'd been something exposed about him that first visit to Woodlands over four years ago, when Judy Chapman had interviewed her for the post of piano tutor. As there had probably been in her own demeanour, for she'd so desperately wanted another pupil. And after that interview at Woodlands she'd seen Peter Vincent for the first time. Who would have guessed that she'd end up marrying him and giving up teaching? Now she picked up the photograph of Philip and examined it. One of his eyes was green and the other brown, although that didn't show in the picture. This unusual combination, together with his frightful stutter and sensitive disposition, wouldn't make life easy for him now he was at boarding school.

She began to play the Chopin prelude again. Music was always an escape, or a refuge, and things had a way of sorting themselves out in her head while she played.

As soon as she'd finished, Peter stuck his head around the door. 'You've been writing to the *Burford Advertiser* again. It's a good letter. I couldn't help seeing it next to the typewriter. I didn't know they were still thinking of building that caravan park at Jingera.'

'They're not. It's going to Dooleys Beach. That was a copy of my old letter. It got published two months ago, just before the proposal was knocked back. That's what happens when you're a nosy porker. You get things wrong if you don't read the date as well.'

'Nosy *parker*. A porker is a pig.'

'That's you too,' she said, laughing. 'And a pig is a policeman and a policeman is a bobby and –'

'Only in England is a policeman a bobby.'

'Tea for two?'

'Is that a real offer or something you're going to play for me?'

'The real stuff. In a teapot, before bed.'

'Just my cup of tea,' he said.

'Terrible pun.'

'One of my better ones, I thought.'

'Have you seen Lorna's father lately?'

'Tommy Hunter? No, not for some months. He called into Ferndale a while back. You were out.'

'Did he say where they were living now?'

'No, and I didn't ask. We talked about other things. I just assumed they were still at the Wallaga Lake Reserve.'

After Ilona told Peter about Lorna's letter, he said, 'You know it's going to be really difficult to arrange a meeting.'

'I know, but we have to try.'

'Well, the first place to check is Wallaga Lake.'

In the attic, Zidra was sitting up in bed, still wide awake although the hall clock had long ago chimed midnight. Thoughts of Lorna churned in her head. The Hunters would surely be desperate for news from their daughter and longing to see her again. Ilona was always saying how much she missed Zidra if she went away for only a night or two; imagine how Lorna's mum must feel.

After pulling open the curtain above her desk, she gazed out at the dark shapes of pine trees silhouetted against the white band of stars stretching across the sky. Unable to resist climbing out of this window the night that she'd first moved into the attic bedroom, it was only the slipping of one of the slates that time that prevented her doing it again. Not that the drop was far if the slates fell, but she had a perfectly good set of stairs that were hers alone and no one ever stopped her coming and going.

The image of Lorna crawling out of the Gudgiegalah boxroom roof light stuck in her mind. The tale gave her hope for her friend; a girl who could subvert punishment by escaping. The girl who could turn solitary confinement into a reward.

Zidra imagined Lorna now, perhaps sitting on the roof above the boxroom at Gudgiegalah Girls' Home, watching a night sky not dissimilar to this. A sky that appeared to their eyes as a hemisphere swathed with an infinity of stars.

CHAPTER 3

Pushing the telescope along the rails was straightforward. Although the instrument was heavy, its platform ran easily down the tracks that George Cadwallader and his younger son, Andy, had constructed the previous autumn. It had been Andy's idea to modify one side of the shed in the back-yard to incorporate sliding doors, and to lay a pair of rails from the shed floor out into the garden. From that position, George was able to gaze unhampered at what he termed to himself the celestial hemisphere. His favourite time for stargazing was around midnight. By then most of the lights in Jingera had been turned off, apart from a few street lamps. Naturally it would have been much better if there were no lights at all, although Jingera was still sufficiently small, even with that new housing development opposite the cemetery, that the streetlights were not a serious problem.

While rolling the telescope back into the shed was easy, locking the door afterwards proved to be more difficult. George couldn't find the key, which he knew he'd been holding just a moment before. In his haste to locate it, he loosened his grip on the torch. It fell to the ground and its beam was extinguished. That meant the bulb had broken and he swore under his breath.

He could hear the metallic clunk of the torch as it collided with one of the rails but it was impossible to see where the torch had rolled. Turning, he tripped on a rail and fell heavily to the ground. He seemed to be clumsier than he used to be, and stiffer too. That must be old age creeping up on him, or too much standing behind the counter of Cadwallader's Quality Meats.

Having established that he was uninjured, George began crawling along the ground in the direction the torch had rolled. Still, I'd rather be crawling about my own backyard in the dark, he thought, than all round the boathouse. That's where he'd initially intended to install the six-inch telescope that he'd bought four years earlier. But his boathouse was on the far side of the lagoon. With his gammy leg, that would have meant a fifteen-minute walk there and a twenty-minute walk back. As well, there was the worry about security. So in the end he'd followed Andy's scheme of converting the shed. Andy was such a practical lad, full of good ideas, though nowhere near as bright as Jim, George's older son.

George, having by this point found the torch on the ground next to the rails and the key in the pocket of his dressing-gown, locked the shed door. For a moment he leant against the wall and stared up at the sky. All the detail of what he'd seen earlier could only be guessed at now. Such a clear view he'd had tonight of the constellation of Grus, the whooping crane. Stargazing always put into perspective his own concerns, and brought him harmony too, perhaps because it reminded him once more of his own insignificance in the bigger order of things. While that might depress some people, it brought him only happiness. And he loved the way the sky changed as the earth went spinning around the sun, so the only way you could manage to find the same star on consecutive nights was to know the shapes of the various groups or constellations.

He wondered now what could be seen with an even more powerful telescope. A ten-inch one perhaps. Or a radio telescope like the one that had just been opened at Parkes. One of these days he'd like to go there and take Eileen and the boys too. But he'd have to be able to afford a car first. His work van was not a vehicle in which Eileen was prepared to travel long distances – she hated driving about labelled as Cadwallader's Quality Meats – and it would be a nightmare getting to Parkes and back by train and bus. There was no doubt that transportation concerns lay behind her decision not to go to Sydney this year for Jim's speech day, although she wouldn't admit it.

'Andy and I went last year,' she'd said when he raised the issue with her the previous evening. 'I'll go next year when Jim will be leaving school.'

There was no way George was going to miss Stambroke College Speech Day though. In early December, he would travel on his own to Sydney and lodge in the cheap guesthouse in Rushcutters Bay where they'd stayed last year. Sometimes he felt almost as if Jim's achievements were his own. Maybe they were, for Jim was his son and now he'd grown so tall he even looked a bit like George in his younger days, when he'd been better-looking and had more hair. Their colouring was the same: green eyes, olive skin and dark straight hair that had a mind of its own.

George would never forget the morning that Jim first left for Stambroke College, not long after the pub and the bushland surrounding Jingera had been destroyed by bushfires. George had travelled to Sydney with Jim that day. Waiting at the bus stop in Jingera square that morning, George had watched his son saunter down the road leading to the lagoon, which was shimmering through the burnt-out bush. New growth had already started appearing and the blackened tree trunks had looked almost woolly with their covering of young shoots. Apart from his new school uniform, purchased too large to allow room for growth, you'd never have thought the boy was about to leave home. He'd looked too relaxed. So relaxed that he was affecting a funny walk. But George had known that Jim was far from tranquil. It wasn't an easy journey that he was embarking on, and George had always been determined to smooth the way for him. Whenever he could he conducted him to and from school, and had been present at every Speech Day.

In some ways everything had changed since Jim left for Stambroke College, and yet nothing had changed. Jim had always been mature beyond his years and seemed almost like a young man, though he was barely sixteen. Once he'd share things with his father but now there was a reticence. That was only right, kids had to grow up and grow away. But there was a class gap there too that George tried not to think about. What he'd done in encouraging Jim to go to Stambroke was right but this distance still hurt.

Sometimes George wondered if his wife's coolness to him might have been different if he'd been a solicitor rather than a butcher. *Wash your hands, George!* she still said to him every evening when he got home from work, even though he washed them before he left the shop as well as after he got home. Straight into the laundry he went but her response to his homecoming was automatic, even as he sluiced his hands noisily at the laundry tub, rubbing at them with hard soap and a scrubbing brush till they were almost as red and raw as the meat he served. It was over five years ago now that he'd heard her tell the boys: *Wash your hands after handling money. You never know where it's been. Maybe at the butchers.'* Jim had intervened at that point, though he'd only been ten. 'Dad's shop is the cleanest in town,' he'd said.

For weeks now George had been counting off the days until this year's Speech Day, and there were only another nineteen to go. Jim's successes were to be celebrated, not taken for granted, and George glowed with pride at the thought of all the prizes Jim had taken the previous year. There would be more this year, no doubt about that. They weren't just for academic work either; he was good at everything, including rowing, cricket and swimming and, in the winter, athletics. Not rugby though, he wasn't the right build for that. You had to be shaped like a cube to be good at rugby.

Evidently Andy was developing too, in his own way. Only yesterday he'd told his father about his success at woodwork, coming top of the class for a joinery project at Burford Boys' High School. 'Well done, Andy,' George had said heartily, slapping his younger son on the shoulder, before returning again to the topic that obsessed him: travelling to Sydney for Stambroke College Speech Day.

CHAPTER 4

'It seems very quiet,' Zidra said, as her mother stopped the car under a flame tree some twenty yards before what appeared to be the boundary of the Wallaga Lake settlement. 'I'd expected masses of people.' The only person in sight was the elderly Aboriginal woman sitting in a faded deck chair in front of the first building, a dilapidated fibro shack. She was wearing a loose-fitting floral dress and a red-and-yellow-striped woollen beanie. Although there were a couple of dogs lying on the ground next to her, they seemed too tired to take any interest in the visitors.

'Be very friendly,' her mother said, and Zidra sighed. As if she needed to be told.

Smiling and waving, her mother got out of the car, and walked across the rough grass. She was wearing her old brown dress and clutching the orange raffia handbag that had recently arrived from David Jones' mail order. Zidra followed, with an assumed nonchalance that covered her nervousness. Not only was she terrified that the Hunters wouldn't be here but she felt strange to be entering what Mama had described, only a few moments before as they drove across the causeway, as a place of incarceration.

'Good-day', Mama cried, in her poor imitation of Australian diction. The more she tried, the odder it sounded.

'G'day,' the woman replied, unsmiling.

'G'day,' Zidra echoed. The woman looked at her and grinned. Zidra beamed back. One of the dogs, a cream Labrador-cross, bared its teeth at her. 'Good dog,' she said hopefully, at which the Labrador summoned enough energy to wag its tail.

'Won't hurt youse,' the woman said. 'Lookin' for anyone?'

'We're friends of the Hunters.' Zidra's mother now became rather voluble as she clarified the connection. Eventually she concluded, 'Where do they live?'

The woman pointed to a shack some fifty yards further down the point. Beyond it, between the tall gum trees, Zidra could see the surface of the lake rippling in the strong easterly breeze.

'Are they in today?'

'Gone away.'

Zidra caught her breath at this news, but her mother simply said, 'Do you know where?'

'No.'

'Where's everyone else?'

'Rob Lowe takem big mob in truck. Alex Fraser takem other mob. Pickin' beans an' corn.'

'Are you sure the Hunters aren't with them?'

'Yairs. Bin gone months.'

'I'll leave a note under their door.' After thanking the woman, Mama headed towards the shabby cottage she'd indicated.

Zidra waited behind. Her expectations dashed, she couldn't think of anything to say to the elderly woman, who anyway appeared disinclined for conversation. To occupy herself, Zidra patted the cream dog.

Later, as they drove back onto the Bermagui road, Mama said,

'What frightful conditions they live in!'

'The views are lovely,' Zidra murmured. She couldn't bear the burden of her mother's disappointment as well as her own.

'Views!' her mother exploded. 'What are views when one is living in an internment camp?' She drove unusually fast over the single-lane wooden bridge, narrowly avoiding a car that had stopped too close to the end, and accelerated along the causeway towards Bermagui.

Zidra held her breath. Her mother had spent years in a concentration camp during the war, and some years afterwards in refugee camps, and yet she never spoke to her of these. While Zidra occasionally thought of asking her, at the same time she didn't really want to hear. Desiring information was one thing, but you couldn't predict how you might be affected by that knowledge. And anyway she knew there'd be reasons for her mother's silence. Including that Zidra's grandparents had been selected for the gas chambers while her mother hadn't.

Her mother added, 'Is not this place like apartheid in South Africa, Zidra? Or the Deep South in the United States?'

'We're trying to help Lorna meet up with her parents, Ma. That's all we can do.'

'We'll see about that, my dear. We'll see about that.'

Zidra knew what this meant. More letters to the newspapers, more letters to politicians. Her mother's preoccupation as she drove south meant she was already composing them.

After a while, Ilona said, 'I never imagined the Hunters wouldn't be at the Reserve. Next time I go into town, I'll try asking at that camp just north of Burford. Maybe someone there will be able to tell me where they are. And then there's that meeting in the New Year about the new housing development for Aborigines. There's bound to be somebody who knows.'

Feeling reassured by this, Zidra said, 'Anyway, there's still a lot of time before the Jervis Bay trip.'

'But it *is* the picking season. Beans and corn and who knows what else. The Hunters could have gone anywhere to do that. But we shall find them, never fear.'

'Can we stop at the Bermagui shops, Ma? There's a Christmas card I need to send urgently.'

In the newsagency, Zidra rifled through the displays of Christmas cards, trying to find one with an appropriate verse. All she wanted was something that would indicate to Lorna that she should dismantle the layers of card to read a message concealed there. Nothing was appropriate though. She'd planned to glue together the two layers of card after writing '*Jervis Bay is on*' inside, but there was little point in doing that if Lorna would never see the words. Anyway, she felt she shouldn't raise Lorna's hopes *too* much, in spite of what she'd told her mother. Maybe they wouldn't be able to track down her family before the Gudgiegalah excursion. Mama had already decided that she and Zidra would go anyway but that wouldn't make up for Lorna not seeing her family.

Perhaps it was better to go for a more straightforward message – although still subtle enough that the censors at Gudgiegalah wouldn't notice. Eventually, in the religious section of the display stand, she found a card that she thought might be suitable. On the front was a Bethlehem scene. Inside, the printed message was the first part of Psalm 121.

I will lift up mine eyes unto the hills, from whence cometh my help.
My help cometh even from the Lord: who hath made Heaven and earth.

She'd always liked that, the first line in particular. Although perhaps the message was a little obscure for her purposes, it would do.

While queueing to pay for the card, she caught sight of a cellophane-wrapped packet of animal stickers displayed on a shelf close to the till. She picked it up and shook it a little. Yes, there was certainly an elephant in there. Not a green elephant but this grey one would suffice. She could colour it the same green as that toy wooden elephant that Philip Chapman had given her all those years ago at Woodlands. She in turn had handed it on to Lorna, in exchange for that flat pink shell that she still had on the bookshelves at home. There was no way that Lorna would miss this message. As soon as she saw the green elephant she would know who the card was from.

Next Zidra chose a bright green pen. After paying for all three items, she went up the hill to the Bermagui post office. At the counter, she eventually found a pen that worked and carefully wrote inside the card: *Happy Christmas and holidays with best wishes from St Andrew's Sunday School, Jingera.* There was no St Andrew's in Jingera, only St Matthew's, and Lorna would remember this.

On the blank page next to the verse, Zidra pasted the sticker of the little elephant and coloured it with the green felt-tip pen. Next she sealed the card in its envelope and carefully printed on it Lorna's name and address. After this she purchased a stamp and posted the card in the mailbox outside. Lorna would have it before Christmas Day.

Mama was waiting by the car next to the row of palm trees lining one side of the park. On the far side of the lawn, beyond a row of Norfolk Island pines, blue water sparkled and seagulls swooped around the tables and benches scavenging for scraps from the people lunching there.

'I've bought Peter's Christmas present from the bookshop,' she said. 'It's Patrick White's new novel, *Riders in the Chariot*. He will love it.'

He would love whatever her mother gave him because it was from her. That they were so devoted only occasionally made Zidra feel left out. Although most of the time she was glad not to have the full focus of her mother's attention. 'Now we'll have a swim, Zidra, in the tidal swimming pool.'

This was the treat she'd talked about on the drive from Jingera to Wallaga Lake that morning. Her mother had been obviously nervous about the long sections of dirt road and they'd both been apprehensive that they wouldn't find the Hunters at the Reserve. And they hadn't. Nothing had been achieved.

Zidra got into the car and looked away when her mother stalled the engine. Slowly they drove around the headland to the steps leading to the pool.

As they walked down to the water, her mother said, 'There was nothing like this when we lived in Bradford. It is perhaps just as well you don't remember that dreary weather and the endless rain.'

Zidra had no recollection of emigrating to Australia. Her mother and *Our Papa*, both refugees, had met in Bradford. She'd been far too young when they left England to remember anything about the place. Her mother was the New Australian and she wasn't, that's what she preferred to think, anyway. That way she would blend in better.

Although she didn't really feel like a swim, she understood that her mother wanted to drown her disappointment swimming endless laps. What she lacked in style she made up for in persistence. Zidra occupied herself by counting the different varieties of fish in the pool – there were nine – and afterwards seeing how long she could hold her head under water before being forced to come up for air. After her fourth attempt, she trod water while looking around for her mother. Nowhere to be seen and her heart skipped a beat; she might easily have got washed out of the far side of the pool over which waves were already crashing with the incoming tide. But no, there she was, sitting on the concrete edge of the pool at the sheltered end, her hair darkened by the water and her arms clasped over her chest in a protective gesture. She looked older than usual, and forlorn, as if the swimming hadn't been reward enough. Zidra breaststroked over and tickled her mother's foot.

'Love you, Ma,' she said.

Her mother smiled down at her and the years dropped away. Her darling mother, whom Zidra couldn't bear to lose, exasperating though she sometimes was.

———◆———

It had rained overnight again. You couldn't ask for more than that, Ilona thought, as she rode with Peter towards the southern boundary of Ferndale. The early morning sunlight, slanting across the wet grass, illuminated beads of water so the paddocks sparkled, and the leaves of the bush beyond the furthest fence glistened as they gently turned in the breeze. To the south the sky was a deep purple, heralding more rain later, or so she hoped. It might fill the new dam that Peter had had excavated at the start of last winter. The contractors had thought it ambitiously large but they'd been proved wrong. Its location was perfect, the catchment area was good and already it was nearly full. In time rushes would grow around the edges and maybe ducks would nest there.

Now Peter stopped, and she watched him rescue a bleating sheep that had somehow managed to get its head caught between the wires of the fence to munch the grass beyond. After he'd mounted his horse again, they took a small detour to the eastern boundary and paused there for a few minutes, to watch the waves washing around the offshore pinnacles of rock. The usual population of black cormorants, perched on the furthest rock, seemed to be surveying their domain. To the south she could see row upon row of headlands, with Jingera just beyond the second. How lucky she was to have Peter by her side, day after day, sharing his life. Sharing the running of the place too, for she did the accounts and settled the bills and organised the paperwork that, until his marriage, he claimed had always been a mess.

At twelve noon they would return to the homestead to have lunch in the kitchen; today it would be leftover casserole from dinner last night. In the first year of their marriage, Peter had tried to learn half a dozen new Latvian words every lunchtime. He had a poor ear in spite of his love of music, and had struggled with the language. Initially he'd felt an obligation to learn it, though she herself had thought it was a waste of time, it would never be needed where they were living, *beyond the black stump*. Wait till I show you *back o'Bourke*, he'd countered, then you'll really know what living in the sticks is like. Although he hadn't taken her there yet, he still intended to. Once Zidra left school it would be easier to get away. But after that first year he'd abandoned all pretence at learning Latvian. What he termed his tin ear just wasn't up to it.

Now she caught sight of the line of flame trees, still in flower, their vermilion petals glowing. God only knew why Peter's grandparents had planted these trees where they had, along the edge of one of the paddocks closest to the road, or how they'd guessed they might survive here. Peter certainly didn't know why, and had never thought to ask them when they were alive. Now she remembered the splendid flame tree near the entrance to the Wallaga Lake Reserve. She sighed. She still couldn't believe that the Hunters were no longer at the Reserve. You shouldn't have expected them to be there, she told herself. Nothing is constant. People come and go, and wax and wane. Only the laws of physics remain the same.

Perhaps she should have told Zidra yesterday that finding the Hunters mightn't be all that straightforward, but she hadn't wanted to worry her. *Someone will be able to tell me where the Hunters are,* she'd said. *There's bound to be somebody who knows.*

Yet now she wasn't so sure. It was very easy for people to disappear, particularly if they had no reason to stay.

And her own history had taught her that they could disappear even if they had a reason to stay.

PART II

Sydney
December, 1961

CHAPTER 5

Spears of light glanced off the harbour. The skiff danced over the wake of a ferry while the boys continued to pull in unison. The boat sliced faster and faster through the water, turning eventually around the buoy and heading back to Rose Bay. The early morning sky, the palest of blues, was rose-tinted to the east. Jim Cadwallader's heart was pounding so hard he could hear blood thumping in his ears, and his early morning tiredness dissipated as adrenalin kicked in. Never before had rowing felt this good. They were moving so fast they had to be breaking their own record.

'Maybe you've even got a chance of winning the Regatta next year,' said O'Brien, the coach, when they were back at the boat ramp and pulling the craft out of the water. 'As long as you buggers don't slacken off.'

'That's what you tell all the boys,' said Eric Hall, gold hair glinting in the sunlight, freckled fair skin reddened by exertion and sixteen years of sunshine.

O'Brien laughed. Jim knew he'd forgive you anything at all as long as you were good at sport.

Afterwards, back at school, Jim had a quick shower to sluice off all the sweat and salt, with his body feeling so alive he felt he could do anything, fly if he wanted to. He'd dreamt of that plenty of times. Feet firmly on the grass, he would start sprinting, more and more rapidly he would pound, and soon his running feet would lift him off the ground, his legs pumping the air as if at bicycle pedals, and before long he was thrusting himself off trees and up into the sky. In these dreams he could do anything he wanted to, anything.

At Stambroke College he could do anything he wanted to, as well, except to walk out the front gate of school. That was an expellable offence.

Walking to the school chapel for prayers before lessons began, Jim could see the glittering harbour through the tall trees bordering the damp green lawn. As always, he was sitting next to Eric, his best friend. He'd met him on the day of the scholarship exam, when he'd never imagined he would see the boy from Walgett again, let alone that they would become close. Although Eric professed his stupidity, he had a natural cunning and an extraordinarily good memory that served him well academically. Jim opened his hymnbook and began, with the others, to sing Psalm 23. *The Lord is my Shepherd* belted out by a thousand voices – there was something rousing about this, however agnostic you might be feeling. The sense of wellbeing Jim had experienced after that morning's exercise returned and began to expand, so that he now felt almost that he was floating above the chapel floor.

That afternoon after lessons had finished, Jim found two envelopes in his pigeonhole at Barton House, one of the four boarding houses arranged in a row not far from the dining hall. He took them outside to read. A few boys were idling around at the far end of the verandah. Ignoring them, Jim sat on the sandstone balustrade and opened the fat envelope from Jingera

40

first. It contained a page from his mother and two from his father. His mother wouldn't be coming to Speech Day, but his father would. Hopefully that meant Andy would be coming too. It had been good last year when they'd gone to Bondi Beach after Speech Day, and Andy had been as excited as if he was seeing a beach for the first time, instead of just about living on one. There wasn't much information in his parents' letters. Dad wrote loving descriptions of the weather and Cadwallader's Quality Meats, and his plans for a new type of sausage with herbs in it. That sort of stuff didn't appear in Mum's letter, which was mainly about how the hens weren't laying and that their yard needed attention. The chookyard was his responsibility, and he could see right away where her thoughts were heading. That would be a nice little job for him when he returned – not that he minded.

The second letter was from Andy and had a Burford postmark. Posted on a weekday, it bore evidence of being written on the bus; Jim smiled at the sight of the untidy handwriting lurching across the page, the occasional word scrawled through and others whose meaning he'd have to guess at.

Dear Jimmo,

Can't wait for you to come home. Only two weeks to go now. I got top marks for my woodwork project. It's a coffee table that I thought of giving to Mum and Dad for Christmas. They haven't seen it yet, although they know I came first. Maybe I'll do an apprenticeship in woodwork or joinery or something. I'd like to do something with my hands. Mum says I have to stay on at school for my Leaving Certificate but I'm not so sure that I even want to sit for the Intermediate Certificate next year. I'm a manual sort of guy and not much good at the academic stuff.

You're a hard act to follow, Jimmo. It might have been better for all of us if I'd been the firstborn and you second, then I wouldn't have to live up to you!

Suppressing a sigh, Jim looked up from the letter. The late afternoon sunlight filtering through the trees cast long shadows over the lawn in front of the boarding house. Everything seemed so peaceful, but surface appearances were deceptive. He'd been looking forward to news from home but when it arrived it was unsettling. He continued reading:

It was rash of you to invite Eric to stay without first squaring it with Mum and Dad. It worked out all right in the end, although not before they had an argument. Seems they thought they'd have to buy Eric's plane ticket from Walgett the way the Halls bought yours and as usual, there's no money. All the more reason for me to start an apprenticeship. But all resistance vanished once they got Mrs Hall's letter saying that Eric was coming south anyway, to visit some relatives near Eden. They'll be dropping him off at our place afterwards so you can return to school together. But I expect you know all about that. Mum said I've got to shift into the sleepout on the back verandah so that you and Eric can share our bedroom. I'd already decided that in any case. It's only for a week and we'll have lots of fun.
See you soon. Andy

Jim couldn't believe his crassness in not checking with his parents first before suggesting the trip to his friend. It simply hadn't occurred to him that they might feel honour-bound to provide Eric with a plane ticket. He glowered at the pages of Andy's letter as if it was himself he was glaring at.

'Not forgetting dinner, are you? The bell's just gone and you didn't budge an inch,' Eric said. '*Billets doux* or just the oldies?'

'The oldies and Andy,' Jim said, stuffing his brother's letter back into its envelope.

'Better get a move on or we'll be last served. There's nothing worse than cold mutton. Ask the boy from Walgett, he's an expert.'

'It's Tuesday so it's going to be sausages and mash,' said Jim, laughing. 'The boy from Walgett should know that after all these years.'

They joined the others in the procession to the dining hall. As they walked past the music rooms, Jim thought he heard the sound of a piano, although practice time was long over. The sound abruptly ceased as the second bell rang for dinner.

CHAPTER 6

Philip Chapman's practice time had ended half an hour ago but there'd been no one else waiting to use the piano so he'd just carried on. Earlier he'd noticed someone in the room next door stumbling over scales and five-finger exercises but mostly he'd heard nothing of what was going on elsewhere at Stambroke College. This was the only time of the day when he felt at peace, isolated in a cell in the row of music rooms. Sometimes he thought that music was the only reality and the rest was a dream, and a bad dream at that. If he could escape for even an hour each day he could pull himself together enough to survive the rest of the time.

Evening prep might have given him some peace if he didn't always find the homework so dull, though at least there was no one taunting him then. The younger boarders were the worst, the boys who were only a year or two older than him, like Keith Macready. Now, after shutting the music book, Philip stared out of the open window, trying to decide what to play next. Maybe the Chopin sonata that he'd started learning some months ago. The third movement brilliantly expressed the yearning he was feeling. The funeral march, his piano teacher called it. But for a moment he allowed himself to be distracted by the view.

Through the row of dense trees bordering the lawn he could see the late afternoon sunlight illuminating Barton House. If you didn't know better, you might think it beautiful, built of that warm red brick with a wide verandah edged by a stone balustrade.

Life would be more bearable if he were a day boy here and not a boarder. The day students were friendly enough. He'd struck up a friendship with one of them, Giles Mellor, who'd invited him home for a free weekend not long ago. That had been the highlight of the term, being in someone else's home with a father and mother and sister who were all nice to him and didn't mock his stutter.

Though he sat next to Giles in the classroom, and this insulated him from the unpleasantness of Stambroke life as a boarder, Giles went home once lessons were over. Philip often imagined him making that journey. Through the leafy streets of Vaucluse, around the park at Nelson Bay, maybe stopping for a few moments to look at the waves lapping against the sandy beach as they had on the walk that Giles had taken him on that free weekend. Then up a steep hill and through the wrought iron gate and into his home, with a welcoming mother and a sister who, although occasionally argumentative, was never nasty. There would be hugs and kisses for Giles, and freedom to do what he wanted, to play with toys, read a book, do his homework when he felt like it and not in some regimented prep time.

It couldn't always be that good, though. Giles was lucky with his parents, and that was another reason to envy him. Philip's mother was never to be called Mum. Her name was Mummy. When he'd called her that at school the day he first arrived the other boys had laughed. Only it wasn't Mummy that he'd said but M-m-m-m-mummy. And they had taken this up and exaggerated it to M-m-m-mum-m-m-m-my. Until he couldn't bear to hear it, until they'd moved onto the next taunt. The latest was p-p-pretty b-b-b-boy, and he hated that even more. Boys were not pretty, they were handsome. It was his blond curls that made them say that. He ran his fingers through what was left of his hair, before resting them again on the edge of the piano.

A few days before, Macready and some of the other juniors had dressed him in a frock raided from the properties box in the drama room, and had forcibly made him up, using a bright red lipstick that had come from God knows where. Only when Dave Lloyd had given the warning that the housemaster was coming had Philip been able to escape. After that he'd chopped off his curls, though he knew his mother would hate this new look. When both his parents collected him from school at the end of term – which happened only infrequently, for it was usually only his father and Mr Jones the chauffeur who came – everyone paid Mummy special attention. He'd observed the headmaster, Dr Barker, transform himself from a frightening figure into a rather fawning one, or at least that's how his father had described him afterwards. 'Your glamorous mother,' the headmaster had said about her once, forgetting the need to keep a distance between head and pupil. 'Always in the social pages and on so many charity boards. You must be in a real social whirl over the holidays.'

As he was, of course, at least to begin with. If she collected him, she would take him around for the first week of the holidays, exhibiting him like a poodle. Then she would grow tired of him and send him back to Woodlands with his father who got restless after a few days in Sydney and as desperate as Philip to head south. Once Mummy had even summoned Mr Jones all the way from Woodlands to take him home, after Daddy had decided to fly to Queensland to view a stud bull he'd heard was for sale. She would stay on a few days more, partying in Sydney, until eventually even she grew fatigued by her Eastern Suburbs' friends and returned home.

Sighing loudly as he recalled what his mother would say, Philip abandoned all thought of playing the Chopin piece. 'Such a frantic social life, darling, but all for such good causes. I've raised thousands, literally thousands. But I just had to come home to spend some time with my darling boy before he goes back to school again. So have you been learning how to run the place? Your father's showing you the ropes? But not every day I hope! Maybe just between practising.' Laughing as if this was a joke, although he knew she was proud of his playing and would listen to him for hours. He loved that about her, the way she would lie back on the green brocade chaise longue with her eyes shut and listen to him play. Then he would be in a bubble of happiness, just him and his mother, far away from the outside world.

At this point Philip started to play some scales. Up and down the piano his fingers tripped, faster and faster, as if they had a life of their own quite distinct from the thoughts whirling through his head. His mother never would pay attention when he tried to say he hated farming. He h-h-h-hated b-b-boarding but he would hate f-f-f-farming even more. He'd struggled to spit out the words but she was too impatient to listen. His stuttering made him slow and she couldn't stand slow people. They were boring, and that was the worst thing she could say about anyone. So she took in nothing of what he was trying to tell her.

When the second dinner bell rang Philip stopped playing, but he stayed for a moment longer in front of the piano. Only after hearing the sound of boys' voices, as they thronged into the dining hall, did he shut the instrument lid. Yesterday he'd written his father a letter, which he'd drafted and re-drafted over the past few days. Tomorrow he would send it. The words were stuck in his head and he kept going over and over them. He hoped he'd got the spelling right, his father was a stickler for that. No point sending you to Stambroke College if they're not teaching you reading, writing and arithmetic, he'd say. But he was also as likely to add, you're going to have to stay on at Stambroke until they do teach you how to read and write.

<hr />

Near the top table in the dining hall he saw the friendly face of Jim Cadwallader, who waved. Between that table and the door was a sea of juniors. He was glad that no one else took any notice of him; he would sit near the door with a few of the nicer Barton House boarders. He knew the juniors in Coombs House would never forgive him for getting transferred to Barton a week ago, even though they hadn't been expelled for what they'd done to him.

He thought of it as a *tarring-and-feathering*, what people did in the old days, they'd read about it in history. But that would have left marks and someone would have been blamed. It was only a bit of fun, one of them said afterwards. Just a bit of glue and some feathers that they'd pulled from a dead currawong found on the lawn of Coombs House. The house-mistress had seen Philip afterwards as he'd crept along the corridor to the showers. He wouldn't tell her what had happened but she was kind and took him into her own bathroom and left him to have a soak there. Not long afterwards he'd been moved to Barton House.

Now he sat down next to a junior he hardly knew, a fair-haired boy called Charlie Madden who was in the year ahead at Barton House. Madden smiled and offered him a glass of water. Philip took it, examining it closely but in a way that Madden wouldn't notice, to see if there was anything unpleasant in it like spit. There didn't seem to be, so he took a cautious sip.

'Sorry about what happened to you last night. They do that to nearly everyone who starts at Barton. Everyone smaller than them, that is.' Philip didn't point out that this was the second time in a week that he'd been routed out at night. This last time had been a disgusting experience. Keith Macready and his friends had made Philip take off all his clothes, and he'd known that was to shame him. Afterwards Macready had taken down his own trousers and pants, and Philip had nearly wet himself in fear, and to his astonishment Macready had put potato chips in his clenched bum crack. How the other boys had laughed at that. After this, Macready's friends made Philip squat down behind Keith and eat the chips, one by one. Philip had felt so sick he could hardly chew, and at the end Keith had farted noisily in his face and he'd thought he was going to throw up. *Arse-licker*, they'd called him after that. *Arse-licker, you tell anyone what we've done to you and you're dead. Or worse.* As soon as they let him go, he'd gone into one of the bathrooms and rinsed his mouth out with water, and brushed his teeth for several minutes, and even after this he'd felt dirtied.

As Philip was taking another sip of water, a latecomer lurched by the bench on which they were sitting and knocked Philip's elbow hard. The glass tilted and the water spilled down the front of his shirt and onto his shorts.

'Sorry, pretty boy. Oh, look, you've wet your pants!' It was Keith Macready. 'Arse-licker,' he added, and grinned before carrying on to the next table.

'Here, use this handkerchief,' Madden said, tugging at the pocket of his shorts.

Although Philip had a perfectly good handkerchief of his own, he took what was offered and mopped up the water with it.

Keith Macready had deliberately bumped into him, he knew, but with Madden next to him he began to feel slightly less alone than he had when first entering the dining room.

After taking back his handkerchief, Madden began to talk about where he came from, a sheep station west of Charters Towers up in Queensland, and miles from anywhere. While he'd never attended school until starting at Stambroke when he was nine, he'd had a few years of School of the Air so he hadn't come completely unprepared. Though the School of the Air hadn't equipped him for some of the things that went on here. Philip gratefully absorbed these words and the kindness that was being offered. Finally Madden said, 'Too bad we're the first bunch of kids in the Wyndham system.'

'W-w-what's . . .?'

'When they make us do six years before the final exams instead of five. I'm in the first intake and you'll be in the second. Older boys still only have to do five years.'

Six years of torture instead of five. Both seemed far too long. Though he wouldn't be going into secondary school for another year, he shuddered at the prospect.

That evening, in the prep period after dinner, Philip opened his English exercise book. 'An Evening at a Restaurant' was a stupid title for a composition; the teacher was running out of ideas again. Slowly Philip began a story of a couple dining out. Two sentences located the restaurant in Double Bay and his characters within it, and now he felt free to devote the rest of the essay to a catalogue of what they were eating. It was safer to record the menu than to attempt to describe what might really be going on; those thoughts and looks that words could never express. He concluded the meal and the composition with ice-cream and chocolate sauce.

With nearly half an hour to spare, he took a quick look out the window. Nothing to see but the reflection of rows of boys sitting at desks, heads down, pens scribbling. He'd never forget the last time he'd gone to a restaurant; he wouldn't want to put that into a composition. It had been in the Easter holidays, just after his parents had collected him from school in the new Bentley and taken him to the Hotel Australia for a few days. The Woodlands' best Hereford bull, called Hamish after a distant cousin to whom the animal bore a faint resemblance, had won second prize in the Easter Show. To celebrate, his father had taken him and Mummy to a special restaurant. His father had drunk so much wine and talked at such length about cattle that soon Mummy had started yawning and trying to change the subject. When she'd finally said, 'Don't be so boring, darling,' Philip had caught his breath and glanced at his father. His face had changed shape so it looked distorted, almost as if a veil had come down over it. On the way back to the Hotel Australia afterwards, his parents had quarrelled. Not much, they were too well mannered for that, but it was the closest thing to a proper argument that he'd ever heard from them. He couldn't bear them to have differences. Seated in the back of the car, he'd stuck his forefingers in his ears and wiggled them about so that the rasp of skin against skin would be a distraction from their voices. It was true that his father could be tedious when he talked about cattle but it wasn't every day that Hamish won a prize. Mummy could be hard to take too when she put on that frightful gushing tone that he hated so much and which turned her into another person.

He hoped they wouldn't argue about him once Daddy got his letter.

Smothering a yawn – his unhappiness was making it hard to sleep at nights – he slowly read through his composition. It was a bit short, so he added a sticky date pudding at the very end, with custard. There was no reason why the hero couldn't have two desserts in a story even if he wouldn't be allowed to in real life.

At this point he glanced at the clock on the wall of the prep room. There was enough time to check again what he'd written to his father. He pulled the letter out of the back of the exercise book, in which he'd tucked it for safety.

Dear Daddy,
I hate it here. I am very very unhappy. The other boys use me
as a skate goat and I want to come home. Please take me out of
boarding school. You can send me to the local school. I will learn
more there than here and be happier.
Can't wait to come home.
Your loving son,
Philip

For a moment he wondered if he should address it to both his parents. It would be easy to add Mummy to the letter. Yet she'd always said that it was his father's idea that he should go to Stambroke so he was the one to convince. Once more Philip read the letter. Something about it seemed wrong. He couldn't work out what it was. Eventually he opened the pocket dictionary that he kept in his book bag and flicked through it to the letter S. Skate goat. There was no such thing. He turned back several pages. Finally he found what he was looking for. Scapegoat: one blamed or punished for the sins of others. Carefully, he corrected the word in his letter, and read it once more before sealing it in an envelope.

Now that he had all the words right, his father would surely take notice of his request and let him come home.

CHAPTER 7

Why he should feel slightly nervous as he approached the gates to Stambroke College, George Cadwallader couldn't understand. He had nothing to be ashamed of. He was every bit as good as these rich people with their confidence and expensive cars that lined each side of the road leading to the school and filled the car park. Money didn't mark your worth, it was kindness and compassion that did that.

Looking down at the school grounds, he could see groups of people scattered across the lawn in front of the Assembly Hall, the men in dark suits and the women in bright dresses, with boys in college uniform weaving between them. At the top of the sandstone steps descending to the lawn, he paused for a moment, in order to brush an imaginary speck of dust off his lapel and to see if he could detect a whiff of camphor. When he'd lifted his suit out of the case the night before, he'd thought it smelled faintly of mothballs, but all he could identify now was the scent of newly mown grass and the frangipani blossoms of the trees flanking the steps.

Putting his hesitation down to shyness, he wished that Eileen had travelled to Sydney with him. Everything was much easier when there were two of them instead of one. He adjusted the new blue-and-red-striped tie that he'd bought in Burford the week before, and began to limp down the stairs. At the bottom he paused again, his attention caught by the beauty of the scene in front of him. The kaleidoscopic colours of the moving figures on the lawn. The Moreton Bay fig trees with their buttressed trunks bordering the edge of the lawn, and beyond that, the glittering blue of the harbour across which a ferry made its way, leaving a wake that appeared almost solid.

And not one familiar face in this sea of strangers.

At this point masters began to marshall the boys into the Assembly Hall. Soon after, the guests were rather less coercively encouraged to move by anxious-looking prefects. George found himself towards the front of the queue and was able to choose a seat reasonably close to the stage. It was impossible to pick out his son from all these blazered boys but he'd see Jim soon enough when it was his turn to go up onto the platform. Once all the parents had seated themselves, the school orchestra began to play. That was when George recognised Philip Chapman at the piano, a small boy compared to all the others in the orchestra. He'd done something funny to his hair; George couldn't help smiling at the sight of the ragged crew cut. Lads were always the same when they got away from their parents, they all wanted to change their hairstyle.

Now the boys in the audience stood up. Their parents rather tentatively followed suit, with the hesitation of infrequent members of a church congregation who could only imperfectly recall the rituals. As the music swelled, the procession of black-robed teachers began to advance at a ponderous pace down the central aisle of the hall and up the stairs onto the stage. There they took their places in a serried display behind the headmaster. At his signal, everyone seated themselves again, accompanied by the orchestra and a rumbling of chairs.

The headmaster began a speech about the school's achievements over the past year and its plans for the future. In spite of his best intentions, George found his attention wandering. There was a row of large wooden boards hanging above the trophy cabinets. These boards, which he hadn't noticed on previous visits, chronologically detailed in gold lettering past heads, past prefects, past athletes, past duxes of the school. In his mind he was already seeing, on the list of duxes of the school, *1962 James Cadwallader.*

He mustn't get his hopes up though, or put any pressure on his son. While Jim was good at everything and could choose any career he wanted, he didn't yet have a vocation. That's why he was doing so many subjects this year, but he'd have to cut out some next year, the school insisted on specialisation for the Leaving Certificate. George still dreamt sometimes that his son would do science and eventually astronomy but Jim had expressed no preference for anything yet. All he'd decided was that he'd go to university but it was almost as if he didn't care what he'd study there.

Now, after a fanfare from the orchestra, a federal politician was ushered onto the stage. From the Liberal Party, naturally, you'd hardly expect that a Labor Party politician would be chosen by an institution representing the establishment. George felt a twinge of disappointment nonetheless. You'd think they'd pick a guest speaker divorced from politics, he thought. Especially just days before the federal election. A judge or a scientist or an admiral, rather than this parliamentarian. Admittedly the man was an Old Boy, so presumably he'd been selected as a role model, though the speech was a self-serving outline of the man's career and achievements. Boys, if you strive hard you too can represent your fellow Australians, you too can be like me. In his irritation

George began to fidget with the program and found that he'd dog-eared the corners when his intention had been to keep the booklet pristine.

Eventually, after the man droned to a conclusion, the headmaster took over the microphone. Next he would call up the lines of boys whose hands the Member of Parliament was to press. Every boy was to receive a certificate of varying degrees of merit, with the older boys last, so there was a considerable time to elapse before it was Jim's turn. George already knew that Jim wouldn't be given every prize for his year, although he'd topped every subject. This spirit of egalitarianism was to be applauded, George told himself. It was petty to want everyone to know that the boys getting those other prizes had only come second. Anyway three prizes were to go Jim's way: first in form, science and history. And as well there was that other award that had been bestowed on Jim a few weeks ago by the Law Society for his essay on human rights. That had been in a competition right across the state, and his was chosen as the best.

As Jim ascended the steps, George felt as if his heart would burst. Tears filled his eyes when his son shook hands with the politician and accepted the prizes. That's my boy, he might have said to the women sitting on either side of him had he not felt too choked with emotion. Instead, he blew his nose very hard. Whoever would have thought that the butcher's son from Jingera would get this far? That he was also going to be made a prefect next year was the icing on the cake.

Afterwards George wandered around the lawn, several times trying unsuccessfully to engage people in conversation. Eventually he joined the queue for tea. He didn't immediately recognise the woman in front of him, distracted as he was by her hat. It was a yellow thing with a large black feather pointing backwards, which threatened his nostrils every time she moved. When she turned, he realised who she was: Mrs Chapman of Woodlands, mother of the boy playing the piano.

'Mr Cadwallader,' she exclaimed at once. Her hair was almost as red as her lipstick. 'How lovely to see you here. You must be so proud of Jim winning all those prizes! And he's grown into such a good-looking boy, he must have all the girls running after him!'

In the face of this effusion, George had no idea what was expected of him. To play safe, he simply grinned and nodded and fiddled with his program.

Perhaps she didn't expect any answer, for she continued almost at once, 'Philip plays the piano. You would have seen him in the orchestra. He played on his own in the school concert but we couldn't go. Poor Jack is kept so busy with the bulls and the rams and whatnots that we don't get to Sydney much, although I do sometimes sneak away. He barely misses me at all, do you, darling?' Here she plucked up the sleeve of her red-faced, white-haired husband. Like George, he made no response apart from smiling and nodding.

The headmaster, sweeping by, caught sight of Mrs Chapman. Approaching with a speed that was almost undignified, he took Mrs Chapman's hand and bent so low over it that he might have been about to kiss it.

'Very good to see you here, Mrs Chapman,' he said. 'Very good. The sun always shines more brightly when you grace us with your presence.'

'How sweet of you to say so, Dr Barker. That's quite the nicest compliment I've had all day.'

It was another language, George thought, embarrassed for them both. At that point he noticed Philip Chapman standing behind his father. So distracted were the Chapman parents by the headmaster they seemed to have forgotten about him. 'Hello, Philip,' George said, smiling. 'Didn't see you standing there.'

'H-hello, Mr C-C-C . . .' The boy gave up on the name as a lost cause and began another tack. 'J-J-Jim has d-d-done really w-w-w . . .'

'Well,' George finished. 'Done well. You've done well too, Philip. Really well.'

'Only at the p-p-piano.' There was a long pause while he struggled to get the next words out. 'D-duffer at everything else.'

Philip's parents, having now been served tea, nodded goodbye before drifting across the lawn, accompanied by the headmaster who seemed intent on keeping them in his party. Trailing several paces behind, Philip chewed at a sticky bun.

After collecting tea and a rock cake, George looked around. No sign of Jim anywhere. He would wait in the dense shade of one of the Moreton Bay fig trees until he could see his son and then he'd emerge. His elation had now quite worn off, replaced by loneliness and a sense of inadequacy. He never felt alienated like this in Jingera, where he knew almost everyone and it was easy to strike up a conversation with those he didn't. But here his simple manner wasn't welcome. He appeared shabby, he knew. His suit, although still serviceable, was old. It was his only suit; he'd bought it for his wedding in 1945. It still fitted him, or at least did now that Eileen had let out the waistband. Double-breasted suits were no longer in fashion, but that wouldn't explain why, apart from the Chapmans, the few people he'd tried to talk to had basically brushed him off. They'd sized up who he was, or probably who he *wasn't*, and hadn't bothered to offer more than a perfunctory *yes* or *no* to his conversational gambits. He was a fish out of water in this crowd, no doubt about that.

But he wasn't going to let that upset him. The sight of Jim receiving those prizes would become one of his most precious memories.

'Hi, Dad,' Jim said. 'I've been looking for you everywhere. Why are you hiding over here?' Under his arm were the three books he'd received as prizes.

'I'm not hiding,' George said. 'Just observing.'

They shook hands, slightly awkwardly, with George balancing the half-eaten rock cake on the saucer. Once upon a time they would have hugged one another but not anymore, not now that Jim was taller than he was. He must have grown an inch or more since the start of term and his shoulders seemed to have broadened.

'Why don't you talk to some of the other parents instead of skulking around on the sidelines?'

George was too pleased to see Jim to let what amounted to an accusation bother him. However there was a slight pause before Jim added, 'Sorry, Dad. Thanks for coming. Here, have a squiz at my prizes. I'll hold your cup of tea.' After they'd made the exchange, he added, 'Why didn't Andy come?'

'He's at school, obviously, that's why.'

'He came last year. I thought he'd be here this year too.'

'Your mother was able to come last time and that's why we brought Andy.' He realised at once how tactless that sounded, and added, 'He can't really afford to miss too much school. Your mother didn't come this year because of all the travelling. Riding about in trains and buses disagrees with her. She'll be coming next year though.'

'And Andy.'

'Yes, if he wants to. Seeing it's your last year.'

'Of course he'll want to come.'

Perhaps he should have offered to bring Andy, George thought as he inspected the three books. He ran his hand over the cover of the top book. It was beautifully bound in leather, with the school crest and title of the prize engraved in gold lettering on the cover and spine. He'd just started to flick through the book, about the history of science, when they were joined by a tall boy with wavy ginger hair and a freckled complexion. It was a moment before George recognised Jim's friend Eric Hall. Though they'd encountered one another a couple of times before, Eric had been transformed in the interim from a boy into a handsome youth. A bit of a ladies' man was how Jim had described him last holidays. Quite how you could be a ladies' man when you were boarding at an all-boys' school in term-time, and living on a property on the Walgett plains in the holidays, was beyond George's understanding.

'Good to see you again, Mr Cadwallader. Thanks for inviting me to stay in the holidays. I'm really looking forward to it.'

'It's a modest town,' George said, although actually he meant their house. 'Not like this part of the world.'

Eric said at once, 'I hate Sydney. Too many people and not enough space.'

'My sentiments entirely,' said George, warming to the young man's charm. 'There's nothing like visiting it, though, to make you appreciate what you've got at home.'

'I can't wait till the holidays start,' Eric said. 'Nearly two months of freedom.'

'Neither can I,' said Jim. 'I can't wait to get home.'

At this, George's initial feeling of alienation from his son quite vanished.

—•—

Dad's late, Jim Cadwallader thought. Fifteen minutes before their train was due to depart and there was still no sign of him under the clock on the concourse where they'd arranged to meet. It wasn't as if he had to come far, the guesthouse he'd stayed in was closer to Railway Square than Stambroke College was.

Jim and some of the other boarders had been conducted by coach to Central Station. They were at first unusually subdued. Their day had started far too early and their sleep the night before too late. End-of-term celebrations had gone on until all hours, with the juniors ragging and the seniors disporting themselves like juniors, and only the prefects maintaining any sense of decorum. Now the boys, blazered and boatered, stood about in small groups that peeled off one by one as trains and platforms were announced.

There was still no sign of Jim's father. To fill in time, Jim inspected the indicator boards. Trains going out west, over the Blue Mountains and on to Dubbo and Broken Hill. Trains heading south to Goulburn and Canberra and Albury. Trains heading north to Newcastle and Coffs Harbour and beyond. Only one train south to Bomaderry.

There was something exciting about being at a railway terminus. Maybe it was the announcements over the loud-speaker, the signs saying Country and Interstate Trains, and the bustle of people hurrying on and off the platforms. He loved the great arch of the barrel vaulting above the concourse, the corrugated iron sheets curving over the elegant metal trusses. Sunlight flooded through the transparent panels at the top, illuminating the groups of boys and giving their farewells added significance.

At this point Jim began to wonder if he'd been unkind to his father the day before. It was true that he'd been annoyed with him and hadn't bothered to disguise it. And it wasn't only because Andy hadn't been offered a trip to Sydney. Being honest with himself, Jim could admit now that he'd been shocked at how shabby his father had seemed in that shiny black suit. Having catalogued the failures of yesterday, Jim next began to wonder if his father might be lost. Unused to making his way around the city, he could have ended up anywhere. Maybe he'd got on the wrong bus or even been mugged. His father had taken three days off work to come to the Speech Day and he deserved better treatment than what his son had doled out to him. Shabby his father undoubtedly was, but Jim's conduct had been a good deal shabbier. Dad was a better man by far than most of the other adults Jim had come across. He was someone to be proud of, not ashamed of.

Just as he'd arrived at this conclusion – with only five minutes before the train was due to leave – he felt a light tap on his shoulder. His father stood there, puce in the face and panting. 'So much traffic,' he gasped. 'I didn't imagine the bus would take so long.'

'Thank God you're here, Dad. We've got to hurry.' Jim grabbed his father's case as well as his own and sprinted towards the platform.

Once they were settled in their carriage, the train began to puff out of the terminus. His father immediately shut his eyes. Although exhausted, Jim didn't follow his example. Instead he inspected his father. He was out of that terrible suit, thank God, and with some surprise Jim noticed for the first time that he was rather handsome, in spite of the slightly sagging cheeks. Skin as olive as Jim's own, but meshed around the eyes with fine lines. Even in repose, one of his eyebrows was slightly raised. In the space of just one term, his hair had receded further. Why this discovery should so abruptly fill Jim with tenderness he didn't understand. Quickly he looked away.

Once they'd terminated at Bomaderry some hours later and transferred onto the bus to Burford, Jim began to feel as if he was almost home. He knew this was an illusion though. There were still many miles to travel. Through tall forests, past dairy farms, down the main streets of little towns whose names he could run through in his head like an invocation. Next, the changing vegetation that would indicate they were almost in Wilba Wilba Shire. The tall straight trunks of eucalyptus trees, dappled white and grey, and the cycads growing between them.

He couldn't wait to get home.

Yet within two months he knew that he'd be looking forward to returning to Sydney. There was only so much you could do at Jingera, but you could always take away part of it in your head.

CHAPTER 8

'W-w-what d-d-d-did you th-think of m-m-my
l-l-letter?'

Ever since school had broken up three days ago,
Philip had been hoping to get his father alone and only now had
it proved possible. Side-by-side, they stood on a jetty at Circular
Quay waiting for the ferry that would take them to the Valencia
Street Wharf at Hunters Hill. They were to visit his father's sister,
Auntie Susan, and her husband Uncle Fred, for afternoon tea.
Mummy had pleaded a headache and they'd left her lying, with
a cold compress over her eyes, in a darkened room of their suite
at the Hotel Australia. The warm air now seemed to be pressing
down on Philip like a light blanket. Seagulls wailed and ferries
hooted, and still his father hadn't answered his question. The
heaving of the jade green harbour water was starting to make
him feel a bit queasy, or it could have been the thought of what
else he wanted to tell his father.

For the past two days his parents had become inseparable as
they never were at home. Philip might normally have been content
to be alone in his room, instead of in a dormitory with eleven
other boys, had he not been so eager to talk to his father about
leaving Stambroke. He couldn't stay on there; this much was clear.

He couldn't stand another term of that anxiety, that waiting for one of the gang to persecute him. Head down the toilet bowl because his hair looked like it needed a good shampoo, or at least that's what Keith Macready had said. Later that fuss about the boot polish on the toilet seat that had got itself all over his shorts.

If it hadn't been for Giles Mellor, he might have run away before the end of term, but the trouble was that he didn't know where to run. He had little idea of the geography of Sydney. He'd always travelled to and from school by car and never taken much notice of the roads, which seemed to wind around in a very confusing way. You couldn't live in ignorance all your life though. After term ended and they'd checked into the Hotel Australia for a week, he'd made a point of finding a map of Sydney. The layout of the city was much clearer once you understood that the road system was set by the shape of the harbour.

His father seemed to have forgotten his question, so he repeated it. 'W-w-what d-d-did y-you think of m-m-my l-l-letter?'

'A nice letter. The spelling was perfect.' His father didn't look at him though, he just carried on staring towards the Harbour Bridge as if he was willing a ferry to appear. 'Good, here it is at last. You've got to remember, Philip, that education's everything these days. I know you're homesick at Stambroke, but it's all for your own good.'

How having his head shoved into the toilet bowl could be for his own good, Philip had no idea. He started to try to explain the bullying but the words refused to form themselves, let alone emerge from his mouth in a sentence that his father could understand.

'Don't get so het up, son,' his father said, putting an arm around Philip's shoulders in a gesture that might have reduced him to tears if he hadn't been so intent on getting his message across. 'I'm not quite sure what you're saying but one thing's clear. You've got to learn how to stand up for yourself and be a man.'

At this moment, the ferry pulled into the wharf. Two men jumped onto the jetty. After slinging thick ropes around metal bollards, they began to guide the passengers onto a rather rickety looking wooden walkway. It was impossible to talk further until they were on board.

'Th-th-they p-p-p-pick on me,' Philip said after they'd found a seat. He tried to explain what happened each night but it proved impossible, the words deserted him.

Some moments passed by before his father said, 'I know teasing goes on at school but it passes. Once you get a bit bigger they won't pick on you anymore. Hang about with your own group of friends. You've got to learn to stick up for yourself in life and this is as good a training as any. Stambroke'll teach you to defend yourself, just as it did me. My days there were some of the happiest of my life.'

Philip watched the light sparkling off the water. It made his eyes hurt. If only he could speak properly. If only he could describe the things that happened, night after night, and the endless anxiety that kept him awake. But he said no more, fearing that tears would come and this would make his father think even less of him than he did already. Anyway, revealing what had happened might make his father think he was a weakling who needed much more time at boarding school to build his character.

So upset did Philip feel that he couldn't take in what he was seeing from the ferry. Already the holidays were ruined with the thought of having to return to Stambroke College at the end.

He barely noticed getting off the boat, or the tree-lined street they walked up to reach his aunt and uncle's house.

But Auntie Susan, waiting at the front gate of one of the sandstone houses, was smiling so broadly it was impossible not to smile back. It was a year since he'd last seen her; she was browner than he'd remembered and her eyes a brighter blue. In spite of being sister and brother, she and his father were different colours. His father's face was probably so red because of all the outdoor work he did. To distract himself while they talked about something dull, Philip wondered what his own brother or sister might have looked like if he hadn't been an only child. Maybe they'd be fair like him. His father had been fair-haired once, before he went white, but his mother's hair remained remarkably red in spite of the passage of time.

Auntie Susan was much older though. Her husband, Fred, waiting on the front verandah, was older still, although not retired yet; he was a solicitor somewhere in the city. Tall and thin, he wore square glasses and hair arranged in strands across his shining scalp. He shook Philip's hand as well as his father's, and asked after the *young man*. It was only a prompt from his father that made Philip realise that he was the person in question.

Fortunately his relatives seemed content to let him sit in silence during afternoon tea. They were absorbed in talking about the Prime Minister, Mr Menzies, who yesterday had narrowly defeated Mr Calwell in some battle to run the country. While their words swirled around him, he took in very little of what they said. He ate nothing either, while he struggled against the feelings of hopelessness that his father's comments had induced. *This is as good a training as any. You've got to learn how to stand up for yourself. You've got to be a man.* Wistfully he stared at the open piano in the far corner of the living room. If it were in another room he could ask to play it, and that would distract him.

When at last they were about to leave, his aunt showed him a music score. 'This is for you. It's a sonatina for the piano. I know you love to play and I thought you mightn't have come across this. It's by an Australian composer called Sculthorpe.'

He looked at his aunt properly for only the second time this visit. She had such a kind face, with those clear blue eyes that seemed to stare right into you. 'Th-th-thanks,' he said, and next surprised himself by managing to add, with only the tiniest stammer, 'It's v-v-very th-thoughtful of y-y-you.'

She put the sheets of music into a manila envelope and handed it to him. 'Come and see us any time,' she said. 'You know where we are. I'm sorry we couldn't invite you here for a free weekend last term but we only got back from London a few weeks ago. Next term you must definitely come to us.' She leant forward and kissed his cheek.

Philip and his father walked to the Valencia Street Wharf without exchanging a word. After boarding the ferry, they sat on a slatted wooden seat at the back of the boat. The sky that had earlier been a brilliant blue had become suffused with a strange yellow light. Staring at the harbour water, which was now dark green and choppy, Philip began for the first time to question his father. Only inwardly, naturally. He'd never have the courage to challenge him openly, or be able to mouth the words.

By the time the ferry reached Circular Quay and his father had finished reading his newspaper, Philip had decided on a new tack. He would work on his mother instead. Not while they were in Sydney, she wasn't herself here, but after they went home to Woodlands. Maybe there she'd have the patience to listen to him. Though he knew she probably wouldn't, not unless he could think of some novel way of getting her attention.

In the meantime he wouldn't talk about his unhappiness to his father. He wouldn't talk about anything with his father. They disembarked, still in silence, under a sky that was now bruised-looking. After hurrying up George Street, they arrived at the hotel just as the first fat raindrops started to fall.

PART III

Wilba Wilba Shire
December, 1961 to February, 1962

Chapter 9

Zidra had been meaning to find out about newspaper cadetships for weeks but there never seemed to be an appropriate time, what with leaving for school so early and returning so late. A few days before term ended, she took a day off school. These days her mother was very good about providing a note for the odd day's absence, even when Zidra wasn't ill. Sometimes one needs a *sickie*, she would say, to allow one to put things into perspective. The notes to the form teacher were no problem for her. 'Zidra was indisposed,' she might write, 'but after a day's bed rest she has been sufficiently restored to return to the fray.'

Zidra had spent part of this morning reading in bed. Tiring of this, she'd taken the box of combs and brushes out to the paddock where her chestnut horse was grazing. Although Star seemed surprised by her appearance several hours before midday when she should have been at school – his sense of the passage of the days was as sophisticated as any human being's, Zidra told him – he'd seemed to enjoy the extra grooming as much as she. Afterwards she'd saddled him up and they'd galloped to the far side of the property and back. By the early afternoon she was ready to begin writing a history essay but when she heard the back door slam shut and soon after her parents' voices outside, she peered out of her attic window. Good, they were heading towards the dam. Now was the opportunity she'd been waiting for to phone Sydney without her mother breathing down her neck.

She retrieved several back copies of the *Sydney Morning Chronicle* that were kept on a shelf in the dresser in the kitchen. After taking them into the hallway, she dumped them on the floor next to the telephone table. Quickly she began to sort through the papers, resisting the temptation to read interesting-looking articles. Instead she checked the names of the editorial team. They were all men, except for the editor of the social pages. Flicking through these, she saw photographs of ladies lunching, photographs of smiling couples at exhibitions and race meetings, and read the glib text underneath each photo. *Mr and Mrs Simon Blythe at the races. Mrs John Symonds and Mrs Peter Wenborn at the new opening at the Hoffman Galleries. Miss Ruth Paton, 18, and Miss Vanessa Bowen, 17, spotted lunching at Vivaldi's.* Zidra scanned the gossip column, idle chitchat of no interest apart from to those whose names were mentioned. There was shipping news too: who was arriving at Sydney Harbour on what ship, who was departing on what other ship. As if anyone cared.

Next Zidra gave the operator the telephone number of the newspaper. For a moment she wondered if Mrs McGrath from Loganbrae next door – it was a party line – was listening in, but she didn't care. She got through and asked to speak to the social editor.

To her surprise, she was immediately connected. Once the preliminaries were over, she said, 'I want to be a journalist. How do I become one?'

'I got started with an arts degree from Sydney University.' The woman's voice was friendly.

'How do you get off the social pages?'

There was a loud laughter. 'My dear, if you're a woman you never get off the social pages.'

'Do you have internships on the paper?'

'There are cadetships. How old are you?'

'Fourteen.'

'Try calling back again in a few years time, darl, and we can discuss the matter further.'

Zidra put down the receiver and sat cross-legged on the floor. *If you're female you never get off the social pages.* Surely it couldn't be the case that being a woman disbarred you from proper journalism. That was old-fashioned, like the marriage bar. She wouldn't be deterred though. She wrote well and she wrote quickly. Mrs Fox the English teacher had told her that these were just the skills needed in journalism, and she'd know, her husband was editor of the *Burford Advertiser*. Zidra began to examine the pages of the newspaper more closely. While many of the articles had no names on them, some did. They were all male but one, Felicity Butler. If Butler could do it, so could she. Again she gave the operator the *Sydney Morning Chronicle* number and this time asked to be connected to Felicity Butler.

'Sorry, love, she's just gone overseas,' the switchboard operator said.

'Is she the foreign editor?'

'No, she was a politics writer but she's actually left the paper. Got a job at the *Daily Courier* in London.'

This discovery gave Zidra fresh hope. A transition from Sydney to London seemed even more interesting than from Jingera to Sydney. After hanging up, she glanced at her reflection in the oval mirror above the telephone table. The caption to this picture was easy. *Miss Zidra Vincent, 14, caught relaxing at Ferndale, decides that she will see the world.*

A degree from Sydney University, she decided, that would be the way into journalism. Or from any university; it was hard to get into Sydney, Jim had told her. Her test results had improved dramatically lately, though. *Making good progress academically,* the last school report had said. That she had a talent for algebra and geography had come as a bit of a surprise. Chemistry remained a closed book, however; there was something about the periodic tables and compounds that put her to sleep. Her conduct reports weren't up to much though, and she knew they never would be. *Cheeky. Inclined to answer back. Shouldn't loiter in the corridors between classes. Inclined to lead others into mischief.*

The reason for the improvement in her grades Zidra had kept to herself. The truth was that she was frightened. Frightened that nothing would ever happen in her life. That the days would continue to pass by endlessly without event. There was always that same old routine: getting up early in the morning, waiting at the gateway for the school bus, all day at school, afterwards home again and, if she were lucky, time to groom and ride Star for half an hour. It sometimes seemed that she was always waiting for something profound to occur, but nothing ever did.

Over the months she became convinced that she would have to get away. Not yet, not until she'd finished school. The only route out of here was to obtain a place at university. Once she'd realised this, she began to work harder at school. After a few months she'd seen, not that much was possible, but rather that *something* was possible.

Over dinner that night, her parents began to discuss the election results. This led, after some minutes, to Zidra's father saying, 'The papers publish a lot of lies. Whatever's released to them by the government they publish, as if it's the truth instead of some fiction.'

'That's a bit harsh, Peter. At least there *is* an opposition.'

'There was one in the McCarthy era too in the United States. But anybody could be denounced as un-American and no verification was required, or none to speak of. The opposition there didn't stop any of that erosion of civil liberties.'

'Newspaper editors can sway public opinion,' her mother said. 'It's they who decide what gets published. They've got incredible power to influence what people think and who they vote for.'

'I'm sure that newspaper reporters don't even check the facts a lot of the time,' Peter said. 'One paper publishes some gossip and the others pick it up without bothering to verify the source.'

'At least in a democracy the opposition can establish when the government's lying and let the media know. Not like in the Soviet Union where no opposition's brooked.'

'Journalism's important in a democracy.' Zidra knew she sounded pompous but she was getting fed up with all this negative talk about journalism. Something positive had to be said about reporters otherwise she'd never be able to reveal her ambitions. 'Journalists can present both points of view and afterwards let the public make up its mind about what's the truth and what's fiction.'

'Zidra's right, that's what the best investigative journalism should do. Present both points of view, giving all the facts. But as well they should explain why they favour one rather than the other.'

'That's what opinion writers might do, but don't forget that neither point of view might be the truth,' Peter said. 'Both might be fiction. Both might be based on misinformation.'

'Even so, I still want to be a journalist.' There it was, out in the open at last, and Zidra nervously waited for the reaction. To begin with there was none, unless you counted the prolonged silence.

'It's a cut-throat job and all you'd deal in would be lies,' Peter said at last.

'Don't be so negative, Peter. We all need dreams.'

'It's not a dream,' Zidra said irritably. 'It's what I'm going to do. I'm good at history and I'm good at English. Mrs Fox said I'd make a good journalist.'

'You write beautifully, darling. If I could write half as well, maybe more of my letters to the editors might get published.'

After this, there was another long pause, until Peter said, 'There's the public service too, Zidra. Or even the diplomatic service. They might be better places to work.'

Before Zidra had a chance to reply, her mother said, 'Both are even more male-dominated than journalism. Or at least the Commonwealth public service is. They've still got a marriage bar.'

At this point Zidra observed the swift exchange of glances between her parents. She hated it when they did this. They had their own private language, or so they thought. She knew how to translate it though. Don't destroy her illusions, her mother was saying, and willing Peter to go along with this. Suddenly Zidra felt angry with them both; it was as if they were conspiring against her. Yet she knew that all those silly rules of society weren't their fault, those rules that said women were good at running a home and having kids and nothing much else. Not that there was anything wrong with running a home, it was just that it didn't pay. No one ever sat down to calculate how much you'd have to pay someone to do what her mother did. Financial independence was everything, and you'd only have that if you could earn your own money. And if you were good at that, no one would want to marry you, or at least that's what they'd have you believe. But anyway, she wasn't even sure if she wanted to get married.

What she hated was that, in spite of the fact that she was brighter than most of the boys in her class, many people viewed her achievements as a liability rather than an asset. In case she hadn't already understood this, only last week when she'd dropped into Sally's house, Mrs Hargreaves had said, *My my, Zidra, you are doing well at school now, but you be careful you don't go putting the boys' noses out of joint.*

Yet Zidra didn't care whose nose she put out of joint. She was going to live her life her way.

'I could write about Lorna,' she said. 'I could do a series of articles tracking the lives of half-caste kids who've been taken away.'

The words were out before she'd given them any conscious thought. They hung in the air while she and her parents contemplated them. They were good words, she decided. This was a good ambition.

'That certainly needs public documentation,' her mother said thoughtfully. 'And far better than writing letters to newspaper editors.'

'And then there's the comparison with apartheid in South Africa,' Zidra added. 'You know, we were talking about that and the civil rights movement the other day on the way back from the Reserve.'

'We were indeed.' Her mother sighed and began to stack the plates. 'And that reminds me, I must call into that camp near Burford soon. We've got to find out where the Hunters are.'

CHAPTER 10

For days Zidra had been looking forward to Jim's return for the Christmas holidays. As always, he'd phoned Ferndale his first night home, and they'd arranged to meet this morning; this beautiful clear morning, when Zidra had been dropped off by her mother in Jingera. Now here she was, at ten o'clock on the dot, standing by the war memorial. Jim hadn't arrived yet, the lazy thing, when he'd only a couple of hundred yards to walk and she'd come nearly ten miles.

She brushed a smudge of grey dust off her navy blue shorts and picked off a few of Spotless Spot's hairs that had managed to attach themselves to her white cotton shirt. After taking off her straw sunhat, she sat on the steps on the beach-side of the memorial, so she could keep an eye on the street leading down to the water as well as on the road up which Jim would come. Surreptitiously she inspected her brown leather sandals. They looked almost new, though purchased at the end of last summer, and showed to advantage her toenails that she'd painted the day before with her mother's pale pink pearlescent nail polish. Soon tiring of this contemplation, she stared down the hill. Though the water was inviting and it might be fun to rent a canoe, there was no sign of Hairy Harry yet. Two summers ago he'd opened his canoe-hire place next to the lagoon. It was just half-a-dozen upside down canoes on the strip of land that the council had started mowing six months before. Soon after the canoes had arrived, a shower had magically appeared, a bit of bent pipe like a gibbet with a shower rose on the end. Only cold water, but at least you could wash the sand off before heading home.

Hairy Harry could spot a business opportunity all right, Mrs Blunkett had said, it was just a shame that he didn't seem to know how to run it afterwards. The trouble was that if he got the urge for a beer or felt like an afternoon's fishing or a burn-up on his bike, he'd shut up shop. After the last canoe came back in, he'd run a steel cable through the cleats at the front of each craft and bolt them to the sign saying *No Speed Boats on the Lagoon*. Then off he'd go. It didn't matter if there was a queue of kids waiting. It didn't matter that the holiday brochures stated they were for hire throughout the school holidays. If Hairy Harry felt like it, canoes were off.

'Zidra!'

She started. 'Where did you come from?'

'The headland.'

Jim sat down next to her. She deliberately bumped his arm with her shoulder, the closest they'd ever get to the hug she'd like to give him. The holidays had officially arrived; this was what she always felt when Jim returned to Jingera.

'I got here a bit early so walked up to the cemetery,' Jim said. 'Tried whistling to you but you didn't hear. You were miles away.'

'It's the surf.' They sat in silence for a few moments, listening to the endless roar of the ocean. She noticed that his legs below the baggy khaki shorts were lightly suntanned, presumably from all the sport he did, and covered with fine dark hair that she'd never really observed before. Glancing at his face, she saw that he was inspecting her legs. Fortunately he was much too well-mannered to comment on the fact that she'd used her mother's depilatory cream on them yesterday. Feeling self-conscious now about this new hairlessness, she rubbed her hands up and down her calves. He looked away but not quickly enough for her to miss his grin. To hide her discomfort, she leant forward and pulled out a weed that had somehow managed to germinate between the memorial plinth and the bitumen road surface.

'You've changed your hair,' he said.

'Yeah. Had a haircut last week and got them to do a fringe too.'

'It suits you.'

'Thanks.'

'Makes you look younger.'

This wasn't what she wanted to hear at all, and she told him so.

'Sorry,' he said, grinning again. 'It makes you look much older and extremely sophisticated.'

'That's more like it.'

'Only one problem though.'

'What's that?'

He leant towards her and plucked some fragments of blossom and twigs out of her hair.

'Oh, that,' she said. 'My hair's like a mop. It picks up flora and fauna whenever I go into the bush. Spot and I were playing there first thing this morning when I was waiting for Mum. No spiders, I hope?'

'Not many.'

'That's all right then.' But she ran her fingers through her curls just to check.

'What would you like to do?'

'What about the usual? Sit under the fig tree in your back garden. Or maybe we could go for a walk along the lagoon. Ma's collecting me at one o'clock on her way back from Burford.'

'We could hire a canoe.'

'Yeah, but Hairy Harry isn't there yet and we don't really want to hang around waiting all morning.'

'I could get the key to the boathouse and we could borrow Dad's boat.'

'Sounds a bit damp if it leaks as much as it used to, and I didn't bring my swimmers.' If he'd been a girl that wouldn't have mattered though. They could have rowed around the bend in the river and swum in their underclothes. Even a year ago she would have been willing to do this, but the Bradley boys had made her self-conscious. That was the trouble with growing up. 'Let's go for a walk.'

They strolled in silence down the hill. There was now a slight awkwardness between them that she couldn't remember ever noticing before. Desperately she struggled to think of something to say. Surely they hadn't grown apart just in the space of one term. No, that was impossible; they'd known each other far too long for that. They'd always be good friends; it was just an initial shyness. Or maybe he felt embarrassed about walking down to the lagoon with her, now that he looked so adult, and she was two years younger and always would be, the same age as his brother, Andy.

They stopped in the middle of the footbridge and watched the translucent green water rippling under it: the Burford River and all its tributaries, including Stillwater Creek. A black bird swooped under the surface with a splash and a moment later was on its way again.

'A cormorant,' Jim said, keen as ever to display his knowledge.

Zidra laughed and resumed her inspection of the straps of yellow weed, anchored firmly to the sandy bottom of the river. They bent with the direction of the tide that was slowly inching in. Somehow staring at the lagoon, in this place where she'd spent so much time with Lorna that first summer in Jingera, made it easy for her to begin telling Jim about Lorna's letter, and the plan for Jervis Bay in February.

'I'm sure you'll find out where the Hunters are before then,' Jim said. 'It's still a long time away. Tommy's probably taken them off somewhere. It's the season for fruit picking.'

'Ma's going to ask today at that camp.'

'Which camp?'

'The one near Burford that the council's threatening to move on.'

'I didn't know there was one there.'

'You wouldn't see it unless you went on the back road. It's quite new. The Aborigines get moved on regularly.'

After this, Zidra found that their conversation began to flow as easily as the water under the footbridge. Once the sun on their backs became too hot, they walked on to the Cadwallader boathouse. There they sat in the shade of a dense stand of she-oaks, and told one another about their lives over the past term.

Afterwards, she thought of how some things would never change; important things like her friendship with Jim. It was almost as if he were her brother. That's what she felt for him, sisterly love.

After calling into the bank in Burford to deposit some cheques, Ilona drove on for several miles before turning onto the side road that led through the hills towards Swampy Creek. The Aboriginal settlement was next to an old rubbish tip. Not the council one but the other one, the illegal dumping ground where people got rid of stuff that the town tip wouldn't take, or when they couldn't be bothered driving the few extra miles into Burford.

Rounding a bend in the road, she mightn't have noticed the settlement if it hadn't been for the plume of smoke from a camp fire spiralling up through the still morning air. Beyond the wrecked cars and other detritus flanking the road was a collection of shanties, ringed by trees. For the most part, the shelters were fabricated from packing cases and rusty corrugated iron, and roofed by the same material or by strips of old carpet held in place by stones. She stopped the car at the side of the road, next to the carcass of what had once been a Holden ute. The morning was starting to feel hot; she wiped her brow with a handker-chief before pulling on the old sun hat that she kept in the back of the car.

As she walked along the verge towards a narrow track leading around the wrecked cars, the smell hit her. Old rubbish and latrines, the stench of temporary encampments. No birds called; she heard only the sound of silence. You might think the camp was deserted if it weren't for that column of smoke signalling otherwise. She rounded the last mound of rubble, a pile of old bricks and concrete bound together with weeds. Only now did she notice the circle of elderly Aborigines sitting cross-legged in the shade of a tree. There were no young people or children around; this had to be the reason that the place was so quiet. She approached, nodding and smiling. Two mongrel dogs growled as she walked towards them but didn't bother to get to their feet. The hostility of the group was almost palpable.

Beads of moisture that had formed between her shoulder-blades and under her arms, trickled down into the waistband of her skirt. She flinched when a gang-gang cockatoo flew overhead, screeching like a rasping door hinge. Preparing to mouth those words she'd been rehearsing, she took a deep breath.

'Hello,' she said. 'My name's Ilona Vincent. And I'm *not* from the Aborigines' Welfare Board.'

There was a brief pause. The elderly woman closest to her spoke first. 'You from the church?'

'No, I'm not from the church. I'm from Ferndale. That's a property a few miles north of Jingera.'

'I knowem. You missus bossman there.'

Another woman said, 'You're not from the trade union?'

At this, Ilona guessed that the camp had been visited recently by the labour alliance investigating Aboriginal poverty. 'No,' she said. 'And I'm not from the Liberal Party or the Communist Party either.'

They all laughed. She squatted on the ground, regretting that her skirt was too tight to allow her to sit cross-legged.

'Wantem pickers? Young 'uns all gone.'

'No, we don't have crops, only sheep and cattle. I'm looking for Tommy and Molly Hunter. They used to be at Wallaga Lake.'

'I was evicted from Wallaga Lake last year,' said one old man. 'Couldn't pay me rent. No job, no work, no pension, no rent. Them Hunters still there when I left.'

'You've not seen them since?'

'No.'

'If you do see them, please tell them I'm looking for them. It's about their daughter, Lorna.'

At this point the expressions of everyone in the group became guarded.

'I swear I'm not the Welfare Board,' she said again. 'Please tell the Hunters if you see them that I'm trying to organise a meeting with their oldest daughter.'

'That girl in Gudgiegalah. Never see nobody.'

'But a meeting might be possible.' Ilona didn't want to say anymore than this. She would hate anything to happen to jeopardise Lorna's trip to Jervis Bay. Yet she could see the scepticism showing on the faces of everyone.

Eventually the woman who'd spoken first said, 'We'll tell em if we see 'em. But won't be here much longer.'

'They're trying to move us on,' said the old man who'd been evicted from Wallaga Lake.

'Who is?'

'The council. The boss next door wants to lease this bit of land. Not the rubbish, but the land behind the tip and this bit of Swampy Creek.'

'Where will they move you?' She waved away the flies now buzzing around her face.

'Anywhere but here.'

'I see.' Indeed she saw only too clearly. Apart from the dump, this was good land and some farmer was bound to want it, and to get rid of its present occupants. The Aboriginal workers were good for picking. They were cheap and willing to work twelve-hour days in the season. But the season only lasted three months, so they weren't needed for the rest of the year.

Driving back through Burford, she pulled into the grounds of the district hospital on an impulse. Maybe no one had seen the Hunters because there'd been an accident, or perhaps a family illness. After eventually finding a parking space, she locked the car and headed into the main entrance. The hall was dark after the harsh sunlight, and reeked of floor polish and disinfectant overlaid with a faint odour of cabbage.

The woman at the desk looked up reluctantly from her paperwork. 'Visiting hours aren't until two o'clock,' she said, peering at Ilona over the top of half-moon spectacles.

'I'm not here to visit anyone. I want to find out if a friend was hospitalised recently.'

'How recently?'

'Any time over the past year.'

'That's a long time. Not a close friend then. What was the name?'

'Tommy or Molly Hunter.'

'Tommy *or* Molly. Not both?'

'No.'

'You'll need to be a bit more specific than that. You need to know which. But anyway I can't release that sort of confidential information, not unless you're family.'

'The Hunters are Aborigines.'

'I see,' the woman said, inspecting Ilona more closely. 'Not relatives then, I suppose. Your accent isn't from around here anyway, is it? New Australian, aren't you? Don't get many of those around here, though there are plenty up Cooma way with the Hydro scheme.'

'I've been here for years. Mrs Vincent's the name.' She wasn't going to expose her first name to be judged by this woman. 'The Hunters are missing and no one knows where they are.'

'Well, you should go to the police for missing persons, not the hospital. Report it there and they'll let you know. But the Abos are always going missing. A shiftless lot. Walkabout, they call it. Not working for you, are they?'

'No. They're friends.'

'I see. Well, try the police station, dear. There's nothing

more I can do to help.' With that, the woman went back to her paperwork.

Back at the car, Ilona kicked the front tyre hard to vent her frustration.

'Glad that's not me you're kicking, love.'

So irritated was she by her encounter that she hadn't noticed the burly young man weeding the garden bed next to the car. 'I'm glad too,' she said. 'You look as if you could give a pretty hard kick back.'

'Never to the ladies,' he said, grinning. 'You've got a bit of style there, but. Maybe we should sign you up to the local footie team.'

'I'll bear that in mind,' she said, managing a laugh. 'I'll be turning up next season for the trials.'

On the drive back to Jingera, she thought about the morning's encounters. The police wouldn't be the slightest bit interested in the Hunters, she knew. The Aborigines were people to be moved on, people to be shunted out of town by six o'clock unless they had a piece of paper to show they were deserving. People to be avoided, or to be locked up if you couldn't do that.

Tracking down the Hunters wasn't going to be easy. Her hopes of finding Lorna's family before Christmas were beginning to evaporate.

CHAPTER 11

The following morning, Jim hung around with Andy at the edge of the lagoon, hoping Hairy Harry would turn up so they could hire a canoe. Eventually, one of the O'Rourke tribe, heading towards the footbridge over the lagoon, said he'd seen Harry having a liquid lunch at the pub. That was when they decided to give up. Andy didn't want to surf and Jim didn't want to swim in the lagoon, so they mooched around, kicking a rock up and down the street. There was no one around, although most of the summer cottages were let out. Everyone must be on the beach; there was certainly a small forest of beach umbrellas planted on the sand, and stick-like figures darted in and out of the waves.

At that moment Andy kicked the rock so hard that it clanged against the hub cap of a car parked a few yards away. Immediately a cottage door opened, and a man in singlet and shorts came out.

'You throwing rocks at my car?'

'No, it just accidentally hit the tyre. Sorry. No damage done.' Andy smiled in that ingratiating way of his and removed his canvas hat as if paying his respects. Thickened by salt from an early morning swim, his sun-bleached hair stood up like straw.

Jim, not yet used to his younger brother being almost the same height as he was, noticed for the first time that his skinny limbs looked oddly stretched and out of proportion to his knobbly joints.

Singlet man was unaffected by Andy's winning smile and doffed hat. After inspecting the hub caps, he walked around his car again, checking the duco. 'You'd better kick your stone somewhere else,' he said finally.

'Sure thing.' Andy picked up the rock and he and Jim strolled up the hill. Thirty yards on, Andy turned around. Singlet man was still watching.

'Don't do it,' Jim warned.

He was too late. Andy's arm circled so quickly it formed a disc in the air and the rock shot forward. At the same moment there was a resounding ping from the metal sign forbidding speedboats. 'Out for a duck, I reckon,' Andy said, grinning. 'Got to keep up the cricket practice, even though it's not term time.'

'You're looking for trouble, Andy. Lucky you didn't get a canoe or a car.'

'Nah. Just can't resist a good target.'

'Or an audience.'

They wandered up the hill, and followed the road leading up to the headland. The primary school had in front of it a freshly painted sign, *Jingera Public School, Established 1890*. A new row of trees, shrouded in plastic against the children and the winter winds, stood sentinel around the edge of the playground. Although the former school mistress, Miss Neville, had moved to Sydney at the same time as Jim, to him she would be forever associated with this building. He'd visited her in Sydney a few times, even stayed with her for one of his free weekends, in the terrace house she shared with Mrs Bates.

He owed his Stambroke College scholarship to her. Without her efforts he would never have sat for the exam, and never have topped it either.

Now Jim and Andy wandered across to the far side of the cemetery on the top of the headland. Beyond the white painted fence bordering the graveyard, a narrow track led under twisted shrubs and along the cliff edge, before dropping to a ledge below. The ocean was spread out in front of them.

Jim took off his hat and massaged his head. The slight headache he'd woken up with that morning had almost completely gone. This was the second day of the school holidays and the second morning he'd slept in until nine o'clock. He might have slept in even longer if his mother hadn't routed him out.

Andy now pulled a crumpled packet of cigarettes out of the pocket of his shorts and lit one. He sucked hard at it and afterwards coughed so much that Jim had to bang him on the back.

'How long have you been smoking these things? Mum will kill you if she finds out. Dad too.' Jim had to speak loudly to be heard above the breakers crashing onto the rocks below them.

'She won't find out. Dad wouldn't mind, he's smoked a fair few in his time. Anyway, he never notices anything I do. He's only interested in what *you* do. I could fall off this cliff or win the lottery or be selected to play for Australia in the Ashes and he wouldn't bat an eyelid. He'd just pat me on the back and say "Well done, son," and carry on with whatever he was up to.'

Jim knew there was some legitimacy to this, but said, 'He was really proud of your woodwork prize. He talked about that for ages on the train trip home.' This was untrue, he'd mentioned it briefly once. Jim hadn't wanted to enquire about it because he knew the table was to be a Christmas present.

'He didn't even ask me what I'd made. After I told him I'd come top, out came the standard response. "Well done, son" without even a question about what it was. Don't you think he'd be curious about that, even if he does think I'm not that bright? You'd think he'd want to encourage me to do something I'm good at. And it's a beautiful table.' Andy stubbed out his cigarette and stared gloomily out to sea.

Jim hadn't seen the table yet. Mr Blake, the woodwork teacher at Burford Boys' High, had agreed to mind it for Andy until closer to Christmas. He said, 'Dad's proud of the shed. That was a terrific idea of yours, to open up one wall and put the telescope on rails. He'd never have thought of that on his own and neither would I. And he uses it all the time. Mum told me that every clear night, he's out there in the garden, pushing the telescope up and down the track.'

Andy's face took on a tender look. 'Staring at the night sky,' he said. 'It doesn't take much to make the old man happy, Jim. I'd do anything to get him to smile but he just doesn't seem to notice me. He was pleased about the shed and that made me glad, but he didn't give me much credit for it. It's as if anything I do or say he discounts because I've done it and not you. He just doesn't think much of me, never has. And I won't be able to change that, no matter what.'

After a while, Andy continued. 'I want to leave Burford High, Jim. I can't take it anymore. It's not just Dad, it's everything. I feel so shut in here, and I'm not much good at lessons. One of the teachers told me about the Army Apprentices' scheme. He reckons I could get in. They take you at the minimum school-leaving age, that's fourteen. I sent off for some information last week. Carpentry and joinery, that's what I'd really like to do.'

'In the army, though?'

'Yeah, why not? They cover all the trades. I'd join the army to do my apprenticeship, and then I'd serve it out for a few years.'

'How long?'

'Nine years altogether.'

'That's a long time, Andy. Mum would hate it.'

'Dad wouldn't though. He served in the war, don't forget. He'd be really proud of me.'

'Does he know?'

'Not yet.'

Jim chewed his thumbnail while he thought this over. It wasn't just that Andy needed to get away, he wanted to do something his father approved of too. Their father sometimes talked about the war as if his time in the army in the Northern Territory had been a great adventure, yet that wouldn't necessarily mean he'd want his son to join up. Joining the army certainly made sense twenty years ago when the Germans were rattling around Europe and the Japanese threatening Australia and the Pacific, but it didn't seem to now. Jim remembered the Communist threat that was reported in the newspapers. 'What if there's another war?' he said.

'Unlikely. Anyway, if there is I'll see a bit of the world. And it's not like I'd be carrying a gun. Only a hammer and chisel.' He laughed.

'Or a hammer and *sickle*, that's the Communist flag. I'm not sure about this, Andy. Melbourne's a long way away.'

'So is Sydney, Jimmo, and it doesn't bother you.'

'But it's in the opposite direction.'

'I know, but what else can I do? An apprenticeship in Burford? What's the future in that? Anyway Mum thinks I should stay on at Burford High rather than go to the Tech there. It's not much good, she says. And if I did go there, she'd worry about money because my apprenticeship wages wouldn't cover my board, but the Army Apprentices' scheme pays wages *and* board. It would be beaut, Jimmo. Just like you at boarding school.'

For an instant Jim wished this had all been decided before he came home. There could be rows all through the holidays once Andy mentioned it, just like all those arguments between his parents when he'd sat for the scholarship and afterwards. But he was being selfish. This probably was the right choice for Andy to make.

Yet a void began to open up inside him as he realised that this could well be the last summer they would spend together. He gazed at the four headlands to the north, layered like cardboard cut-outs and receding into a distant haze from which Mount Dromedary rose. He'd thought he would be the first to leave Jingera permanently and that Andy would always be here. Not just next year and the years after but right into the future: Cadwallader and Son, Quality Meats. There was continuity there.

Though now he thought of it, there'd never been any mention of such a venture and he couldn't imagine his father and Andy working together. It had been an assumption that he'd made about Andy's future and it had been wrong. He wondered how many other assumptions he'd been making that he didn't even notice, let alone question. That Jingera was the best place in the world? That he'd be Dux of Stambroke next year? That Andy didn't resent his successes?

CHAPTER 12

'Don't slam the car door!' Ilona called to Zidra, but it was too late.

'Need to tell her before, not after,' Peter said, flinching slightly.

'Sorry, Ma.' Zidra grinned through the car window and adjusted her sunhat. She had a striped beach bag slung over one shoulder and a patch of white zinc cream on her nose that Ilona felt sure would be wiped off as soon as she was out of sight.

Sally Hargreaves was already waiting near the post office. 'Isn't it a lovely day!' she said. 'Hairy Harry's renting his canoes this morning, so I thought we could take one out.'

'I'll need some extra money, Mama,' said Zidra.

Ilona dug into her handbag to find a few coins. 'See you at four, Zidra,' she said. 'And don't go wandering off if we're a bit late back.'

'Give my love to the Chapmans and Mrs Jones,' Zidra called. Mrs Jones was the housekeeper at Woodlands, with whom Zidra had struck up a close friendship in the days when Ilona gave Philip Chapman piano lessons there.

Getting to Woodlands was now a very different experience, Ilona reflected. Before marrying Peter, she was chauffeured in the Woodlands' car. Afterwards, Peter drove her but today she was chauffeuring Peter, and soon they would be sweeping up the drive in the Armstrong. The advantage of gravel was that one could *sweep* at any speed, even as low as ten miles an hour. Ilona was enjoying the driving now that Peter had stopped giving such intricate instructions, and she was beginning to feel more confident. She was starting to love the old car almost as much as he did; its smell of leather, the way it handled, the long bonnet stretching in front of her, and all that shiny chrome.

The road snaked ahead of them, up through the low hills, greener than she'd ever seen them after the recent rain. Soon she would turn to the right, at the sign for Woodlands, and over a cattle grid. The dirt road would wind up the hill and over the rise and at that moment they would see the dense trees crowding around the homestead and, behind them, the escarpment. Peter would say, as he always did at this point, Wiley's Woollen Mills meet Woodlands Stud Farm. No sign of the woollen mills, she'd said the first time, and he'd replied that you mightn't see them but they're still here, providing a lot of the *dosh* to maintain the stud farm.

Once they arrived at Woodlands, Peter would vanish with Jack Chapman somewhere down by the stockyards. Judy Chapman would kiss Ilona, the standard form of greeting since she'd married Peter, and would soon retire with a book to the breakfast room. After that Ilona would make her own way into the drawing room.

Today Philip didn't notice her opening the door. Bathed in a shaft of sunlight angling through the French windows, he might have been spotlit on stage. Sitting at the grand piano, he was playing a dark piece she'd never heard before. She stopped, unwilling to interrupt his concentration. That a ten-year-old could play so well did not surprise her. At the Conservatorium in Riga, where she'd learnt the piano, there were many gifted young musicians. It was the ferocity that he brought to the music that moved her, that anguish in his soul. Only when he'd finished playing did he look up.

'S-s-s-sorry. D-d-didn't s-s-s-see y-y-you.'

She held out her arms, and he ran into them. After smoothing his short fair hair, she gently pushed him away from her in order to take his long-fingered hands in her own. His hands had grown much larger and it would be easier for him now to play more ambitious pieces. 'You look different,' she said. 'Older of course; it's been four months or so since I saw you last. It must be the hair.'

'I c-c-c-cut it . . . l-l-later M-m-mummy t-t-took me to her h-h-hairdresser.'

She laughed but immediately regretted it when she saw the hurt expression on his face. She guessed that he'd been teased at school and that was making him look so guarded. Of course he should never have been allowed to attend with longish hair. Those thick blond curls combined with the delicate features of his mother, and the full red lips, made him appear quite girlish. Judy Chapman had other ideas, though. The curls made him look so *distingué,* she'd said.

To distract Philip, Ilona began to talk about what she'd been doing. How she was driving a lot nowadays, because Peter had become fed up with it, and that he preferred to ride a horse rather than sit behind a steering wheel. And how bad she was at riding; the first time she got onto the horse Peter had bought for her, Zidra's horse Starless Star had sauntered up to her and bitten her on the thigh. If that wasn't bad enough, only a week ago, when she'd been walking across one of the further paddocks where she normally never went, she'd twisted her ankle in a wombat hole. While it wasn't a serious injury, it had left a tremendous bruise, and here she exhibited the yellow and purple mark on her ankle. Consequently, she hadn't been able to drive for a few days and they'd missed the Christmas dance. She'd thought that Zidra would care about that, but she'd actually been pleased because there was some boy from Burford High School pestering her. Anyway she hated jiving, or at least that's what she'd said, although having collected her from a party only two weeks ago, and seeing her whizzing around the floor, she herself thought otherwise.

Here Ilona paused for breath and struggled to think of what else she could say that wouldn't require more than a nod of the head in response. Her monologue seemed to have made Philip slightly more at ease. Although not exactly smiling, he no longer looked as if he might weep. 'Perhaps you'd like to play something for me,' she said.

'I've wr-written a . . .' and there was a long pause as he struggled with the next word, '. . . s-song.'

'How lovely,' she said. In the days before Philip went to Stambroke College, she'd spent time coaching him in singing. His stuttering was virtually non-existent when he sang, although whether this was through the altered vocalisation process or his familiarity with the music she couldn't tell. 'Is it your own composition? Just nod or shake your head.'

He nodded.

'I'll lie on the couch and rest my ankle while I listen.' Slipping off her shoes, she stretched out on the dark green brocade chaise longue. Philip found a cushion for her to lean against and she smiled at him. He seemed tense again. Probably worried that she wouldn't like his music. He sat at the piano and played through a few bars before beginning to sing in a clear steady voice.

Night after night after night after night,
Once the house master has turned off the light,
Boys from the year ahead
Start to climb out of bed.

Philip Chapman's the one they seek.
It happens at least once a week.
Down the toilet they stick his head
After that they pee on his bed.

Now son Philip wants to be dead
Keep him here at Woodlands instead.

Horrified, Ilona sat up and patted the sofa next to her. 'Does that really happen to you, Philip?'

Nodding, he sat down beside her.

'I understand the song, Philip. It's for your parents.'

'M-m-mummy.'

The song was a clever way of getting Judy's attention, communicating verbally without the clutter of the stuttering. Although there was writing too, of course. Perhaps he should write out the song as a poem.

Gently she began to ask questions but soon stopped because he was crying too much. She took his thin body in her arms and held him close, while rocking him to and fro. Staying on at Stambroke was madness for such a sensitive boy. People in institutions didn't tolerate differences, but it was tolerance that allowed talent to flourish. Boarding wasn't for everyone. Ilona looked at the delicate planes of his face, still pale in spite of the intensity of his grief. Although unblemished, he was not unscarred. Tenderly she began to suggest what he might write in a letter to his parents that could accompany the poem. Smiling at her now, he appeared almost like the boy she'd known before he'd been sent away.

But this might not be enough, she knew. After kissing Philip goodbye, she knocked at the door of the breakfast room. Judy was curled up in the only armchair and waved Ilona to one of the chairs arranged around the table.

'I need to talk to you about Philip.'

'Terribly talented, isn't he? We're so lucky Stambroke arranged lessons at the Conservatorium. We'd never be able to get someone locally as good as that. Oh, sorry, darling, I didn't mean to cause offence. You've been absolutely marvellous to Philip over the years, and it's thanks to you that he's got as far as he has.'

'Thank you. No offence taken. He's a gifted boy, and there's nothing more I can teach him.'

'But there's something you wanted?'

'Yes. Philip seems very unhappy and –'

'Unhappy?' Judy snapped, before Ilona could finish speaking. 'He's delighted to be home again, I can tell you. He was badgering us for days to leave the Hotel Australia and get home to Woodlands. He adores it here. I would have preferred to stay on in Sydney for a bit longer, but we came home earlier just for his sake. We are *martyrs* to his happiness.'

'I was going to say that he's very unhappy at Stambroke College, not at Woodlands.' Although Ilona had guessed that this conversation wouldn't be easy, it was turning out to be even more difficult than she'd imagined. She continued. 'It's clear he's being bullied there and for a boy with his sensitive soul it must be quite dreadful for him. Also his stutter cannot make it easy for him to defend himself.'

Judy made a face. 'Oh, I see, that's what you're worried

about.' It was unclear what irritated her more, the sensitive soul or the stuttering; or perhaps it was simply Ilona's tactlessness in drawing her attention to both. 'His father did tell me he was teased a bit last term, the poor darling. But that's life for you, Ilona. You have to be trained to withstand the hard knocks of this world, Jack says, and there's no better place for that than at a boys' school. Although of course my heart bleeds for poor Philip, I simply cannot get Jack to change his mind. He went there himself, you see.'

Ilona wondered if Judy had even tried. She put about the story that she adored her son, but the adoration didn't extend to spending much time with him. It was far more conducive to her social life to have him at Stambroke College, giving her an excuse to spend time in Sydney. 'I think it's doing him real psychological damage.'

'Nonsense, darling. It's character building, surely you can see that. Anyway, and I know you'll forgive me being so outspoken, I really don't think it's any of your business, do you? I don't tell you how to bring up Zidra, nor should you tell us how to educate Philip. I invited you here not only because we simply love to see you and Peter, such dear friends both of you, but also because I know how much Philip adores you. But I certainly don't want to be lectured by you. Philip just experienced a bit of teasing last term, a bit of good-natured fun. And next year, all will have been forgotten.'

At this moment she looked out of the window, distracted by the car that was now pulling up in front of the house. Her relief was obvious. 'Oh, here are the first of our guests arriving for the weekend. Was that all you wanted to tell me, darling?'

Ilona could hardly trust herself to speak, so angry did she feel at this diminution of poor Philip's anguish. 'Perhaps you will listen though, when he tells you himself.'

'Of course, Ilona. I always listen,' Judy said, standing up so that Ilona felt compelled to do the same. 'I really must go now, darling, and welcome our guests,' Judy continued. 'They telephoned only last night to say they'd be arriving early. It was so good of you to make time to come and see us this morning in your busy routine. Dear Philip does appreciate your visits hugely. You must come again soon. No hard feelings, I promise you. I know you mean well.'

There was to be no occasion to speak to Jack Chapman alone. He and Peter were already talking to the guests, a smart-looking middle-aged couple.

Although Ilona told Peter about what had happened on the way home in the car, he had no further advice to offer her, only his reassurance that she'd done the best she could. 'In a way, Judy is right,' he added afterwards. 'He's their child, and they make decisions about him.'

'I thought they mightn't know about what's been happening to him, yet clearly they do.'

'I don't think there's anything more that we can do. But that's a terrific idea of yours to invite him to come and stay with us for a few days.'

My heart bleeds for poor Philip. Maybe Judy had meant those silver words that slid so easily off her tongue, although Ilona doubted that she meant them for more than a few minutes. Ilona felt she'd failed in making Judy see the harm that Stambroke was doing to her son. *A bit of good-natured fun* might be all right for a boy of robust disposition but not for Philip.

Perhaps the boy's poem would melt Judy's heart, Ilona thought, as she navigated the car around the hairpin bends before Jingera. Surely a mother couldn't fail to be moved by it.

CHAPTER 13

If you had to choose a single moment to capture the essence of a summer morning, this would be it, Jim decided. The sky was an enamelled blue, cicadas thrummed against the distant pounding of the surf, and he could smell the scent of newly mown grass and feel the warm sun on his skin. Sauntering up the hill towards the town square, he saw Zidra's mother in front of the war memorial. Even though she'd been Mrs Vincent for years now, he still thought of her as The Talivaldis. That was the name he'd come up with when she and Zidra had first arrived in Jingera: the *Spotted or Herbaceous Talivaldis,* the sort of name you'd find in a book of exotic birds. That suited her better than plain old Mrs Vincent, he thought.

Wearing a purple dress with orange flowers printed on it, she was now gazing intently at the names inscribed on the obelisk.

'Hello, Mrs Vincent,' he called.

'Good morning, Jim,' she said, straightening up. 'Come and look at all the names here – five Peabody boys killed in the First World War. The entire male side of that family must have been wiped out. Have you ever met a Peabody from this area?'

'Never.' Jim looked at the names engraved in gold lettering on the polished grey granite. He hadn't noticed before that there were so many Peabody deaths although he'd often read the long list of names on the sides of the obelisk, the casualties from two world wars. Had recognised most of them too – the Beatties and the McGraths and the Kirbys and the Leighs – families who still lived locally.

After blowing her nose loudly, The Talivaldis returned the handkerchief to the pocket of her skirt. Her fair hair, loosely pinned up at the back of her head, was escaping from its constraints and falling in wisps around her face.

'How's your foot?' he asked.

She held it out for his inspection. There was a dark greenish-yellow mark around the outside of her bare ankle. For the first time he noticed what shapely legs she had, just like her daughter.

'The bruise has almost gone,' she said. 'Peter said I was lucky not to break it. It kept me out of action for a few days though. I thought twice before I walked anywhere but it's better now. So tell me, Jim, what are you up to over the holidays?'

'Just hanging around, mostly. Andy and I are fixing the chook-yard next week. One of my school friends, Eric Hall, is coming to stay for the last week of the holidays.'

'That will be lovely for you both,' she said. 'Is he from Sydney?'

'No, he's from a property near Walgett.' Seeing her blank look, he added, 'That's in north-western New South Wales.'

'*Beyond the black stump,*' she said.

He liked the way she pulled out these colloquialisms as if they were some novelty. '*Out at woop woop,*' he responded.

'I haven't heard that one before,' she said, smiling.

'Did Zidra come to town with you today?' Jim avoided looking at The Talivaldis while he asked this.

'No. She caught the bus into Burford. She's doing her Christmas shopping.'

I could have gone with her, Jim thought, if she'd bothered to let me know. It seemed he always phoned her, never the other way around. He kicked rather harder than warranted at a pebble on the pavement and stubbed his toe.

It now appeared that The Talivaldis was thinking of something else, for her expression was slightly distracted and her brown eyes looked through him rather than at him. 'Zidra would have told you about our trip to Wallaga Lake,' she said.

'Yes, she told me the day after I got home.'

'Wallaga Lake is so very beautiful,' she said, 'but the Reserve upset me too, and it wasn't only because we didn't find the Hunters. In fact, I still haven't been able to find out where they are. You will phone me, won't you Jim, if you hear anything about them?'

After he promised, just as he'd promised Zidra, she continued. 'Afterwards I realised what disturbed me about the place. We read in the newspapers about apartheid in South Africa and we condemn it, or the liberal-minded among us do. Yet we have a similar system operating right here on our doorstep. We just don't notice it because there are so few Aborigines around, but it's here all the same.'

'There are lots of Aborigines at Walgett,' Jim said. 'They live in camps. I saw them when I went to stay with the Halls last summer holidays.' He'd been unprepared to see so many of them and the squalor in which they lived. They were a strong presence – in the shanties by the river, in the streets. But they were an absence too. Absent from certain areas, banned from certain areas – some of the shops, the hotels, even the town swimming pool.

'Why?' he'd asked Eric at the time.

'Don't know,' Eric had said. 'Never really thought about it. Just the way it is, I suppose.'

Just the way it is. But you needed to question the way things were. The Talivaldis was always asking why. That was partly because she was foreign and had a different slant on things but she also had a curious mind. Jim was supposed to be clever but he wasn't questioning enough. He should work on his critical faculties more. It was no good coming top of everything, pulling out the answers that everyone wanted to hear. He had to learn to do more than that. He had to learn to question everything in order to try to understand it.

At this point, he noticed his mother coming out of the general store next to the post office, with Mrs Llewellyn, the wife of the man who ran the pub. Mrs Llewellyn was large-boned and hearty. Her short grey hair looked as if it could be taken on and off like a beanie. It was rumoured that she used to like a drop or two, and this was why Taffy Llewellyn never let her near the bar. Got to keep the old girl away from temptation, he'd confided to someone not long after they'd first arrived, a secret that had spread rapidly through the town. This didn't reduce attendance at the Brownies' group she'd started up though, or so Jim's mother had reported.

The two women strolled across the square towards Jim and The Talivaldis, still standing by the war memorial. That his mother and The Talivaldis had become quite friendly had at first surprised him. Once she used to call Zidra and her mother the reffos, along with the rest of the town, but she'd forgotten all about that after they'd changed their name to Vincent. He guessed that she was suspicious of anything new, but when it was no longer novel she would incorporate it unquestioningly into the fabric of her everyday life.

After greetings had been exchanged, his mother surprised him further by saying, 'Would you both like to pop in for a cup of tea? I was about to go home and make some.'

'Thank you, Eileen. I'd love to.'

'I'd love to as well, but I've got to supervise Taffy supervising the kitchenhand,' said Mrs Llewellyn with a smile.

Soon after, Mrs Llewellyn returned to the hotel, while Jim's mother and The Talivaldis headed off for what The Talivaldis was now referring to as a *cuppa*. For a moment Jim watched the two of them, Zidra's mother with her shopping basket and that clashing purple and orange frock, and his mother in her floral dress of muted tones of blue.

Adults alter too; this thought came to him like a revelation. He'd grown up conscious of his own development but with a lack of awareness that his parents were also changing. Only now did it occur to him that they would be maturing just as he was, and that this would continue to happen. He'd observed only the small physical changes in his parents: some new wrinkles, a few more white hairs among the dark, his father's hair receding. Yet there would also be an evolution in their thinking and in their views of the world, of which he was unaware. Everything was in a state of flux. Not even memories were fixed points.

The crying of two seagulls swooping low overhead interrupted Jim's reverie. He strolled across to the post office to buy a stamp for his letter and joined the queue of people waiting to be served by Mrs Blunkett. After this he'd go to the library at the front of the church hall that was open two days a week. He'd ordered a book from the Burford library that was supposed to be coming in that morning.

As Jim came out of the post office, he saw Sally Hargreaves walking up the hill from the lagoon. He'd met her a few days ago on the footbridge leading to the beach. He and Andy had been heading to the beach and she and Zidra had already been swimming, but they'd stopped to talk for a few minutes. He'd liked the way she laughed a lot, as if everything he said was funny. He stopped now, and waited for her to catch up. Her dark silky hair fell over her bare shoulders and her sundress was a pale shade of green. She was even prettier than he'd remembered.

'Hello, Sally.'

'Hello, Jim.'

After this exchange he could think of nothing more to say and neither, apparently, could she. It had been easy to talk to her the other day when Zidra and Andy had been present. If only Zidra were here now. Desperately he scoured his mind for a topic.

'Lovely day,' he said.

'Sure is.'

There was another pause, which stretched and stretched. Searching for something to say, he remembered his earlier exchange with The Talivaldis. 'Come and have a look at this,' he said. 'All the Peabody names on the war memorial.'

Conversation flowed without much difficulty after that, although nowhere near as effortlessly as it did with Zidra or her mother. That was only because he'd known them longer. Or perhaps the real reason was that he was too easily distracted by Sally's looks that, he now decided, were the acme of female beauty.

Only later in the library did he begin to think of the witty anecdotes he might have told her but hadn't. At that moment he remembered the phrase they'd learnt in French last term, *l'esprit d'escalier*. The conversation you think of on the way out when the occasion is already behind you.

With several books under his arm, he headed home. The lounge-room door was open and he was surprised to hear that The Talivaldis was still talking to his mother. Stopping outside the door to the bedroom he shared with Andy, he listened for a moment to their conversation. The Talivaldis was describing the system of apartheid in South Africa and was further developing the arguments she'd made to him earlier. So eloquent was she that she might have been giving a lecture. This proselytising was not a side of her character that he'd noticed before.

'Well, how would you improve things for the Aborigines?' his mother now asked.

'Better housing, better education, better integration. That would be a start.'

'But suppose they don't want to be integrated?'

'Ah, their different culture and the different rhythms,' The Talivaldis mused. 'And different insights. Can we not learn from that?'

'Different hygiene too. They're filthy.'

'That's only a few of them and it comes from poverty. And exploitation.'

'How can lack of hygiene come from exploitation? Anyway, I've never exploited anyone in my life.'

'Don't take it personally. We can't generalise from one case – you!'

Jim held his breath, waiting for an explosion from his mother, but there was only silence.

'We've taken their land from them, Eileen. Their livelihood and their self-respect. And what have we given them in return? Nothing but disease and alienation. We've got a lot to apologise for. Not you personally, but all of us.' There was a pause. 'But I must go now. I mustn't hold you up anymore and I've got some more errands to run. I have enjoyed talking to you. It's sharpened up my ideas.'

'Like a sounding board.'

The Talivaldis laughed. 'You make me see flaws in my arguments and that leads me to make improvements.'

'Always improvements,' his mother said. 'You're like Jim. But sometimes in this world you just have to make do with second best.'

At the sound of teacups being placed on a tray, Jim dumped all the library books but one on his bed, before swiftly heading into the back garden. He made straight for that favourite spot: the little hollow under the figtree where he couldn't be seen from the house. Despite opening the library book, he didn't read it. He was puzzled by his mother's comment about making do with second best. What could she mean? Was it Jingera? She'd always seemed reasonably content with her life here, apart from the shopping, or lack of it. Somehow he doubted it was him or Andy. While she favoured Andy more than him, she would not view either as second best. Surely she couldn't mean Dad. He would do just about anything for her. And he was a good man, straightforward and honest. She just didn't appreciate him enough.

While a seed of doubt had been planted in his fertile mind, he didn't pay any more heed to it for there were other more pressing things to dwell on. Not his library book, certainly, although it was the one about the Copernican revolution that he'd been waiting so eagerly to read. Instead he began to think again of Sally Hargreaves, and her dark-lashed eyes that were the colour of the sky at midday.

CHAPTER 14

Ilona sat in the car and sorted through the mail. Ten Christmas cards, mostly from Peter's old friends, and three were from people to whom they hadn't sent anything. There was a postcard too; a brightly coloured postcard, a cartoon picture of a small child in a stroller. Running across the top of the card was the message in yellow letters, *Be Good To Your Mother*. Turning it over, she saw the Gudgiegalah postmark, and a few words scrawled in block letters in what had to be Lorna's hand:

IT'S STILL ON. HURRAH FOR ST ANDREWS SUNDAY SCHOOL!

And hurrah for this part of the Jervis Bay trip being sorted out, Ilona thought, smiling. It was such a clever card for Lorna to pick. Being good to your mother was the last thing the people at the Gudgiegalah Girls' Home would want. Forgetting your mother was their goal.

Only now did she remember that she should have asked Mrs Blunkett if she knew where the Hunters were. She'd thought of that on the drive into town and had somehow forgotten it during her various conversations and errands, to the butcher, the mechanic and the post office. That would have to wait until the next time she came into Jingera; the post office had just shut for lunch.

Once Mrs Blunket knew she was looking for the Hunters, it wouldn't be long before the whole town would know. Soon after that there would surely be news of their whereabouts.

Yet there were fewer than six weeks to go before the Jervis Bay trip and so far she'd made no progress whatsoever in finding Lorna's family. No one had seen them. No one had heard of where they might be.

<hr />

As Jim and Andy came out of their front gate, Jim heard his name being called, and saw Zidra running down the hill towards them. He felt his spirits lift; seeing Zidra always had that effect. Now he'd be able to give her the present that he'd hidden in his sock drawer so Andy wouldn't comment.

'Glad I've caught you,' Zidra said, puffing slightly. She was holding a basket awkwardly behind her, and Jim knew better than to ask why. 'I've only got a few minutes,' she added. 'Mama's going to be in a terrible hurry to get home once the pump spare part arrives at Kirby's Service Depot. She said she's leaving then with or without me.'

Andy grinned and winked at Jim before making himself scarce. This winking whenever Jim spoke to a girl was one of the few things about Andy that really irritated Jim. His brother just couldn't seem to comprehend that you could have girls as friends, rather than girlfriends. It was especially annoying when Andy knew that Zidra was like a sister to Jim. Or a brother: Zidra, the honorary boy. Although maybe she no longer wanted to be thought of as a tomboy – that would explain the pink pearlescent polish on her toenails.

'What are you grinning about?' Zidra said.

'Just thinking how glad I am you turned up. I've got your Christmas present inside. Give me two seconds.'

It had become a tradition that Jim and Zidra exchanged gifts on Christmas Eve. When he returned with the small parcel, she'd removed her hand from behind her back and was holding out a package, wrapped in red-and-yellow-striped paper.

'Let's swap,' she said, smiling. 'What's in yours?'

'You can open it now and find out.'

'Are you sure?'

'Yes, if you'd like to. I want to see your face.' That was the only way to make sure it was what she wanted. Her emotions were transparent to him, he thought. He'd known her for so long he could tell right away if she was displeased or delighted, regardless of what words she might use.

With difficulty she tore off the wrapping paper. 'Too much sellotape,' she said. 'I won't be able to use this paper again next Christmas.' She held up the box inside. 'Chocolates,' she said, and he could tell she was surprised. 'How lovely.'

'No,' he said quickly. 'Open the box. It's just for protection.'

She lifted the chocolate box lid. Inside was another box, narrow and long. He watched her face light up. 'It's a fountain pen, a Sheaffer! Oh Jim, how did you guess this is exactly what I wanted!' With trembling fingers she pulled out the navy blue pen with its gold lid and her name engraved in copperplate lettering on the side. 'It's beautiful,' she said, taking off the cap. 'Thank you. What a lovely design for the nib. The top bit runs right up the shaft, so the nib looks diamond-shaped.'

'For your writing,' he said, embarrassed now by her enthusiasm.

She laughed. 'Of course. What else for? Not for stirring my tea, is that what you're telling me? I'll write to you with it, and use it for my essays. Now it's your turn.'

His parcel was a little larger. It also seemed to be a box of some description, and when he turned it over it rattled loudly.

'You'll never guess what it is.'

Though tempted to suggest it was a box, after glancing at her eager face and glowing dark eyes he refrained from doing so. Quickly he removed the wrapping paper, to reveal a black lacquered container with five brightly coloured figures painted on the top. A regal figure sat on a raised platform and appeared to be sniffing a rose, while four courtiers looked on. 'What a beaut present!' he said. 'Where's it from?'

'The opportunity shop in Burford. I saw it there the other day and thought it would be just right for you. Mama thinks it's either Chinese or Middle Eastern. The box looks Chinese but the figure on the dais looks a bit like a Turkish sultan.'

'It's perfect.' And it was, so much so that he felt almost moved to tears. It was a lovely exotic thing, unlike any gift he'd ever received before.

'Open it.'

He lifted the lid of the box and laughed when he glimpsed what was inside: the largest gumnut he'd ever seen, it must have been at least an inch across. 'Where did this come from?'

'Dad's stock and station agent friend brought some back from Western Australia. I kept one for myself, and this one's for you.'

'It's magnificent. What lovely presents, Zidra. Thank you so much.' He lifted the box to inspect the frieze around its base. A few hares and deer were shown lolloping between trees, and behind them reared a range of mountains.

'You can store pencils inside it.'

'Yes.' But he wouldn't, he'd keep letters in it. It was just the right size for envelopes. He'd put Zidra's letters in it, and the letters from his parents and Andy, and maybe in the future there'd even be a postcard from Sally. At that moment he glanced up the road and caught sight of The Talivaldis waving frantically from the square.

'Better go,' Zidra said at the sight of her mother.

She turned and ran up the hill, fast and graceful. Holding his box in the empty street, Jim stared after her. At the top of the street, she turned and waved, and Jim raised a hand in farewell. Why he should abruptly feel sad puzzled him.

An image sprang into his mind of Zidra going into the Burford opportunity shop. Maybe her attention had been caught by the beautiful black lacquered box in the window; or perhaps she'd discovered it in the back of the shop, tucked behind junk or under a pile of used clothing. How like her to have found something out of the ordinary, even in Burford. He wondered how the box had got there. It looked quite old. Maybe its owners had brought it back from China, or from Turkey years ago, perhaps after a business trip selling or buying maize or wheat or whatever. They'd loved the box and kept their treasures in it, and when they'd died their relatives had passed it on, finding no worth in it. And it had sat for years in the back of the op shop until Zidra had wandered in and seen right away that it was right for Jim.

Though he'd given a lot of thought to the present he'd bought her, a fountain pen certainly wasn't exotic. Even the very special one he'd chosen after learning of Zidra's ambition to be a journalist. Of course reporters used typewriters rather than fountain pens, but his gift was more of a symbol. And also, he had to admit, an encouragement for her to keep writing letters to him. He'd given her something to write essays and letters with, and she'd given him a box in which to keep letters. There was something nicely complementary about that.

CHAPTER 15

Christmas Eve at the Vincent household would be the way Zidra had always known it, and as it had been at the Talivaldis household before. Late dinner, and then reading and listening to Christmas music on the radio or gramophone. Zidra predicted that her mother would play Mozart's Requiem tonight. A new recording had arrived and would be decreed suitable for the occasion in spite of its more sombre purpose.

Someone had already switched on the lights of the Christmas tree in the living room. There were no presents laid out there for her to inspect or feel though. After returning from Jingera that afternoon, she'd rewrapped the fountain pen that Jim had given her and she now lay this under the tree. It was one of the best things she'd ever received. That and Jim's reaction to her gift; you couldn't fail to see how touched he'd been by the black lacquered box with its enigmatic illustrations.

The clock struck seven. She was starting to feel cooped up in the house. Dinner wouldn't be for ages yet. Just a few minutes earlier she'd checked in the kitchen; her parents were sitting at the table discussing the vagaries of water pumps, as far as she could tell, and the leg of lamb was still sitting in the baking tray waiting to go into the oven.

Unnoticed, she collected a carrot from the vegetable drawer and went outside onto the back verandah. The dogs appeared without her needing to whistle for them, and she sauntered across the home paddock to give Star his Christmas Eve treat. 'Too late for another ride, old boy,' she said, patting his well-groomed glossy coat. 'Tomorrow instead.' Afterwards she strolled on towards the dam. Peter had got the pump working again and she could hear its reassuring humming. A white bird with spindly legs and a black curved beak cocked its head as the dogs approached, before taking to the air with an effortless flapping of its wings, as if that had been its intention all along. Zidra found a stick and tossed it to the dogs. Rusty was uninterested but Spotless Spot would never tire of retrieving it.

Daylight was fading fast, and a scattering of stars had become faintly visible. As she threw the stick again and again, she thought of Lorna. Of course she would be in Gudgiegalah for Christmas. Those 'boarders' there would never go home from that place that was like a prison. Perhaps Lorna was locked in the boxroom even now.

Ha ha, she'd written defiantly in her letter. Yet being shut up could never be fun even if you could climb onto the roof. Maybe she was sitting above the roof light now and watching the same sky that was arching over Zidra. A deep longing to see her old friend again might have overwhelmed her if she hadn't thought of Lorna's trip to Jervis Bay. There were only six weeks to go.

Spotless Spot nuzzled her hand, and she threw the stick again, as far as she possibly could. Up into the air it rose, higher and higher; she could never have tossed it so far if she'd deliberately tried. Following its progress became difficult. Darkness was falling and the earlier sprinkling of stars had metamorphosed into a white swathe across the indigo sky.

If she were a bird she would take to the air now. She imagined herself rising up to meet the Milky Way, rising above the paddocks of Ferndale. Airborne she would look down on this beautiful land, at its undulating green hills and its rivers snaking from the escarpment to the ocean. She would swoop through the sky and effortlessly travel those many miles to the west, beyond the Great Dividing Range and onwards to the small township of Gudgiegalah.

At this moment she remembered what Lorna had told her years ago about the Milky Way and how it had formed. *Once the sky had been dark, darker than anything you could imagine. Dark until two ancestors had sailed up the river and into the sky, and transformed themselves into stars to shine down on their people. And from that time the spirits of the earth mob after death went up into the sky, and made a river of shining stars. A big mob stars.*

She smiled at this thought. Tonight she and Lorna were both looking at the big mob stars, she felt sure of it. One at Ferndale and the other at Gudgiegalah, they were friends yet, linked by this river of stars across the indigo sky.

CHAPTER 16

Christmas morning, and what could be better than lying in for an extra half hour or so, George thought. Listening to Eileen's steady breathing and savouring the fact that he didn't have to get up and go to the shop. Didn't have to do anything apart from go to Church then afterwards open some presents and watch Eileen unwrap hers. He couldn't wait to see her expression when she opened what he'd bought for her, the crystal water jug and six glasses that she'd admired when they'd been shopping in Burford a few months back. Later he'd gone back alone to buy the set. It turned out to be rather more expensive than it looked but he'd wanted to be sure of purchasing something that pleased her. Wrapped in red paper with holly leaves printed on it, the package now lay under the Christmas tree in the lounge room.

Glancing at his watch, George saw that he'd been lying awake for only ten minutes and yet it seemed like an hour. Funny how he wanted to get up now, even though it was a holiday. He was a creature of habit, that was his problem, or perhaps it was his strength. He was a bit tired, though. Christmas Eve had been even busier than usual. It was well after five o'clock before he and The Boy – the assistant was still known by this name even though approaching middle-age – had been able to clean the shop and lock up for the evening. The feeling of great exhaustion that had almost overwhelmed him last night was now replaced by expectation. Christmas Day with his family and a week off work, now what could be better than that?

He rolled over to look at Eileen, who was still slumbering beside him. Her floral nightgown had slipped off one shoulder and exposed her breast. Gently he pushed at the fabric, so the nightgown slipped further down, revealing the rosebud of her nipple. He was tempted to stroke it; he loved to see it spring erect at the lightest touch. But as Eileen stirred, he thought better of it. There was a time and a season for everything, and he knew that Christmas morning was not Saturday night. For a moment, he watched her peaceful face to see if she was about to wake up. Her eyelids fluttered once but didn't open, and her breathing continued slow and regular. Emboldened by this, he lightly touched her nipple.

'Don't, George,' she said at once, rolling over with her back to him. 'Go back to sleep.'

Happy Christmas to you too, he thought. As always he would make her a cup of tea to drink in bed and that would buy her forgiveness. After shrugging on his dressing-gown, he padded out to the kitchen and put on the kettle. On the table all the vegetables for Christmas lunch were laid out in readiness, and in the refrigerator was the chicken he'd brought home the day before.

While he was pouring tea into Eileen's cup, he heard the boys' voices coming from the passage beside the house. Perhaps they were going for that early morning swim they'd spoken about the night before. He waited for a moment to see what they were up to. Hearing no more, he took two cups of tea into the bedroom.

Normally he let Eileen drink hers alone while he supped his at the kitchen table, but it was Christmas Day after all, and he had as much right to a cup of tea in bed on the first day of his holidays as she did.

She was sitting up in bed waiting. All the pillows, including his own, were arranged behind her. She took a cup and saucer from him and smiled. 'Happy Christmas, George.'

'Happy Christmas, Eileen.'

After putting his own cup of tea on the bedside table, he kissed her. She let him press his lips to hers but there was no answering pressure. For a moment he waited by the bedside in the hope that she might relinquish a pillow but she didn't even think to make the offer.

Feeling distinctly put out, he carried his cup into the lounge room and sat there sipping it as noisily as he could. Although brightly wrapped presents were arranged around the Christmas tree in front of the fireplace, it didn't seem like Christmas somehow. The boys were growing up, that was why. Not so long ago the house would have rung with their laughter and games but not anymore. He and Eileen were going to have to get used to the house becoming quieter and quieter until one day, in maybe ten or fifteen years time, the boys got married and had children of their own.

He'd be close to old age by that time. Sometimes he felt as if he hadn't started living yet.

———⋅◆⋅———

Jim, aware of some tension between his parents, watched them carefully. He might be imagining it but they seemed wary of one another, and certainly excessively polite. Yet there'd been no obvious disagreement the night before and he'd certainly heard no raised voices this morning.

The four of them were sitting in the lounge room. In front of the empty fireplace was the artificial Christmas tree their mother had bought three years ago after she'd become fed up with the real pine branches Dad used to buy, and which dropped needles everywhere. Andy's face was alight with expectation and he too was watching Dad closely. Almost like a dog watching its master, Jim thought for an instant. There was too much need in Andy's expression, and it made Jim feel uncomfortable.

Andy's well-wrapped table lay under the back verandah. They'd collected it from Mr Blake a few days before and Andy had hidden it with a neighbour until this morning. While Dad was making tea in the kitchen, they'd managed to smuggle it underneath the house without being seen. There'd been an anxious moment or two when they'd heard the creaking of the floorboards above them. They'd crawled under the house, into the gap between the sloping earth and the timber floorboards, hoping their father wouldn't come out onto the verandah to see what they were up to. Only when they'd heard his footsteps heading back to the bedroom did they dare to start speaking again. In Andy's case it was initially a fit of the giggles and that had made Jim laugh too, and they'd rolled around in the dust under the house until they ended up in stitches. When Andy had recovered enough to crawl out, his hair was covered with spiders' webs and this had made them burst out laughing again.

—————

Ever since early morning tea, George had been feeling out of sorts. Eileen's rejection of his advances and sequestration of his pillow still offended him. That she'd essentially ostracised him from his own bed certainly hadn't made for a good beginning to Christmas Day. The church service she'd insisted they all attend had been even longer than usual, and he'd thanked God the padre only visited once a month. Now she'd just unwrapped the present he'd given her.

'Lovely, thanks,' she'd said. Although smiling at him, her tone was flat. She barely glanced at the contents of the box, covered with cellophane so the jug and glasses were visible, before putting it on the floor in front of her.

This wholly inadequate response was like a slap in the face. The rational part of him knew that this was an overreaction, brought about only because she hadn't sufficiently exclaimed over the gift that he'd selected so carefully. But why had she raved about the water jug and glasses in the shop in Burford, and not when they arrived in the house? It seemed that certain people always wanted what they didn't have. And when they got exactly what they desired, they treated it with indifference. It was as if things lost all value through shifting from a Burford shopfront into a Jingera lounge room. *Distant fields are greener.*

'Aren't you going to open this, Dad? You've just been sitting here watching the rest of us open our presents.'

George took the small parcel Andy handed him. 'Is this from you, son?'

'No, it's from Mum. See the label?'

George opened the package. Inside were three pairs of green and red argyle-patterned socks. Although he needed new socks and these were in principle very welcome, he hated patterned socks and he didn't know how Eileen could have forgotten this. Or worse, not even noticed his likes and dislikes after eighteen years of marriage.

'Here's my present, Dad.' Jim handed him a book-sized package.

George took his time peeling off the sellotape and stripping back the red-and-yellow-striped paper. Inside was the latest edition of the little book on the constellations of the Southern Hemisphere. How typical of Jim to notice that his copy was falling to bits. 'Thanks, Jim. That's very thoughtful of you.'

'One more to go,' Andy said, grinning.

Both boys now left the room. After gathering together bits of wrapping paper, George shoved them into the wastepaper basket. Then he sat down again in his armchair just as Jim and Andy struggled back with a large parcel wrapped in brown paper.

'Is that for your father or me?' Eileen said, smiling.

'For both of you,' Andy said.

Eileen at once began to undo the parcel, before George even had a chance to sit down next to her on the sofa to share in the unwrapping. It was clear she didn't want him anywhere near her so he stayed where he was in the armchair across the room. She pulled off layer upon layer of brown paper, revealing at last an elegant coffee table.

'I made it,' Andy said. 'It's what won first prize in woodwork.'

So this was what the prize had been for. It was a fine-looking thing, George thought, with an inlay of some blond wood forming a border towards the edge of the darker tabletop. But it was for Eileen, not for him.

'This is sassafras,' Andy said, running his hand gently over the surface. 'With an inlay of celery top pine. There's lots of terrific timbers but joiners don't use the half of them.'

'Is that so?' Eileen said. 'I suppose some are easier to work with than others. Come and sit down next to me. This has to be the most beautiful coffee table I've ever seen and exactly what we need in here too.' She gave Andy a hug and a kiss.

Without really seeing it, George stared vacantly at the fireplace. He felt excluded from the family group: the three others sitting on the sofa, Eileen sandwiched between the two boys, while he was left out on the other side of the room. 'Well done, son,' he said at last, as heartily as he felt able to.

He didn't look directly at Andy as he spoke, and so didn't see the expression of disappointment that appeared only fleetingly on his son's face before it became an impassive mask.

'I'll have to turn the vegetables,' Eileen now said. 'George, you can sharpen the carving knife for me.'

Picking up his new edition of the constellations of the Southern Hemisphere, George trod heavily after her to the kitchen. Before finding the grinding stone, he put the book into the pocket of his jacket hanging in the laundry. Later he would compare it carefully with his old copy to see what had changed between the two editions.

———

Fingering the one pound note in his pocket, Jim stood watching Andy. He was lying on his bed and pretending to read. They'd had guests for lunch, some elderly cousins of their father's, a couple in their early sixties who'd driven out from Burford. Andy had brightened up a bit when they'd given each boy some money. But after they'd left again, once afternoon tea was over, Andy had retreated into their bedroom.

'Let's walk up to the headland,' Jim now said. He guessed Andy was still feeling down about Dad's reaction to the table that morning. Jim had winced when he'd heard the words: 'Well done, son.' Exactly the response that Andy had reported about the woodwork prize. Yet to Jim's ears it wasn't the words so much as the way Dad had said them, in that flat, disinterested way, without even looking at Andy.

On the headland, the sun still felt hot although the shadows were lengthening. The sky to the east appeared pale and washed-out above the darkening blue of the ocean. At the far side of the cemetery they sat on the roughly mown grass, under the partial shade of a young Norfolk Island pine, its needles standing to attention on either side of each branch.

'You must have noticed, Jimmo,' Andy said, almost as soon as they'd sat down. Savagely he plucked at a handful of grass and began to shred it into tiny pieces. 'You must have seen how Dad didn't even give the table a second glance, and he certainly didn't look at me.'

'I think they'd either had an argument or were about to have one. You know how tense Mum gets on Christmas morning. It's because of having the roast for lunch instead of tea.'

'It's more than that. Dad just doesn't care about me, or anything I do, or anything I make. I'll never be able to please him, however hard I try. "Well done, son," is all he says. The stock response when people can't be bothered making an effort to think of something original.'

'It's high praise from Dad. You know what he's like. If he says something's *quite nice* it means it's absolutely fantastic. Understated, that's what he is. "Well done, son," is the best I've ever got from him as well.' But it wasn't, he'd also got eye contact and interest, and poor Andy hadn't received either of these this morning. 'Mum really loved it, you know she did. She said it was the most beautiful table ever and just what they needed.'

'I know she did. But whatever I do, she thinks it's wonderful.' Andy picked a dandelion flower and began to crumple its soft stalk. As the sun advanced down the sky, even the blades of grass were throwing long shadows.

'Maybe it is because she praises you so much that he feels he doesn't need to.' This idea had only now occurred to Jim as a means of cheering Andy but there could be some truth in it. One parent had to balance out what the other did.

'Possibly,' said Andy. 'But he's a practical man himself. He makes things. He repairs things. You'd think he'd take some interest in what I make.'

'Sometimes I think he's only practical because he has to be. But he's a bit of a dreamer really. That's why he likes the stars.'

'That's just an escape. The simple fact of the matter is that, whatever I do, it's not enough to make him interested in me.'

CHAPTER 17

For over a week Woodlands had been full of visitors and Philip felt he'd never be able to get his mother alone. Of course, he'd had plenty of opportunities to play the piano for her. And for any other of the guests who could be induced to listen, although he knew they'd prefer to gallop about the tennis court or sit on the lawn in the dense shade of the oak trees where the temperature was always a few degrees cooler than anywhere else. When he played the piano, Mummy always sat listening, face rapt.But perhaps his talent wasn't enough for what he wanted to do.

Finally, the last guests left, their cars crunching down the gravel drive. He heaved a sigh of relief as Woodlands relaxed once more into its usual peaceful state. The house seemed blessedly empty. You could wander about it without fear of bumping into people who might want to chat to you and listen to your stuttered response. He hated it if they grew impatient and completed the sentence for him. Often they got it wrong. Worse even than this was when they pretended to understand, when he knew all the time that they'd just got fed up with waiting for an answer.

With the last visitor gone, he could open the piano and practise for as long and as loudly as he wanted to, without disturbing anyone who might be reading the newspaper or a book or talking. On no account was he to start playing if guests were in the drawing room *conversing*, Mummy had said. Only if he was already at the piano when someone came into the room was he allowed to continue, or if she specifically invited him to perform. *Simple etiquette*, she called it.

As soon as the Chapmans were on their own again, his father vanished into his study to look at books on cattle breeding or *The Land* newspaper, his favourite reading matter. Now at last Philip would have the opportunity to give his mother the poem that would make her understand that he couldn't possibly be allowed to return to Stambroke College at the end of January. He changed into a clean shirt and washed his face and hands thoroughly – she so liked him to be neat and clean. While drying his face, he inspected his reflection in the mirror. What seemed like a major blemish in term time looked like a mark of distinction in the Woodlands' cloakroom. One green eye and one brown eye flecked with green was the only asymmetry of his face. Once he was sure his parents would let him leave Stambroke, he'd grow his hair again and that would make Mummy happy.

He found her sitting in the drawing room reading a novel. After patting the pocket of his shorts, to check that the poem and letter were still there, he sat on the piano stool. As soon as she put down her book, he would show it to her. Quietly, he opened the piano and began to play.

'Oh, Philip,' she said, before he'd got through more than a bar or two. 'There's something I've been meaning to tell you for days but with all these visitors about there's never been a free moment. Such a lovely Christmas we've had, but I have to confess I'm really glad that at last we've got some time to ourselves. Come and sit next to me, darling, while I tell you about the wonderful little surprise Daddy has lined up for me. He's quite the dearest man in the world.' She swung her stockinged legs off the chaise longue and patted the brocade next to her.

Philip abandoned the piano and sat down beside her, smelling the delicious scent she wore, *Amarige,* she called it. Smiling, he snuggled up to her and leant his head on her shoulder. After she'd revealed Daddy's little surprise, he would give the poem to her. They would have the whole afternoon to talk things over, just the two of them. Later today she would tell Daddy that he simply had to write to the headmaster withdrawing their son from his school. Maybe his parents could hire a tutor for him and he could practise the piano whenever he liked. Somehow he didn't think Mummy would allow him to go to Burford Boys' High once he was old enough for secondary school. Or there was always the School of the Air that Charlie Madden had told him about.

'You'll never guess where your father is going to take me, darling.'

'W-w-w-where?'

'Have a guess!'

'H-h-hotel Australia?'

'Yes, first of all. And guess where to next.'

He couldn't think of anywhere else they might go, except perhaps to see cousin Hamish who lived near Armidale in northern New South Wales. That wouldn't fill her with this much joy though. 'A-a-armidale,' he said anyway, to keep up his side of their game.

She laughed, as he knew she would.

'T-t-tell me!'

'To Europe, isn't that wonderful? Not by flying boat, alas, they stopped those flights after the war. Oh darling, I've always wanted to travel to Europe! Now at last your father has decided he can rely on Hardcastle to run the place while we're away.'

'W-w-what . . . a-about . . .?'

She waited patiently while he struggled to say the words. After a moment he managed to say, 'W-w-hat w-w-will b-become of m-m-me?'

'What will become of you?' she repeated, laughing. 'What a funny question, sweetheart. We'll only be gone for one term, so nothing will become of you. You'll just carry on at Stambroke the way you would have anyway. For Easter you'll go to stay with your Auntie Susan and Uncle Fred in Hunters Hill. You like them, I know. Susan's musical, just like you. Maybe you could go to Giles Mellor's family at Vaucluse for the free weekend. Giles's mother sent me such a sweet note after you'd visited them last term. I'll write you lots of letters of course, and dozens of postcards, and bring you home wonderful presents, so it will be just as if you've come along too!'

'B-b-but . . .'

'It's for my fortieth birthday, darling,' she said, rather more sharply now. 'You can't possibly want to spoil that for me.'

'B-b-but . . .'

'Dearest boy, aren't you pleased for me? It's something I've always wanted.'

'O-o-of c-c-c . . .' The words just wouldn't form themselves. It was as if pebbles were stuck in his throat. He took a deep breath in readiness for singing his anguish but at that point the telephone in the hall started to ring.

'Must get that, darling. Don't you go away.' She removed her arm and kissed him lightly on the tip of his nose before running out into the hall.

How she could she do this to him? She was the most selfish

creature alive. If only he'd given the poem to her earlier, while all the guests were here, maybe that would have shamed his parents into taking him out of school. Mrs Vincent had advised him to tell his mother sooner rather than later. Tears filled his eyes as he realised that it was too late now. He couldn't spoil Mummy's pleasure, he knew that was impossible.

Yet now how would he survive another term at Stambroke? He began to feel dizzy and slightly sick, and his palms were hot and sticky. Slowly he wiped them on the green brocade of the chaise longue. How she would hate to see him doing this. Noticing the whisky decanter on the sideboard, he crept over and took a quick slug. The liquid burnt his throat and he started to cough. After wiping his chin on the back of his hand, he sat at the piano and began to play Mozart's Requiem, the darkest piece of music that he knew. He'd heard a recording of it several times on the gramophone and could easily play bits of it by ear. Oblivious now of his mother talking vivaciously in the hallway, he didn't notice when she shut the door to the drawing room. He felt only a profound unhappiness that manifested itself in sound. He had no control over anything apart from his fingertips as they marched across the keys.

Later he went to the bathroom upstairs and took the nail scissors out of the medicine cabinet. Methodically he worked across his head, cutting off all the new growth, cutting it until it was uniformly half an inch long. His mother would be upset but he didn't care anymore what she thought. She did whatever she pleased regardless of the consequences, and so too would he.

Yet that evening neither of his parents mentioned his hair. Maybe they hadn't even noticed, he was that unimportant to them. For an instant he wondered what further damage he could inflict on himself before they would comment.

At dinner his father began to talk about their plans to go to Europe. Mummy, with a narrowing of her eyes and an almost imperceptible tilt of the head, at least had the good grace to signal him to stop. His father didn't understand her though. She had to say, *Later, Jack,* several times before he got the message.

Daddy was a bit obtuse, Philip decided as he pushed the food around his plate, rearranging it to look as if he'd eaten something. He had no appetite and felt that he'd never eat again. It wasn't just that his father was tactless talking about their stupid trip to Europe without him. It was more his refusal to understand that being picked on at school wasn't character building, or not for someone like him. Now Daddy was wolfing his dinner down as if he hadn't seen food for weeks, or maybe he just wanted to get the meal over with as quickly as Philip did.

'It's so lovely to have the house to ourselves again,' Mummy said. 'Just the three of us.'

'And the rest,' said Philip, as rudely as he knew how. 'M-mr and M-mrs Jones and M-mmary.'

His father laughed but Mummy stared at him with a danger-ous glint in her eye. 'Don't be so *literal*, darling. You know quite well what I mean.'

'Just the three of us,' his father echoed, grinning. He lay down his knife and fork, having polished off everything on his plate and might even have eaten the pattern off the second best Wedgwood if it wasn't glazed on so well. 'Thought I'd take you around the property tomorrow morning, son. It's been a while since we've done that together and it's time you got to know the lie of the land.'

'N-no th-thanks. I already know the lie of the land.' After years wandering over it, Philip knew every gully and paddock, and every rock and fence post even. He avoided looking at his father though. While he wanted to hurt him for not taking him out of Stambroke, he didn't want to see the wound.

Mummy laughed, that tinkling little sound like a xylophone that she could produce when she wasn't at all amused. 'Daddy means that *metaphorically*, darling. He wants to explain things to you.'

'All this will be yours one day, son,' his father said.

Philip flinched. He wanted none of it, apart from the piano.

'So you may as well get familiar with the workings of it sooner rather than later.'

He glanced at his father. Solid and honest he was, and Philip might have felt a moment's pity for him if he wasn't still so upset about having to return to Stambroke.

Then a thought occurred to him, one that was to shift in and out of his consciousness in the coming weeks. If he couldn't hurt his parents, maybe he could hurt himself instead.

There must be lots of ways of doing that.

CHAPTER 18

Unusually, there was no queue in the post office and Mrs Blunkett seemed delighted to see Ilona. Not that she was special, Ilona knew. Any face would serve to release the dammed-up torrent of words.

Before Ilona even had the opportunity to ask for stamps, Mrs Blunkett said, 'Mrs Cadwallader was in here yesterday wondering if I'd set eyes on you. Said she hadn't seen you for a while, so I said there was always the phone, but she said it was nothing special. Expect you've been busy with the school holidays and all that.'

'Have you seen the Hunter family?' Ilona managed to interject as Mrs Blunkett took a breath. 'I need to find out where they're living.'

'Which Hunters is that? . . . Oh, I see . . . Not the farming Hunters but the other ones, the Aborigines. Yes, I remember them. They never came into the post office, but. Their kiddy Lorna and Zidra were friends before she was taken. No, haven't seen them for a year or more.'

Ilona fought down her disappointment. She'd been convinced that Mrs Blunkett would know something. That she didn't probably meant that the Hunters had gone somewhere else, and this could make her search really difficult.

'Well, I can certainly keep an ear open. You know me, soul of discretion, won't ask why. Expect you've got some work for Tommy out at Ferndale. Oh, here's Mrs Smythe. Won't be a moment, Mrs Smythe, just got to finish serving Mrs Vincent. Ta-ta love, that's a good-looking daughter you've got. S'pose it won't be long before she gets a boyfriend, eh?'

Out in the street Ilona paused for breath; listening to Mrs Blunkett did tend to take it out of one. She was beginning to feel anxious that they wouldn't find the Hunters in time. Realistically, her only hope now was that meeting about Aboriginal housing in two weeks time. There'd be lots of Aborigines there and the Hunters might turn up too.

Now she walked down the hill to her old cottage. The hedge had produced its usual abundance of small white flowers, and she inhaled their heady perfume, sweet but not sickly. The orange trumpet flowers growing over the verandah blazed in the morning sunlight, and the crashing of the surf drowned out all other noise as it pounded inexorably on the beach.

Once she'd thought the sea unchanging but how wrong she'd been. Some days it was noisy, others it was quiet. Like people, oceans were in a continual state of unrest. Bending down now to pick up an ice-cream wrapper that someone had left under the hedge of her old cottage, she was saddened by how neglected the place looked. At that instant a small bird flitted out of the dense foliage, maybe the offspring of the birds who'd nested there four years ago. As she straightened up, she decided there was just enough time to visit Eileen Cadwallader before driving on to Woodlands. The challenge of chipping away at Eileen's prejudice was too attractive to pass over, and she could tell her all about the letter she was composing for

the *Sydney Morning Chronicle* about the Gudgiegalah Girls'
Home.

But when Eileen opened her front door her hair was awry
and her face creased in distress.

'What's the matter?' Ilona said.

'Nothing. Well, I'm feeling a bit low actually.'

'Shall I go away?'

'No, come in, please, you'll cheer me up.' Eileen held open the
fly-screen door and showed Ilona into the front living room.

'New coffee table,' Ilona said. 'It's very beautiful.'

'Andy made it.' At this, Eileen burst into tears. Ilona stood
up again and put an arm around Eileen's shoulders. The older
woman recoiled slightly, evidently one of those people who don't
like being touched, Ilona decided. Removing her arm, she said,
'There, there, let me make you a cup of tea, and then you can tell
me all about it.'

'No, you won't know where anything is.' Eileen began to
laugh through her tears, in a slightly hysterical way, Ilona
thought. The occasion called for a tablespoon of brandy but
she guessed that there wouldn't be any in the Cadwallader
household. Eileen added, 'I'd get one of the boys to make the
tea but they're hardly ever here anymore. Even though its school
holidays, I never seem to see them. They're out all the time and
before you know it the holidays will be over.' She fumbled in her
pocket for a handkerchief. 'I think of all the times I've roused
on them and wished them out of the house, and soon they will
be, permanently.'

Ilona sat down. On a previous visit she'd heard Eileen bawling
out Andy: *Don't walk all over my clean polished floor in your
Blücher boots*! Somehow she doubted Andy would be leaving
home for this. It was one of Eileen's more colourful expressions

that he'd probably recall with great affection when he was older.

After blowing her nose loudly, Eileen continued. 'The last straw is Andy saying he doesn't want to stay on at school. He wants to do an apprenticeship. I'd hoped for better things for him.'

'There's nothing wrong with learning a trade, Eileen.'

'It would mean he'd be earning his own wages right away, and probably going to live somewhere else, not that they pay them much, and then I'll be on my own. All alone.' She sat down in the other armchair. 'I'll have nothing to do, no company and at night only George. There'll be no purpose to my life.'

Poor George, Ilona thought. Such a sad thing to be loved by the whole town but unappreciated by his wife. But no, she was being too harsh; Eileen must love George, she just didn't know how to express her appreciation.

'Anyway he's not going anywhere until he's done the Intermediate Certificate,' Eileen said. 'That's what I've told him and I'm sticking with it.'

'That seems sensible,' Ilona said gently. 'But when children do leave home eventually I suppose it could also be an opportunity. For the parents, I mean. To follow new interests.'

'Never!' Eileen said almost angrily.

'Why not?'

'What am I if not a mother? I'm nothing!'

Ilona felt shocked by this revelation. How could Eileen's identity be defined only by motherhood? It was a biological imperative and a source of great satisfaction but it never solely characterised who you were. She said, 'You're Eileen, and unique.'

'But my children are my life's work. I never expected it to end so soon.'

'It's not ending. It's just evolving into something different.

They still love you. They always will. And they're good boys, both of them. They'll keep in touch.'

'I'll be so isolated. And George is starting to drink.'

'George drink? Surely not!'

'Last Friday he went to the pub after work and didn't get home until twenty minutes past six. That's twenty minutes after we normally have tea.'

Ilona resisted the temptation to smile. 'So he was in the pub for just over an hour?'

'Long enough for tea to spoil. It's that drunkard, Mr Hargreaves. He collected George from Cadwallader's at five o'clock, apparently. Hargreaves is in the pub every night until closing time when they throw him out, that's what Mrs Blunkett told me. Don't know why his wife puts up with it.'

This was news to Ilona, although Peter had mentioned that Hargreaves liked a spot or two. But so too did half the township of Jingera, the male half mainly, and she knew that Eileen was occasionally prone to exaggeration. Anyway why begrudge George an hour or two with Hargreaves on a Friday after work? Maybe there was some other reason for Eileen's irritation with George. 'You'll have to find new things to do,' she said. 'For instance, you could come with me to the demonstration in Canberra for Aboriginal rights. The Aborigines have just got the vote, but there's a long way to go yet. The demo's not for some months though, but there's a meeting in Burford about Aboriginal housing I can take you to first.'

'Me in a demo?'

'Yes, why not?'

'But I don't approve of all that.'

'Yes, you do. You said only the other day it wasn't a bad thing the Aborigines got the vote. Just think, most of them are people like you and George.' While Ilona suspected that Eileen would always view whites as superior, part of Ilona's own mission was to erode Eileen's bigotry. She continued. 'Decent people with children they love and who want a good future. Why should we exclude them? Anyway, it might be fun to go to Burford together. What do you think about that?'

Eileen surprised her. 'Maybe I'll take you up on that,' she said. 'And now it's time for that cup of tea.'

'Next time,' Ilona said, glancing at her watch. 'By the way, you haven't seen the Hunters, have you?' When Eileen looked blank, she said, 'The family of that Aboriginal girl, Lorna, who was taken away to the Gudgiegalah Girls' Home, do you remember? She and Zidra were best friends.'

'No, I haven't seen them. Not for ages.'

'Not even Tommy? He used to fish from the jetty in the lagoon here.'

'No. I expect they're up at the Wallaga Lake Reserve, where they're supposed to be.'

Suppressing her annoyance at this last remark, Ilona said, 'They're not there. I checked. If you see them, do let me know. Phone me at any time. It's pretty urgent.'

'Sure.'

Eileen didn't ask why, and Ilona was glad of this. The situation wasn't one she felt she could explain to her. After all, if the Gudgiegalah authorities got wind of a planned meeting they could always cancel the trip, or leave poor Lorna behind.

Yet Ilona wanted everyone to be aware of their search for the Hunters. If this was common knowledge, surely someone would contact her with information. She hoped the family hadn't left the area altogether. They weren't at the Wallaga Lake Reserve, they weren't at the camp outside Burford. And as far as she could tell, they weren't picking at any of the farms with crops either. Peter had telephoned all the local properties and no one had seen them.

It was as if they'd vanished from Wilba Wilba Shire altogether.

Her only hope now was that they'd turn up at the meeting about Aboriginal housing.

CHAPTER 19

'I've heard the news,' Mrs Vincent said, bursting into the drawing room at Woodlands and interrupting Philip's concentration. While knowing she was coming to visit this morning, he hadn't expected her to come unannounced. No barking dogs, no swish of tyres on the gravel, no footsteps in the hall; all sound drowned out as he hammered out a prelude. 'Your mother told me just now. So you are to stay on at Stambroke. Did you not show them your poem?'

'N-n-no.' Removing his hands from the keyboard, he waited. 'Why?'

She stood only a couple of feet away. Hoping she wouldn't come any closer, he held his breath. He didn't want to cry again but if she touched him the tears would spill at once.

'Why?' she repeated.

'I-i-t's . . . s-s-s-silly poem.'

'It was a good poem, Philip, although its quality is hardly the point, as you know. It was the content that mattered. So your mother hasn't seen it?'

'N-n-no.' He lifted his hands into the air and let them hover over the piano. Lowering his hands onto the keys he played a scale in F sharp.

'And your father?'

'H-h-he says s-s-school is g-g-good training.' Now Philip played a swift arpeggio.

'For the hard knocks of this world. I see. Would you like me to speak to them?'

'N-no.' He closed the piano and stared out the window, not wanting to see the kindness that would be in her eyes. Outside, Mr Jones was raking the gravel path to clear it of the cedar needles. The sunlight, filtering through the trees, cast dancing shadows over him as he moved backwards and forwards with the rake.

'Your parents are off to Europe,' she said slowly. 'But it will only be for a term.'

Philip said nothing. There was no point when everything had already been decided.

'So you have only a couple more weeks at home. What are you doing with yourself?'

'P-p-playing.'

'Have you been to the beach yet?'

'N-no.'

'Would you care to stay with us at Ferndale for a few days soon? I know Zidra would love you to visit and so would Peter and I. Would you like that?'

'Y-y-yes.'

'I shall organise it with your parents then. Perhaps you'll be able to come in a couple of days' time.' Gently Mrs Vincent kissed the top of his head, before departing only slightly less abruptly than she'd arrived.

Later, he'd heard the crunching of gravel as she drove away. Afterwards his mother came to find him. When he heard her approaching, he started to play a piece that he knew she wouldn't like; Shostakovich was too Russian, she thought. He pretended not to hear the tip-tap of her heels on the polished wooden floor-boards that became muffled by the Persian rug as she advanced towards him. Perching herself on the chaise longue, she remained silent until he'd finished. He might have played it again if she hadn't started speaking.

'The Vincents have invited you to stay for a few days,' she said. 'So very sweet of them, darling, and she said you wanted to go. That will work out rather well, as I was planning to have Jones drive me to Sydney for a few days. I need to get some more clothes to take away, and there's simply nothing in the Burford shops, nothing. I might have taken you to Sydney with me if she hadn't invited you, but I'm sure this is the best. You'd hate visiting the dressmaker and traipsing around the gown shops with me!' Here she laughed. 'Your father certainly does.'

As no reply seemed necessary, he began to play again the same piece and after a moment or two she left. As soon as the door shut behind her, he stopped. There was no point continuing now he could no longer annoy her. After opening one of the French windows, he walked around the side of the house, avoiding Jones, who'd moved on to the northern end of the gravel path. The scent of honeysuckle filled his nostrils. He picked a flower from the vine climbing up the side of the house and broke the stem to suck out the sweet nectar. But that didn't satisfy him and he bit hard on the stalk before spitting it onto the grass.

Skirting around the gravel area at the back of the house and steering well clear of the stockyards, he headed towards the paddocks behind the white-painted outbuildings. Beyond these, the land rose in a series of hills towards the bush flanking the escarpment. At the top of the first hill, he sat on a granite boulder and looked out over Woodlands.

When his father had taken him around the property the previous week, discussing *man-to-man* the way it was run, Philip hadn't absorbed one-tenth of what he'd heard. All he'd been able to think about was that he wished for nothing to change. He wanted to never grow up, never be left alone. Never have his parents go away. If he hadn't already hated them so much for leaving him at Stambroke, he might have hated them more for leaving the country.

Although he loved Woodlands, he didn't want any of it. If his parents went to Europe and never came back, what would he do? He'd be all alone, but would that be so terrible? He'd leave school, he decided at once, and live somewhere else. In Sydney, probably. That would mean he could carry on his piano lessons at the Con, and this prospect didn't seem too bad. He could practise the piano as much as he wanted, and go to concerts and listen to the crowds and the traffic. And to the tugboats hooting on the harbour, the clinking rigging of the boats moored at the marina, and all those other sounds that he'd never consciously noticed when he was at school. Yet at this moment they emerged from his memory as if waiting for the chance to resurface, already formed into a coherent whole that he simply had to get down before it vanished again.

He ran down the hill and into the drawing room without being seen by anyone. For several hours he scribbled and played the piano.

But afterwards he knew that the composition wasn't right and he tore up the notes he'd written on the lined paper. So angry was he with this failure that he took the matches from the kitchen and set fire to the scraps of paper in the basin in the cloakroom. Slowly he burnt them, a piece at a time. The flames flickered, orange and blue.

It would be easy to burn himself, along with his disappointment. He put a finger in the fire. For several seconds he left it there. When the pain got too intense to bear, he flung the piece of paper into the basin. Perhaps it would be better to burn down Woodlands. He put the last few scraps on top of the burning paper and blew hard. They caught and flared. But in a moment it was over: the flames were extinguished, along with his anger.

All that remained was an intense self-loathing.

CHAPTER 20

Unwelcome sunlight fell on Zidra's face and she pulled the sheet over her head. Several minutes later she felt strong enough to open one eye and squint at her wristwatch; already it was after ten and she'd slept for nearly ten hours. Going to the pictures did that to you, made you relax, especially a film like *Gidget* that she'd seen twice before. She and Sally had giggled about Moondoggie all the way home in the back seat of the Hargreaves' car, until finally Mrs Hargreaves said – though you could tell she was joking – it was definitely the last time she was driving them into Burford.

Later, after a quick shower, Zidra dressed and found her mother in the kitchen. 'I've invited Philip Chapman to spend a couple of days with us,' her mother announced without any preamble. 'Didn't have a chance to tell you yesterday before you went out.' She had her back to Zidra and was doing something complicated with the electric egg beater that involved measuring and whisking simultaneously.

'Hmmm.' Zidra decided to reserve judgement on this announcement until after a cup of tea.

'You will be delighted at this opportunity,' her mother declared, once she'd turned off the mixmaster. Deftly she folded some sifted flour into the bowl. 'Can you believe that he has not yet been to the beach these summer holidays that will so soon be over? Tomorrow we will collect him. It is apparently not convenient for Mr Jones to bring him here.'

'Do I have to come too?'

'Is it not convenient for you either?' She turned to look at Zidra rather sternly, her mouth a horizontal line.

'It's all right.' Zidra knew it was always best to humour her when she was in one of these moods.

'Afterwards I'll drop you both at Jingera Beach for a while and return in the late afternoon. You will need to watch Philip of course. Then we will have a barbecue on the beach. All of us.'

'Can I ask Sally too?'

'Yes, of course. And Jim and Andy.'

'Jim's friend Eric arrived yesterday.'

'Ah, the boy from Walgettt. Yes, we shall invite them all to the barbie.'

'Barbecue,' Zidra corrected. This abbreviation in her mother's accent sounded quite ludicrous.

'It will be convenient for Mr Jones to collect Philip, however,' her mother said, ignoring the interruption, 'after he's stayed with us for several nights.'

'You won't get a look in at the piano, Ma.'

'That won't matter. I can listen to Philip all day and never tire of it. But he will come to us for a little holiday and not to practise all the time. It will be up to us to create distractions for him.'

Zidra eyed her mother with incredulity. She really meant it would be up to *you*. While Zidra was fond of Philip, there wasn't much of the holiday left, and she certainly hadn't planned on spending that time playing nursemaid to a ten-year-old. At that moment she remembered the little green elephant and Lorna.

This, and the cup of tea, put her in a better frame of mind. 'Sure thing,' she said. 'I'll go and do some phoning about the barbecue.'

'*Barbie*,' said her mother, before switching on the electric beater again.

Such a self-contained boy, Zidra thought, sneaking a sideways look at Philip, who was sitting on a striped beach towel laid out on the sand next to her own. The others – Jim and Sally and Andy and Jim's friend Eric – were still in the surf. Philip had become rather beautiful, she thought, with pale skin and short spiky blond hair. It was a striking combination with those asymmetric eyes and dark brown eyelashes. Surreptitiously she felt her own eyebrows. She'd plucked them for the first time that morning and hoped she hadn't overdone it. A slightly surprised look was what her mother, who didn't miss a trick, had said and added that it made her appear *touchingly* innocent. Zidra wasn't sure she liked that. *Sophisticated* seemed more appropriate.

The thing about Philip was that he didn't require you to talk much. In fact, it sometimes seemed as if he'd prefer you not to talk at all. Maybe that was because they'd known one another for so long and had played together sometimes at Woodlands. Nearly half of his lifetime ago, she'd given him the fossil that her mother had found, and he'd told her he still had it displayed in his bedroom. She liked that. While naturally you wanted to be valued for yourself, it was pretty good when your gifts were appreciated too.

The first hour after Zidra and Philip had been dropped off at Jingera they'd spent by the lagoon. It was when Zidra was watching Philip swim in the sheltered water that she'd heard Jim calling her name. So intent had she been on making sure Philip didn't get into difficulties – he was rather a poor swimmer – she'd missed seeing Jim and the others walk over the footbridge. The boy from Walgett wasn't someone you'd easily overlook. Pushing six feet tall, he was spattered with freckles that were golden rather than brown. These and his gingery hair lent him a glowing appearance. Involuntarily she'd pulled up the front of her swimming costume, without thinking that this would draw attention to that part of her anatomy most constricted by the bathers. Only afterwards did the boy from Walgett glance at her face – he had deep blue eyes the colour of the sky – and he'd grinned. When she saw that, she looked away at once, feeling she'd made a discovery, although whether it was about Eric or herself she couldn't say.

Once Philip had tired of swimming in the lagoon, he'd insisted on showering under the standpipe near Hairy Harry's canoes to wash off the salt. Dried again and in shorts and T-shirt, he was at last willing to catch up with the others, who'd already stationed themselves on the beach. Sally had wanted Zidra to go into the surf with them but she'd declined; it was clear that Philip wasn't interested in surfing. He was content just to sit on the sand next to her and observe the waves, or at least that's what he appeared to be doing. And listening to something too – the breakers or the gulls or some inner rhythm – and occasionally jiggling his feet.

Hugging her arms across her chest – the afternoon was becoming cool – Zidra watched the others emerging from the breakers. At once Andy fossicked around at the edge of the waves. Soon he picked up a long strand of seaweed and, flourishing it around his head like a lasso, began to chase Jim and Sally. Eric was not so easily distracted; he marched straight up the beach towards where Zidra and Philip were sitting. As soon as Philip saw him approaching, he lay down on his back on the towel and closed his eyes.

After spreading out a towel, Eric sat down next to Zidra.

'What have you been up to over the holidays?' he said, as if he'd met her beforehand and was resuming an earlier conversation.

'Nothing much.' She might have told him about Lorna if she'd known him well enough to gauge his sympathies. But just because he was Jim's friend didn't mean he'd share Jim's views about Aboriginal people, and anyway some things were too private to discuss with strangers. The approaching trip to see Lorna at Jervis Bay, for instance. She said, 'Reading and riding and relaxing. The three Rs.'

Eric laughed. 'I haven't been up to much either but that's the best sort of holiday, I reckon, Zid.'

Effortlessly Jim's name for her slipped off Eric's tongue and she wasn't sure she liked this. There was a moment's pause, during which she wondered what Jim might have told Eric about her, while Eric ferreted around in the pile of clothes that had been discarded earlier. Eventually he retrieved from the pocket of his shorts a bottle of suntan oil. After spreading some over his arms and legs, he asked Zidra, 'Can you rub some of this on my back?'

She could hardly refuse, although she couldn't help thinking this should be done by someone who'd known him longer than half an hour. Anyway it was now late afternoon and even someone of his colouring would no longer burn from the sun. Yet in spite of these observations she wanted to do what he asked. She wanted to feel the texture of those golden freckles and touch the exposed shoulder blades. After glancing at Philip, still lying on his towel with his eyes shut – whether asleep or awake she couldn't tell – she took the proffered bottle. She poured some oil onto the palm of her hand and began to apply it to Eric's shoulders. His skin was warm from the sun. The golden down covering his back was so fine you would never see it unless you were this close. Evenly she rubbed the oil into his shoulders, over the shoulderblades and the vulnerable bumps of vertebra, stopping occasionally to tip more oil onto her palm. Slowly she worked down his long back towards the waistband of his board shorts. She stopped an inch short of these, and began to rub the oil remaining on her fingers over her bare legs.

Aware that he'd turned to look at her, she carried on rubbing her legs even after the oil had been absorbed. At length she stopped and caught his blue stare. It was impossible to halt the blush that started at the base of her neck and advanced up her face. She averted her eyes. The meaning of this moment was unclear, although it was significant in some way she had yet to determine.

As the others joined them, she wondered why he'd asked her to oil his back. If not for sun protection, it was to draw attention to his very beautiful body. Yet he was hardly someone who needed to adopt such stratagems: she couldn't stop herself from returning to a contemplation of all that radiance, though was unable to decide if she was attracted or repelled by it.

———

Jim's hand had somehow caught hold of Sally's when Andy was chasing them with the skein of seaweed that he was brandishing about like a stock whip. Together they ran along the edge of the surf until Sally tripped and fell to her knees, dragging Jim with her into the ebbing water. Sprawled next to her, he saw beads of water trickling down her forehead and her dark hair spreading like seaweed in the shifting shallows. He was about to kiss her when Andy, confounded pest that he was, jumped shrieking over them both. At once Jim began to help Sally to her feet while Andy started to flail his legs with the seaweed. Grabbing it from him, Jim happened to glance up the beach and was therefore a witness to Zidra's anointing of Eric's back.

His stomach turned. That Eric might use the opportunity of their brief absence to good effect hadn't occurred to him. Eric was far too old for Zidra and Jim should have warned her about him. He could have told her about the last school formal when, in spite of the close supervision, Eric had managed to snog three different girls in the space of one evening. It simply hadn't crossed Jim's mind that Eric would find Zidra attractive. She was two years younger, after all, and Jim still thought of her as younger even than that. Although these holidays it certainly hadn't escaped his notice that her figure had developed, her face still had that mix of proud independence and innocence. Now he thought about it, this was bound to appeal to Eric, who would be certain to rise to such a challenge. All these thoughts sped through his mind as he guided Sally back up the beach towards the others.

He arrived in time to witness Zidra's blush and the intense scrutiny that Eric was giving her, that look that seemed to make even the most clued-up girls go weak at the knees. The fact that no words were being traded gave the little exchange even greater import. Jim's irritation at this tender scene manifested itself in a strong desire to kick hard at something, Eric preferably, even though he was his best friend. Instead he contented himself with hurling the seaweed he'd earlier confiscated from Andy as far as possible towards the sand dunes. Andy, like a determined dog in need of exercise, at once gave chase. You'd imagine Eric would behave himself in front of young Philip, Jim thought, even though the boy did appear to be sound asleep. Jim knew he'd have to keep a close eye on Eric for the rest of the afternoon and evening. That this might spoil his own developing romance with Sally served to increase his annoyance.

'What's up, Jim?' Eric asked, grinning.

Zidra was so obviously avoiding looking at Eric that Jim became suspicious of her feelings; surely she wouldn't be so foolish as to fall for Eric. At this moment she was smiling rather fatuously at the receding tide. Despite the presence of Zidra's chaperone, as Jim now felt himself to be, Eric picked up a handful of sand and dribbled it over her ankles. She laughed and stood up to shake herself.

She is lovely, Jim thought with a sudden shock and realised that he didn't want her this way. He didn't want her growing up; it was one of those Jingera changes that he'd prefer not to happen. The town was diminishing, the old fixed points were changing, and Zid Vincent was no longer an androgynous child but on the threshold of becoming a young woman.

It would have been better for his peace of mind if she'd been more homely.

He sat next to Sally, who'd spread out a towel. She put her hand on his knee, a gesture that five minutes earlier would have filled him with delight. While he responded in a predictable way, and put an arm around her shoulders, he felt no emotional reaction. But there was only one week of holiday left and he needed to make the most of it.

CHAPTER 21

The pine cones in the fireplace in the Ferndale living room ignited easily, and blue and orange flames flickered around the kindling. Philip watched Mrs Vincent as she fed small pieces of wood into the flames. After a while they began to die back. That was when Mr Vincent got up from the sofa and started to rearrange the wood. She didn't seem to mind but stayed kneeling next to him, smiling.

It had been Mrs Vincent's idea to have a fire. There'd been a sudden cold change in the late afternoon and the temperature had dropped right down to fifty-five degrees Fahrenheit, according to Mrs Vincent and the thermometer on the back verandah. 'What a marvellous excuse!' she'd said. The fire also seemed to be a reason to bring them all together. He liked that about her, that she made a real effort for people. And the odd thing was that the sunburn made you feel hot and cold at the same time, so he was even gladder about the fire, though after a while it became so warm that they had to open all the windows again.

Once Mr and Mrs Vincent had got the wood burning to their mutual satisfaction, glowing but not flaming, Mr Vincent sat down again on the sofa. After Mrs Vincent slipped off her shoes and curled up next to him, he put an arm around her shoulders and drew her close.

Zidra had got out the Monopoly set. Philip helped her put the cards in the right places but refused to be banker. He would have preferred not to play, but he could tell she felt responsible for his entertainment. Anyway Mrs Vincent had thought it would be a good thing and he'd got to know her well enough to see that she generally got what she wanted, although in the nicest possible way. Maybe that was because what she decided would happen was what everyone else wanted as well, but they just hadn't quite realised it yet.

So it was with Monopoly. He began to enjoy the game after a while and luck seemed to be going his way. Soon he was amassing a small fortune in property, on all these sites distributed across London. That city to which his parents would be flying next week, the day after they dumped him off at Stambroke College. He tried not to think about it. Instead he focused on the moment, with Zidra teasing him about his property empire, and Mr and Mrs Vincent joining in, while keeping up murmured conversation with one another and slowly sipping at the 'postprandial snorter' that Mr Vincent had poured for each of them.

Philip began to feel almost content. The first day away from Woodlands he hadn't enjoyed so much, apart from that swim in Jingera lagoon and the time sitting with Zidra on the beach when he'd been listening to a piece of music that was playing in his head. Music based on the thumping of the breakers and the wailing of the seagulls against which a melody of haunting beauty had abruptly presented itself. Of course Eric had spoilt it all by making Zidra rub oil on his silly back and she, who should have had more sense, had gone all moony-spoony over him. Jim and Sally weren't much better, and he'd been glad of the arrival of Mr and Mrs Vincent, with a hamper and a portable barbecue, that had put an end to all such nonsense.

Today had been much better. Zidra had taken him for a walk and they'd ended up on the beach near the homestead. He'd loved that, partly because she'd left him alone while she read a book. You're not allowed to swim at this beach, it's too dangerous, she'd said, but he didn't mind that because he hated surfing and much preferred paddling about at the edge of the water and examining bits and pieces thrown up by the waves. When that had palled, he'd inspected the rock pools and those spiky things that Zidra said were sea anemones, and the periwinkle shells stuck to the rocks, and pink starfish and, in a deep crevice, even an octopus. Zidra had intervened only to make him keep his shirt and hat on. Mrs Vincent had given strict instructions to both of them about that, and she'd been right, because he had caught a bit of sun.

After an hour or so, he'd joined Zidra where she was sitting on the sand. By this time the sun had moved over and she was in the shadow cast by the cliff. He began to ask her what she was reading, but she was one of those rare people who seemed to intuit the direction of his thoughts before he'd managed to spit out the first word.

'*Eyeless in Gaza*,' she said, showing him the cover of the paperback. 'Jim lent it to me. Mama thinks it's highly unsuitable, but how else am I to get an education stuck in the wilds of southern New South Wales?'

Since she was smiling, he knew it was safe to laugh.

'I'm going to become a journalist,' she said. 'After I finish university.'

She sketched out her ambitions, to travel overseas and report on major political events, preferably of the more dangerous kind. Entranced, he listened. His stutter and lack of conversation sometimes elicited information that would never be revealed to him if he were able to tell his own stories. Yet she didn't talk *at* him but *to* him, regularly looking into his eyes and waiting for him to nod or mumble something before proceeding.

After a while, she began to talk about what had happened on Jingera Beach the afternoon before. At first that had shocked him, but soon he'd been glad because it seemed that at last she'd seen what Eric was like. *A good-looking boy on the make* was how she described him. 'He has lovely freckles though,' she confided. 'But he was trying to manipulate me and I don't like that. I didn't see it at first, I only realised it later. Imagine if I took off nearly all my clothes and asked someone I'd only just met to rub sunscreen over me. What would they think?'

Philip averted his eyes.

'It's because he's a bloke that he thinks he can get away with it,' she said firmly, shutting up her book. 'But he's not going to get off with me, nor are any of the other boys. Whether they're from Stambroke College or Burford Boys' High, they're all the same.'

Now Philip began to lose the drift of what she was saying and took in only the rise and fall of her voice as she continued with her monologue.

'Of course, some girls aren't so wised up,' she'd concluded. 'They're the ones who end up pregnant. There were two girls from Burford Girls' High who had to leave last year. They got sent off to that home for unmarried mothers on the far side of town. Everyone views them as fallen women now, although it's the boys who are as much to blame. Jim told me last night what Eric's really like. Charming but untrustworthy. Obviously I knew that right away.'

Philip guessed this part of the story was untrue but there was no sense in trying to point that out. Instead he began to push the sand about to make a sandcastle. As he'd hoped, Zidra soon stopped going on about Eric, and became diverted by the failure of his castle to stay upright.

'We need wet sand to do this, Philip,' she said. 'Let's move closer to the water.' That she was able to continue talking while helping him build an extensive castle with battlements and a moat and a keep was testament to her intelligence, he felt. He could only do one thing at a time and speaking wasn't one of them. Eventually he managed to say, with only a little hesitation, 'J-Jim's k-k-k-kind.'

She stopped talking at once, although she managed to continue further excavating the moat. After a moment, she said, 'Jim's the best boy alive, apart from you, that is. He's like a brother to me.'

Then Philip had heard no more about Eric or Jim as she'd became distracted by the shells littering the shoreline that would be the perfect decoration for their battlements.

At this point a log fell out of the fireplace grate onto the marble hearth and Mr Vincent stood up to restore it to the grate. The best thing about the day, Philip thought, staring at the glowing embers, was after he and Zidra had returned from their walk. Mrs Vincent had taken him to the piano and showed him the music of someone called Oleksii Talivaldis – battered sheets of music with handwritten notes and scribbled messages in the margins, in some language he couldn't follow.

'I thought you'd like to read this,' she'd said. 'I've only just started playing it again. At first it brought back too many memories, but recently I was able to try once more.'

To begin with, he'd been struck solely by the music. Ahead of his time, Mrs Vincent had said of Oleksii, but Philip didn't really understand that. All he'd been able to take in was the importance of what he was hearing, this non-repetitive ordering of the twelve notes of the chromatic scale, and the brilliant transformations.

Only afterwards did he realise that Oleksii was her first husband, who'd died years ago before she and Zidra moved to Jingera.

Now it was Mrs Vincent's turn to poke around at the fire, trying to dampen it down a bit as they were all too hot by this point, while Mr Vincent offered helpful advice. Philip acquired a hotel on Park Lane and another one on Regent Street, and the Monopoly game was soon over.

Later, as he lay awake in the spare bedroom in Ferndale, listening to the sound of the distant surf and the wind sighing through the pine needles, he was able to forget what lay in store for him the following week. Soon he drifted into strange and complicated dreams in which twelve-tone scales transformed and transposed themselves in various ways that, even in his sleep, he knew to be impossible.

Waking as the white light of dawn fingered its way through the chink in the curtains, he began to toss and turn. The holidays were nearly over and soon he'd be back at Stambroke College. He began to feel sick at the thought of what lay ahead. Sitting up in bed, he took several sips of water from the glass on the bedside table but this only increased his nausea. How he was to survive the term stretching endlessly ahead he couldn't imagine, and with his parents twelve thousand miles away there was no hope of an early release.

The trip back to Woodlands the next day was to prove worse than disappointing. For a start, Jones was several hours too early, and so Philip hadn't been able to play the particular Talivaldis piece that had haunted him since the previous afternoon. Another source of irritation was that he hadn't even finished breakfast when the Bentley pulled up in front of the house at Ferndale. It wasn't so much the interrupted meal but that he loved sitting at the table in the kitchen listening to the hissing of the kettle on the Aga and seeing, through the door to the walkway, those lozenges of purple and green light cast onto the floor by the coloured glass windows. So far Zidra had only spoken a few words to him – it seemed she wasn't at her best first thing in the morning – and that was another disappointment. He loved to listen to her long speeches and her mimicry – she could do a perfect imitation of Mrs Blunkett – but most of all he wanted her to talk about her father. Her real one, not Mr Vincent. A bit earlier Philip had mentioned to her the name Oleksii Talivaldis – he'd even managed to get out that mouthful of a name with only the tiniest stutter – but she didn't seem much interested in talking about him. Maybe she'd never been all that close to him, just as he wasn't all that close to his father. She seemed to be annoyed with her mother though.

Mr Vincent had been very interested in the Talivaldis compositions though. While Mrs Vincent was making another pot of tea, he'd said he hadn't known Talivaldis wrote music and asked what Philip thought of the pieces. All he'd been able to blurt out was. 'G-g-g-good.' You might almost have thought Mr Vincent was musical himself until you remembered what he'd said the night before about having a tin ear. Mrs Vincent had explained what that meant and they'd both laughed, though Mr Vincent in a forced kind of a way. Philip got the impression that he didn't like Oleksii very much. That was often the way with people, he'd noticed. If they didn't like someone they asked lots of questions about them. Yet sometimes, if they liked someone a lot, they'd refuse to talk about them at all.

Now Mrs Vincent, apparently relaxed about Jones' early arrival, took him on a tour of the garden while Philip hastily packed. Just before Philip was admitted into the passenger seat of the Bentley, Mrs Vincent gave him a big hug. 'Remember that we're just a telephone call away,' she said, kissing his cheek. 'Feel free to phone at any time. It's been so lovely having you to stay.'

'Th-th . . .' But he had been unable to complete this simple word. Not even that trick of thinking of a replacement had helped him, for what could substitute for *thanks*?

Only when the car was beyond Jingera did Jones reveal the bad news that Mummy hadn't returned to Woodlands. She'd decided to stay in Sydney until *You and Mr Chapman are ready to join her,* Jones said.

When Philip asked why, Jones said he didn't exactly know but he thought it was something to do with dress fittings. The person in charge of alterations had proved unreliable, so Mrs Chapman had been forced to stay on in Sydney. Conversation ceased and they travelled the rest of the way to Woodlands accompanied only by the swishing of tyres on bitumen, and afterwards on gravel.

He knew his mother had planned this. She must have, otherwise she would've had to come back to pack her clothes for Europe. She'd planned it and hadn't wanted to tell him beforehand, whether from delicacy or self-centredness he was unable to decide. While unwilling to judge her, it was impossible to stem his unhappiness at the prospect of being without her for the last few days of holiday.

The telephone started ringing as soon as he entered the hallway at Woodlands and no one else was around to answer it. Reluctantly picking up the receiver, he tried to mouth a greeting, but there was no need.

'Is that you, darling?'

He made a noise that might have passed for agreement.

His mother proceeded. 'I'm so sorry I can't get back for the last few days of your holiday, but things have been unbelievably hectic here. Mrs Brown, who does the alterations, let me down. Poor dear, her mother's been unwell but she's back on board now, so all's well that ends well. At least I'll have some glad rags to take away, so I'm not likely to completely disgrace your father. Anyway I expect you're really pleased to have him all to yourself for a bit, and of course you'll be able to practise the piano as much as you like.' Here she gave her musical little laugh before continuing. 'And naturally I'll see you when you come up here. We'll all spend the night at the Hotel Australia before you go back to Stambroke College. I suppose you're getting quite excited about seeing all your friends again. Oh darling, I almost forgot to tell you that I telephoned Mrs Vincent just after Jones collected you. She said how much they all enjoyed having you to stay. So sweet of them. She said you're such a talented boy, but I've always known that of course. Well, my dearest, I mustn't keep you and I've got a lunch to go to. So do give Daddy a great big hug and a kiss for me and tell him I'll phone again later. And do take care of yourself, sweetheart.'

He struggled to make a noise, but already the earpiece had clicked and he was left listening to the unrelenting sound of the dial tone.

After returning the receiver to its cradle, he ran upstairs to her dressing room and threw open the wardrobe doors. Yes, the best leather suitcases were gone, and so too were many of her dresses and shoes. She'd known she wouldn't be coming back to Woodlands before leaving for Europe but hadn't bothered to tell him.

Hadn't been brave enough to tell him.

So angry was he now feeling that he wanted to tear at the dresses, to rip into them with a sharp knife or a pair of scissors. But he wouldn't do that; he was too lacking in nerve, or too frightened of the consequences. Instead he took the scissors from the bathroom next door and ran into his own bedroom, pulling out of the wardrobe those long trousers that his mother had given him at the start of the holidays. *For best, for my little man*, she'd said, and he'd hated them even as she'd handed them over. Fancy pants. Why didn't she let him choose his own clothes?

He tore into the trousers with the nail scissors, mutilating them so that they would never again be wearable. After putting away the scissors, he took the damaged trousers and placed them in Mummy's wardrobe where she would be sure to see them as soon as she opened the door. That this wouldn't be for some months didn't spoil his pleasure in this act of revenge.

Luncheon, served as usual in the dining room, was a rather sad affair, with only his father for company. While trying hard to respond to his heartiness, Philip knew he was failing dismally. He was unable to do more than nod or shake his head. The power of speech had completely deserted him. Eventually his father gave up any pretence at conversation and they each ate quickly, in Philip's case more to get away as soon as possible than to appease his hunger.

After the ordeal by lunch was over, Philip went up to his bedroom and shut the door. It was a large room with a view of the paddocks to the north-west, rising to the escarpment from which trailed wisps of gauzy cloud. Elbows resting on the windowsill, he watched his father, in that uniform of blue shirt, moleskin trousers and riding boots, head towards the stockyards.

The sight of his father moved him almost to tears. If he had the power of speech, would what he longed to say come pouring out?

That you could love and hate someone at the same time puzzled him.

Maybe there were some things you could never express. Even in music.

Once his father was out of sight, Philip opened the cupboard and pulled out the box of wooden animals. He hadn't looked at them for some time, hadn't even given them a thought until Zidra had mentioned that green elephant he'd presented her with all those years ago. After tipping the animals out onto the pale green carpet, he began to arrange them in groups. When this was done, he took out another box from the cupboard, a set of plastic fence sections that could clip together. These he used to box in all these wild creatures: the zebras, the elephants, the giraffes, the lions and the tigers. Just as he was constrained, so too were these animals.

The confinement complete, he left his zoo on the floor and went downstairs to the drawing room. Seated on the piano stool, he took a number of deep breaths, before beginning to play the Talivaldis arrangements that, he discovered without much surprise, he seemed to have remembered perfectly.

CHAPTER 22

The day of the meeting about the Aboriginal housing proposal, Ilona collected Eileen just after lunch, and spent much of the drive into Burford briefing her. Though Eileen knew of the proposal, Ilona suspected she hadn't been closely following the issues, if indeed she'd been following them at all.

'Wilba Wilba Shire council is responsible for the Aboriginal camp near Burford,' Ilona said. 'The local farmers want the Aborigines moved on, for their own good, they say. The papers want them moved on because they're a moral and political embarrassment. The *Canberra Times* only last week had an opinion piece asking how such shocking conditions could be tolerated barely a hundred miles from the nation's capital. Now, as you know, the Anglican Church has stepped in with the offer of land for the construction of ten houses. But there are several problems.'

'What are those?'

'The land's in the centre of Burford.' Before Eileen had a chance to respond, she added, 'You might well ask why that's a problem, and that would be a good question. The answer is that some people think it will create a ghetto. What they're really concerned about, though, is that it will lower property values. The site's right in the middle of a residential area. I saw a letter in the *Burford Advertiser* suggesting that Aborigines need training to live in a house. Training in domestic science, they said.'

She stopped talking for a moment while she overtook a truck going even more slowly than her preferred speed. After this, she said, 'So that leads us to the second problem.' She hesitated, hoping that Eileen might hazard a guess as to what this was. When she didn't, Ilona continued. 'No one asks the Aborigines where they'd like their housing to be.'

Still there was no response from Eileen. After a few moments Ilona added, 'Anyway, I do think the *Burford Advertiser* is trying to stir up community opposition to having Aborigines living side-by-side with whites. The council's partly to blame as well. Of course, if they refuse the development application to let the Aborigines live in town and then issue eviction notices to get them off the land they're camped on, wherever are they expected to go?'

'To the Reserve, that's where.'

'But why should they be treated as if they're aliens in their own country?'

Whether Eileen had no answer to this question, or was simply unwilling to supply one, Ilona wasn't to know. For the rest of the journey they travelled in silence.

The meeting was in the church hall, a red-brick building on a grassy plot not far from the centre of Burford. Ilona eventually found a space in the bottom corner of the car park, under a cedar tree. Once inside the building, she hesitated. Graced with a high sloping ceiling supported by splendid triangular trusses, the hall was already rather full. There was a central aisle with uncomfortable looking wooden seats arranged on each side.

Had it been a wedding, the bride's guests would have been on one side and the groom's on the other, she thought, and perhaps those in the know understood that, if you supported the proposal to build Aboriginal houses you should park yourself on the left, and if you didn't, on the right. At this moment she noticed the large group of Aborigines towards the back. Quickly she looked for the Hunters; surely they'd come to this meeting.

'There're some spare seats towards the front,' Eileen said, taking her arm and guiding her forward, before she'd had a chance to finish her search. 'That might be an interesting spot to sit. I've heard the new rector is worth hearing.'

For an instant Ilona wondered if this was why Eileen had agreed to accompany her, an opportunity to hear the new, and reputedly charismatic, Reverend Cannadine from the Anglican Church providing the land for the proposed housing. That had to be him sitting on the platform, and he was certainly very handsome, in a large red-faced sort of way, although his dog-collar appeared to be several sizes too small and was probably chafing his neck.

Soon after they'd settled themselves in their seats, the Reverend Cannadine got to his feet. There was applause followed by a brief round of heckling, which he ignored as he held aloft what looked to be a large flat board about three feet square and covered in a cloth.

'I have something to show you,' he said. 'Something that will interest you all greatly, as it has me. Something that I found attached to the street sign next to our land.'

With a flourish, he removed the cloth and held up the sign for all to see. BOONG BOULEVARDE was written in foot-high letters and underneath was an enlarged photograph of a drunken Aboriginal man sprawled on the pavement.

Ilona held her breath; whose side was this man on?

'That's right,' a man in the audience shouted. 'They're a bunch of bloody no-hopers and we don't want them as our neighbours.'

'We have our Aboriginal brothers and sisters in the audience,' the rector said, his face flushing a deeper red. 'Let us do them the courtesy of not abusing them.'

All heads now turned to peer at the group of Aborigines sitting towards the back of the hall. Ilona scanned their faces. None of them looked like Tommy or Molly Hunter, but it was hard to see everyone in the hall from this far forward.

The Reverend Cannadine took advantage of this moment to put down the sign before continuing. 'Now permit me to explain why this notice saddened me so deeply when I found it last night. Permit me to explain why I felt compelled to show it to you today. Why would I want to do this? Because the sign is a symbol. It's a symbol of all that is wrong with race relations in Burford. And indeed not just in Burford but in Australia. When white men came to this country, they took away from the original Australians all opportunities to live as equals in this glorious land of ours.' His voice was loud and deep, and reverberated through the hall. 'If our consciences are to be cleansed of this dreadful shame, we must make a start right here in Burford. Through this shocking human delineation that we have created, this needless separation of black from white, we are condemning a part of the human race to a life of physical, social and mental humiliation. Achieving equality for Aboriginal people in Burford is one way of purging our consciences of our shameful history.

'The story of the Aborigines' dispossession is an unjust story. Aboriginal people are human beings like us and yet we haven't treated them so. They're our equals in every respect, and yet we haven't treated them equally. We had the opportunity at Federation and yet we didn't take it. Once this unjust history is recognised, it will surely be possible for us all to move on to express our deep regret about their shameful treatment.'

At this point there was loud clapping from some sections of the audience, and boos and hisses from others. 'Such a wonderful speaker,' Eileen whispered, her eyes bright.

'It's the Abos' fault that they're segregated,' a man in the audience yelled out. 'They simply don't want to integrate.'

'We won't give them the opportunity, that's why!' Ilona shouted, on her feet without even thinking about it. 'And that's what this housing proposal is about, giving them an opportunity.'

'I don't want a mob of drunks on the other side of my fence,' someone else called out.

'Why not let us have the sort of houses we want, where we want them?' cried a white-haired Aboriginal man whom Ilona hadn't noticed until now, although he was sitting in the front row.

'You will be consulted,' said the Reverend Cannadine soothingly.

A man from a few rows back now called out, 'The Abos don't want houses anyway. All they want is a sheet of corrugated iron and a few poles, preferably on someone else's good farming land.'

'Not true,' shouted the white-haired Aboriginal man.

'And they're drunk half the time,' someone else bellowed.

The rector now held up both his hands to quell the rising sound in the hall. When the noise had subsided, he continued. 'No one raises questions about the morality of a white householder who comes home inebriated. No one debates if a white householder should invite his brother or sister to stay. No one asks whether or not white families should be allowed to become our neighbours. Why are we treating our black brethren so differently? It is surely the responsibility of the Burford community to take the initiative in reversing our shameful treatment of the original inhabitants of this great land. And it is surely our responsibility to do it now. Yes, there is a potential conflict right here in Burford. A potential conflict between racial equality and traditional attitudes that *assume* the inferiority of the Aboriginal people. But this is a conflict that we can choose to avoid. Indeed, we must choose right now to move beyond such conflict. We must do this not only to unravel our past unjust treatment, but we must also avoid harming Australia's reputation as a fair-minded people.'

There was a murmuring from the audience. More heckling might have followed, had not a photographer dashed down the aisle. The Reverend Cannadine again elevated the sign, BOONG BOULEVARDE. The camera flashed and an image was created that, by the next day, would be on the front page of both the *Burford Advertiser* and the *Canberra Times*.

On the way out of the hall, Ilona signed up to become involved in the campaign for housing Aboriginal people in Burford. That the campaign would run for years rather than months, she could not have guessed. Eileen hung back from volunteering, although she did manage to shake the hand of the Reverend Cannadine. She'd experienced a conversion to the Reverend rather than to the Aboriginal cause, Ilona decided in slight irritation. Her trouble was that she had no passion to make the world a better place.

While Eileen and the Reverend Cannadine were chatting, Ilona approached some Aborigines standing on the lawn nearby.

She didn't recognise anyone from the camp she'd visited but she did want to talk to the elderly man who'd spoken at the meeting. Engaged in an animated conversation, he didn't at first notice her standing near him. The journalist from the *Canberra Times* had no compunction in interrupting the conversation, however, and Ilona stepped back a few paces until he'd taken several photographs.

Afterwards the elderly man beckoned Ilona over.

'You made a really good point just now,' she said, 'about building the sort of houses you want where you want them. That hadn't occurred to me before, but you're quite right.'

'We certainly need somewhere to live, but we'd like to choose where.'

'And you need to be consulted about the housing designs.'

'We do but I don't think we've got to that stage yet,' the man said. 'The church will be lucky to get planning permission and they won't get it if we're visibly involved. That's the way things work around here.'

After some more discussion about the project, Ilona introduced herself.

'I know who you are,' he said, smiling. 'I'm Jack Wheeler.'

So he knows I'm not from Welfare, she thought, and he may even know whom I'm looking for. After taking a deep breath, she asked him if he knew the whereabouts of Tommy and Molly Hunter and their family.

'Saw them just a few months ago,' he said slowly. 'Haven't seen them recently though. Last I heard they'd gone to a property near Bogong. There's a station owner there who wanted some labour. Are you wanting pickers for your crops?'

'No. We're only grazing at Ferndale.'

'That's what I thought.'

'I need to get some news to the Hunters. Do you know the name of that property?'

'Numbugga Flats. It's out the back of Bogong.'

'The back of Bogong. That's up in the mountains, isn't it?'

'Yes. You have to take the main road and turn off before Bogong.'

'If you see them, do please let them know I'm looking for them. But I think I might take a drive to Numbugga Flats.'

Ilona and Eileen were silent on the drive back to Jingera. This week I shall go to Bogong and find the Hunters, Ilona thought, and perhaps take Peter with me. After mentally packing a picnic hamper, and negotiating a few more miles, Ilona began to think about what sort of housing might suit the Aborigines who were being moved on from the camp outside Burford.

These were people who were used to sitting comfortably on the ground, she thought; people who didn't necessarily need chairs and tables and other paraphernalia. Why should they be rehoused in neat Australian suburban bungalows and not consulted about the type of design that would suit their needs? Maybe this would be something they could raise with the Reverend Cannadine before the next meeting. Maybe someone like Jack Wheeler could liaise with an architect to design houses whose walls could be propped open in good weather and shut when it rained or was cold. Or at least houses with wide verandahs, not like those double- or triple-fronted monstrosities that people were building these days. That new development opposite the cemetery in Jingera was a perfect example of how *not* to build houses.

After dropping Eileen at the Cadwalladers' cottage, Ilona couldn't find anywhere to leave the car in the square in Jingera. The parking area at the back of the hotel was only half full, so she left the Armstrong there. She called into the butcher's shop first. There was a run of customers in front of her, including a woman who'd said she'd come all the way from Bermagui. She bought ten pounds of George's special sausages to freeze: the pork and sage, the lamb and rosemary, and the beef and mixed herbs. For a moment Ilona wondered if she might miss out on her own favourites, the pork and sage, but George got more from out the back. By the time she'd bought a few things at the general store and collected the post and a package of books, some thirty minutes had elapsed. If she hadn't decided to put the parcel into the car boot rather than the back seat, she might not have seen the graffiti at once. But there it was, in bright red letters plastered over the back of the car: *ABO LOVER.*

She glanced around. No one in sight. Perhaps someone was watching her from the pub, but no, that wasn't possible. It had no windows overlooking the car park. She felt slightly sick, hating the thought that someone in Jingera felt such animosity towards the Aborigines, and to her for having associated with them. Was it because she'd attended the Burford meeting? Or was it because she'd been looking for the Hunters?

Perhaps the paint was only poster colour and would be easy to wipe off. She put down the parcel. After pulling out the cloth she kept in the side pocket of the car, she wet it with water from a hosepipe at the edge of the lawn bordering the parking area. She gently rubbed at the first letter. It wasn't going to come off. The paint must be oil-based, though how it could have dried so quickly was anyone's guess.

Now it occurred to her that the words couldn't have been

painted onto the car in Jingera, but in Burford while they were in the meeting. Yes, that must have been it. Someone at the meeting had seen where her sympathies lay and painted the sign on the car afterwards. The Armstrong was the only one of its kind in the area, and she would be easily identifiable as its driver.

When she arrived home, Peter said, 'I don't care about the car so much, or the bigotry of whoever painted those letters on it. But you might be in danger.'

'Of course I'm not in danger,' she said, laughing although she didn't really feel like it.

'I can get that paint off anyway,' said Peter, 'with a bit of white spirit and then my fingernail. It might leave a few scratches but we won't let that worry us. I'd put money on this being ordinary house paint. That's nowhere near as hard as car duco that's baked on.'

'No, don't bother,' Ilona said. 'Leave it as it is. It's a badge of honour.'

'Or a badge of courage.'

'Now this has happened perhaps I won't be so anxious about making a tiny ding in the paintwork,' she said. 'I should be able to park by ear.'

'By touch, perhaps,' he said, and put an arm around her shoulders. 'But I'll clean it off anyway.'

As she exchanged her high heels for the pair of flats she'd left just inside the kitchen door, she pondered over what had happened. It seemed that everywhere there was prejudice. Although Ferndale was like a safe haven, with a fence all around it, it was only because Peter's family had been rich enough and lucky enough to buy it years ago, and had bequeathed it to Peter, that they were able to live here. Yet now she started to wonder if it really belonged to them.

'Did you see the Hunters?' Peter said.

'No. But I spoke to someone who knows where they are. They're at Numbugga Flats.'

'Up in the mountains? I don't like you driving up there on your own, not in an old car like ours. I'll come with you.'

'Good, I thought you might. I'll pack a hamper and we'll have a picnic.'

'I'm a bit surprised they'd go that far though. This is their country, after all. Why would they leave it?'

'We'll soon find out,' Ilona said. 'I can't wait to see their faces when they hear about Jervis Bay and the chance of seeing Lorna again so soon. They'll be really excited. Then the only thing for me to worry about will be how much time they can take off work and how to get them all up there.'

CHAPTER 23

Last afternoon of the summer holidays, at least for those kids at state schools. As the bus swung into the square in Jingera, Zidra saw Sally waiting outside the post office. Even though Sally must have heard the bus chugging down the road – there was no other traffic around – she kept her back turned. After getting off the bus, Zidra saw who was claiming all of her friend's attention: Jim was standing just inside the post office door.

'They're coming canoeing with us,' Sally said, smirking at Zidra as if she'd just won something. 'Jim and Eric both.'

Zidra put her beach bag on the pavement. Jim nodded at her, unsmiling. Not even a *hello*, you might almost think he was sorry to see her turn up on this final afternoon of the holidays. She herself wasn't at all keen on going out on the lagoon with him and Eric. Instead of a leisurely paddle upstream, there'd be flirting and showing off, and anyway she'd decided she didn't want to see Eric again. It was too late though; here he was looming up next to Jim and goodness gracious, how he'd changed colour! Between those coppery freckles his skin was now burnt red and that golden aura had completely gone.

Skin-deep allure was just that, so superficial that a small change in colour could tilt her over that margin between attraction and indifference. It wasn't that she didn't like him, but rather that the desire to touch him had completely vanished.

'Hi babe,' he said in a fake American accent, as he picked up her beach bag. 'What have you got in here? Pretty heavy, isn't it, for an afternoon's boating?'

'Some books,' she said, trying to take the bag from him. Their hands touched for a moment too long. While she let his hand rest against hers, it was only because she didn't want to relinquish the bag. Yet still she couldn't prevent a blush suffusing her neck and face. When he let go she almost fell backwards. 'Just some books Jim lent me,' she said, pulling them out of the bag: *Eyeless in Gaza,* and a book on fossils that she'd struggled through. 'I was planning to drop them into his house before Sally and I went canoeing.'

'I'll take them,' Jim said. 'I'll meet you all at Hairy Harry's.'

'I'll come with you,' Sally said. 'You two can get the canoes.'

Zidra found Sally's peremptory tone and her departure with Jim far more exasperating than being left alone with Eric. It was Zidra who had the special friendship with Jim that went back years. Sally had only met him at the start of the holidays, and it wasn't fair that she could so easily displace Zidra in his affections.

Shocked at the antipathy she felt at that moment for Sally, Zidra used her sandaled foot to destroy a small weed that had the temerity to grow between the pavement and the brick wall of the post office. Intent on this task, she didn't at first hear what Eric was saying, and he had to repeat it.

'Back to Sydney tomorrow, Zid. Can't say I'm looking forward to it. We're doing the Leaving Certificate this year as well as training for the Head of the River. So it's going to be a lot of work.'

'What's the Head of the River?'

'The Regatta on the Nepean River. Hasn't Jim mentioned it? We're both in the eights.'

She told Eric that she never listened to Jim when he talked about sport and that she only skimmed through those paragraphs in his letters. Jim knew this, of course, she'd told him often, but still he persisted. Though now she came to think about it, perhaps there had been something about rowing and the Regatta in several of his letters. 'I expect it's very important,' she concluded, with a touch of sarcasm. 'Team building and all that.'

Eric chose not to notice her dismissive tone, and she was glad of it. He wasn't too bad, she decided, now that she no longer found him attractive in that disturbing sense. At this moment he picked up her bag again. Still unwilling to admit to his courtesy, she might have tussled with him if she hadn't suspected this was what he wanted. Instead she laughed. 'Sure, you can carry it. You can paddle too. Good training for the Head of the River. Maybe we can go right up towards Burford.' Now she knew that travelling with Eric was inescapable, she began to feel quite pleased at the way the afternoon was shaping up. 'We could take the canoe with the double-sided paddle,' she said.

'There's only one of those. Don't you want to paddle too?'

'No, or only coming back.'

He laughed. 'Oh yes, with the current.' But she could tell he was pleased. She certainly wasn't going to reveal that her decision was based on the thought that he should keep both of his hands busy. She felt even more pleased when Hairy Harry refrained from patting her bottom as he normally did at the launching of the canoes.

Jim and Sally turned up some time later; you wouldn't think carrying two books to the Cadwallader house could take them so long. Zidra was already sitting in the front of one of the canoes. Eric, standing knee-deep in the water, had tight hold of both boats. Without any discussion, Jim waded into the lagoon and stepped into the canoe in which Zidra was perched. It rocked as he sat down. Though his bared teeth might have been a grin or a grimace, she couldn't conceal her pleasure, and smiled. Sally was now eyeing Eric in that way she had that made people feel so special. Sally could look after herself; that was one of the things Zidra most admired about her; that toughness that you didn't always see because it was so well camouflaged by the laughter and the smiles.

A gentle wind had sprung up and light sparkled off the flickering surface of the lagoon. Zidra and Jim started paddling. Seated facing forward, Zidra watched the water flow past and listened to the regular splash of the paddle slicing into the water. The distant laughter of Sally and Eric faded as their canoe lagged behind and Eric struggled with the double-sided paddle. Jim didn't say a word and Zidra didn't feel like talking either. She guessed that Jim wanted to wear himself out. She often felt like that too, when angry or upset; only physical exertion could distance you from the misery. Perhaps Sally had said she wanted to travel with Eric and that had distressed Jim. It would have to be that, rather than the other way around. Sally was much too pretty for anyone to want to dump her.

'Are you all right, Zidra?'

In surprise, she turned. 'Of course I am.'

'You seem unusually quiet. Do you mind that I kidnapped you?'

'Is that what it was? I thought you might have been sacked.'

He laughed. 'No, it was by mutual consent. Anyway, we weren't really going out together.'

'No? You could have fooled me. You don't think Sally needs protection from Eric?'

'She can fend for herself. You know that, Zidra. Anyway, I wanted to talk to you. We've had hardly any time together these holidays.'

'We've had about what we usually have.' Glancing around at him again, she caught her breath. His face was set. That she couldn't bear to look at him for more than a split second was only because she was afraid her expression might give her away. She stopped paddling. The new emotion that she was feeling confused her and at first she couldn't put a name to it. Trailing a hand in the water, she pondered what it was. More than affection, she decided, it was closer to tenderness.

Jim paddled the canoe towards the edge of the river where the water was still and shaded by the long shadows of the she-oaks. After a moment, when Zidra felt calmer, she turned around to sit facing him, rocking the canoe as she did so.

'Sure you wouldn't rather be in Eric's canoe?'

'Not really,' she said. She wasn't going to make things too easy for him. 'You didn't need to warn me off him, you know. I'm quite able to work things out for myself.'

'You have to watch out for some boys.'

'You think I don't know that? You're as bad as Mama. Boys and men. They're always ogling. Their eyes drill right into you.' She noticed that Jim at once changed his focus from her face to the river beyond. 'Not you, though,' she said, smiling. 'Or anyway, only at Sally.'

After he'd restored eye contact, she said, 'I can't decide if it's a good thing or a bad thing to be suspicious. Perhaps it's good.

I'm quite a guarded sort of person.'

'Well, that didn't stop you trusting Eric. Not that Eric isn't trustworthy, it's just that . . .' He paused. 'It's just that he's rather inclined to make passes.'

She laughed. 'How old-fashioned you sound! Are you jealous, Jim, just because I rubbed his back with oil?'

'No, I just want to make sure you don't make a fool of yourself.'

After she'd flicked him with water, he added, 'And to protect you.'

'I know and I'm glad of it. That's what you said just before you went off to start at Stambroke. I'll never forget the morning you left here for the first time.'

Zidra stared into the water, dark green at this point. She would never forget either that night before Jim had first left Jingera. She'd spent it tossing and turning and occasionally checking the clock with her torch; it had seemed that morning would never come. Eventually she'd slept for a few hours and, at precisely six o'clock, had awoken with a start. So anxious was she to say goodbye to Jim that she'd dashed out of the house without even having a drink of water or telling Mama. Hidden in her favourite place under the hedge, she'd waited for him. Once he'd arrived, they'd walked down to the lagoon and back, watched by Mr Cadwallader who was waiting at the bus stop with Jim's suitcases.

'That's when you told me your mother was going to marry Mr Vincent,' Jim continued. 'And that he was going to adopt you. You were so excited. And for a moment I had a mental image of you in flowing white christening robes with a bonnet on your head. I don't know why I was confusing adoption with christening. Maybe it was just because I'd seen newspaper photos of babies being adopted and they were all so small.'

'That was when you asked me to write to you,' Zidra said.

'No, you asked me to write to you.'

'No, it was the other way around. But while we're on the subject of writing, can you do me a favour, Jim?'

'What?'

'Leave the sport out of your letters, all except the rowing.'

'Okay, but can you do me a favour too?'

'What's that?'

'Cut out the descriptions of Star. Everything else you write is beaut. But no horses.'

She laughed. Horses would continue to appear in her letters but she'd make the telling briefer, and all to be written with the new fountain pen he'd given her. 'Surely you realise that horses are very interesting,' she said. 'Do you know that the name Philip means *lover of horses*?'

'Well, I'm sure that's not something he'll be telling the boys at school.'

'*Lover of music* would suit him better. You will look out for him, won't you, at Stambroke?'

'I promise.'

'Funny that children don't have any rights. Lorna was taken to Gudgiegalah against her will. Philip was sent to Stambroke against his will. How do you decide who should have rights and who shouldn't?'

'That's what my essay for the Law Society was about. What are you grinning about, Zidra?'

'Have you any idea how funny that sounds? Makes you sound thirty instead of sixteen. You'll be an old man before you're twenty.' When he looked startled, she flicked him with water again to show she was only teasing. 'Anyway, what did your essay have to say about who should have rights?'

'One approach is to say that incompetent people shouldn't have rights. Children are incompetent at many things and so shouldn't have rights.'

'But plenty of adults are too, and they don't have the right to choose taken away from them. Philip's clearly not looking forward to going back to Stambroke and I think he should have the right to choose not to.' She paused for a moment, thinking of how she'd grown fond of Philip in the few days he'd stayed at Ferndale. 'You know, I was really annoyed with Mama at first for inviting him to stay,' she continued. 'I thought he'd be a drag. But he wasn't, and he's a terrific listener.'

Jim said nothing, as if to illustrate his own listening credentials, and Zidra flushed as she realised that Philip appeared to pay such close attention because he could barely talk. She continued. 'Mama got out a whole lot of music when Philip was visiting that I didn't know she had. Handwritten stuff. She showed it to Philip.' Zidra hesitated; while she wanted to tell Jim about this she knew it would be painful. 'It was written by my father, my real father, Oleksii. Philip played it, and do you know what? She'd never showed it to me before. Never. Yet it was my father's.' So distressed had she felt at this concealment that she'd barely been able to talk to her mother for several days.

'Maybe it was too upsetting for her.'

'I don't know. I was never really close to him anyway, not like I am to Peter. My real father wasn't like Peter. He was miserable. I hated him coming home from work. The atmosphere in the flat changed the minute he walked in the front door. I've never felt guilty about not missing him. He's the one who should have felt guilty. He was so grumpy all the time.'

'I expect the war made him like that. Try to think about it from his perspective.'

'Why should I try to see it from his perspective?'

'It might help you understand him better.'

'But Mama survived the war and Peter survived the war. I'm not going to feel guilty about what the war did to *Our Papa Who Art in Heaven*. I'm fed up with the war and with hearing about it.'

'You're angry.'

'Angry?' Only after she'd spewed out the word did she realise that Jim was right. She was angry with her father, and now with Jim for pointing it out.

Yet how futile resentment was when there was nothing she could do about it. Perhaps she should concentrate on her luck in having a new father and Ferndale. Anyway you could love people *as if* they were your father, even when they weren't. And to be honest, she hadn't even liked her father's music when Philip had played it. It was too harsh, too dissonant. Maybe that was why Mama hadn't shown it to her. Zidra knew she lacked musical discernment. She'd never felt the slightest interest in music, and although she'd reluctantly continued practising the piano, right up until she was ten, she'd insisted on giving it up after that. Yet Philip had understood her father's music, that had been obvious, and that had pleased her mother. Even if Zidra couldn't appreciate Papa's music, at least she could be glad that others did. It took away from his grumpiness.

'When are you going to Jervis Bay?' Jim asked.

'In two weeks.'

'It seems like an odd time of the year to take the Gudgiegalah girls on a trip.'

'That's what I thought too, but Peter says they won't be missing any school because that's when the Gudgiegalah Show is on, and Mama says that the guesthouses offer cheap rates when the holiday season's over. I'm getting really anxious about it.'

'Why?'

'We still haven't located the Hunters. Imagine Lorna's disappointment if we can't find them in time. Mama's getting really worried about it too. She doesn't say so, but I can tell. She's got another lead though. She's heard they're living at Numbugga Flats, up on the plateau. She and Peter are going to drive up there next week.'

At this point Eric and Sally caught up, and soon after they turned the canoes around and began to paddle back. Past the she-oaks stands they glided, and the dead eucalyptus tree on whose bleached branches cormorants perched, with their wings spread to dry. Then the craft caught the faster-flowing current in the middle of the river, and they used the paddles only to steer the canoes.

How curious it was that a few words here and a few words there could make you feel so connected, Zidra thought, to people and to the past. Just a few words could do it, could give you a sense of continuity and allow you to take as well as to give. Jim was her past and her present, and that thought brought her some peace.

———◆———

Afterwards, when Jim and Eric had seen Zidra onto the bus north and escorted Sally home, Jim took Eric up to the headland and through the cemetery. Beyond the gravestones and the white-painted fence, they sat on the narrow strip of recently mown grass. Below them stretched Jingera Beach, that long sweep of white sand rising into high sand dunes backed by dense bush.

I won't see my family and Zidra for another term, Jim thought. He was growing away from his family though. Moving away, growing away. He realised for the first time that he'd miss Zidra more than his family. But that was natural. She had similar interests to his. That was all there was to it.

Yet he knew he was kidding himself.

In the late afternoon light, the flickering ocean was iridescent. To the south a bank of indigo-bottomed white clouds became faintly tinged with gold from the sinking sun. That Zidra had become beautiful was neither here nor there. She was one of his best friends, and would stay that way. Or would she? Today she had become more than that. Maybe she'd been more than that for a long time.

Yet perhaps he would be growing away from her too, as his adulthood beckoned, and this thought saddened him.

'It's been terrific staying with your family,' Eric said.

So long had they been sitting in silence that Jim had forgotten he wasn't alone. He didn't really want to talk but knew what was expected of him. That's what Stambroke taught you, if you didn't know already. 'Great to have you,' he mumbled.

'Being away from home and school has helped me decide,' Eric said.

'Decide what?'

'I don't want to go to university. I just want to go on the land.'

'Why?'

'I miss it. I'm homesick.'

'Even here?'

'Yes, even here. It's beautiful but too hilly and too green. And Sydney's too crowded. I belong to the black plains.'

'How do you know where you belong when you were sent away to school so young?'

'I just know. When I go home to all that space I feel my soul spread out and when I go back to Sydney I feel it being squeezed into a tight mould again. I'm going to help Dad run the property. Eventually I'll marry some nice girl I'll meet at a polo match.' He laughed, as he always did when talking about life up north. 'She'll have blue eyes and brown hair and a sense of humour.'

'Sounds like Sally.'

'Yes, or someone like her. There'll be lots of Sallys before then though.'

CHAPTER 24

At the Ferndale stop, Zidra struggled off the bus with the beach bag and the parcel Mrs Blunkett had given her, inwardly cursed her luck in being caught by the postmistress in Jingera. Now she was going to have to walk all the way along the drive, from the entrance-gate to the homestead, juggling the package as well as her bag. Mrs Blunkett had appeared at the door of the post office when she and the others had been hanging about at the Jingera bus stop, and had beckoned her over. 'Something for your mother,' she'd said, nodding her head so vigorously that her white curls shook. 'Another box from David Jones, I wonder what this time. She's a great one for the mail order, but that's what you've got to do when you're on the land like, and I suppose she thinks twice before venturing far in the car. Back to school tomorrow, eh? Bet you're looking forward to it, the school holidays seem to go on forever when you're young.' Only Jim's shouting that the bus was coming had given Zidra an excuse to get away, and she'd dashed across the square with barely a minute to spare, while Mrs Blunkett called after her, 'Mind you're careful with that package! It's fragile.'

So intent was Zidra now on not dropping the parcel – how stupid of her to agree to take it when her mother could easily have collected it in the car – that she didn't see her mother standing at the entrance-gate until she was almost upon her. 'What's the occasion?' she said. 'Or have you come to help carry?'

'Yes. Mrs Blunkett telephoned, so I thought I'd meet the bus.' Her mother took the parcel from her.

'What's inside?' Zidra said. 'Mrs Blunkett was so consumed with curiosity I'm surprised she didn't open it.' She mimicked the postmistress: '*Another one from David Jones, I wonder what this time. Your mother's a great one for the mail order, but that's what you've got to do when you're on the land like.*'

'Some books and records. Anyway, Mrs Blunkett now knows what's inside because I told her on the phone. Thanks for collecting them.'

Looking at her mother's smiling face, Zidra realised she'd forgiven her for not telling her about Papa's music. That's what talking to Jim had done; it had allowed her to see what had happened in a new light. And she'd also begun to wonder if Papa wasn't far more than just a grumpy man who'd never had two words for her. Although she'd felt she had only one good memory of him, that time he'd taken her to the circus and they'd eaten fairy floss, there must be other good stuff too.

In time, she'd ask her mother to tell her more about him but not yet. What she wanted to do instead, as soon as she got into the haven of her attic room, was to replay in her mind the events of the afternoon. Especially that moment on the river when she'd realised what she was starting to feel for Jim.

––—•—––

Ilona, waiting at the front gate when Zidra got off the bus, had noticed with a start how lovely her daughter had become, with those dark curls framing her oval face, and the tawny brown eyes and golden skin. Yet it wasn't only the pleasing proportions of her face, it was a sort of inner glow that she'd recently acquired. Ilona wouldn't be making any remarks about this though. She'd nearly had her head bitten off after her thoughtless comment about Zidra's plucked eyebrows.

It was to be hoped that Zidra's radiance, that was the word that best described it, had nothing to do with Eric Hall, the boy from Walgett. Ever since meeting him at that barbecue on the beach Ilona had suspected that his interest in Zidra was not platonic. 'Did you enjoy your canoeing?' she now enquired, as they strolled back along the drive towards the homestead, nestled in its semicircle of pine trees.

'It was terrific,' Zidra said. 'We went out with Jim and Eric in the end.'

'Yes, Mrs Blunkett told me when she phoned me about the parcel.'

'Of course she would. Anyway, we had a terrific time on the water. We paddled all the way upriver – it took ages – and back again. A lovely afternoon.'

Ilona waited for more but Zidra had nothing else to say. Eventually Ilona said, 'And who was paddling your canoe? Was it you or the boy from Walgett?'

'It was only Jim, Mama. You don't need to worry,' Zidra said, grinning.

The boy from Walgett would be returning to Sydney with Jim tomorrow, and Ilona was glad of it. It wasn't that she disliked Eric, she told herself. Indeed, he was rather charming, but he was clearly too old for Zidra and was probably fast into the bargain. Mothers had a sixth sense for that kind of thing.

CHAPTER 25

Zidra inspected the brightly coloured postcard with the Gudgiegalah postmark and the cartoon picture of a small child in a stroller. Ever since receiving it weeks before, she'd kept it propped against the lamp on her bedside table. Once more she read the words scrawled in block letters in Lorna's hand:

IT'S STILL ON. HURRAH FOR ST ANDREWS SUNDAY SCHOOL!

Yet it wasn't much of a *hurrah* anymore, she thought. There was less than a week to go until the Jervis Bay trip, and they still hadn't located the Hunters. While it would be wonderful to see Lorna when she and her mother travelled north, Zidra couldn't bear to think of her disappointment if they failed to bring Lorna's mother, and failed even to obtain news of where the family was.

Tomorrow Mama and Peter were going on their expedition to Numbugga Flats, while she would be plodding through her lessons at Burford Girls' High. Mama wouldn't think of letting her take a *sickie* on this day. 'We shall find them,' she had exclaimed. 'And bring you home the good news.' The only consolation,

Zidra thought, was that she would be dropped off at school instead of having to take the school bus.

———

They'd be at Numbugga Flats in another half hour at most, Peter reckoned. Ilona could barely contain her excitement at the prospect of meeting up with the Hunters again and seeing their expressions when she told them the news of Lorna's visit to Jervis Bay. Quite how she would get them to the coast next week she hadn't yet worked out, though Peter had said that there was a bus service between Bogong and Burford, and that it would be easy to collect them from the bus station in Burford.

At the top of the escarpment the terrain changed so dramatically that you might be forgiven for thinking you'd travelled to another country, Ilona thought. A country without rain and with infertile soil. The road wound through paddocks littered with sheep and tussocks, and some isolated stands of eucalyptus trees. The sheep and the tussocks were virtually indistinguishable, each casting shadows in the afternoon sunlight.

Before Bogong, they turned off the highway onto a narrow unpaved road that meandered through an increasingly desolate landscape; no stock, no living trees, and only the weathered ringbarked tree stumps indicating that this area had once been forested. How hard the Hunters would find living here, she thought, after the lushness of the coast. Some miles further on, a sign indicated that Numbugga Flats lay to their right. Peter turned the car onto a rutted track that followed the contours around a hill and terminated in front of a homestead, a low weatherboard building. Beyond this was a large corrugated iron shearing shed that looked to be in poor repair. Apart from this, there were none of the usual outbuildings to be found on country properties, except for an apology for a dunny some way behind the back of the house. And the accumulated detritus of years spent struggling to make a living from this land: discarded tractors, ploughs and a couple of decrepit old utes.

A man and several dogs came out of the house; a tall stringy-looking individual, who shaded his eyes as he watched the car come to a halt. The dogs barked and circled the vehicle, but at a whistle from their owner they slunk behind him and lay down in the dust. The man and the dogs were the only living things in sight, Ilona thought. It was hard to imagine a more austere spot.

After Peter had explained where they were from, the man, Bob Fitzgerald, was welcoming, and would have made them a cup of tea if Ilona had let him. And perhaps she should have, for Peter raised his eyebrows when she refused. As if to compensate for her ungraciousness, he embarked on one of those slow conversations at which he was so practised; about the price of wool and superphosphate, and the problems of rabbits and resistance to myxomatosis, while all she wanted to do was shout, *Where are the Hunters?*

Only after a good quarter of an hour of yarning did Peter get around to stating the purpose of their visit. They were looking for the Hunter family, he explained, and they'd heard that Tommy Hunter, and maybe his family too, were working at Numbugga Flats.

'Sorry, mate. Never heard of them,' Bob said.

'But are you sure?' Ilona said. 'I was told they were here.' Perhaps Bob didn't know their names; that must be it. 'They're an Aboriginal family,' she added.

'Abos, you say? No, not seen any around here for years. Someone was pulling your leg, I reckon.'

She hesitated while a range of emotions competed within her. Disappointment that their quest was in vain. Irritation with the dismissive way he said *Abos*. And a growing suspicion that perhaps she'd misheard what the Aboriginal man in Burford had told her. 'I was informed they were at Numbugga Flats near Bogong,' she said. 'That's here, isn't it?'

'Spot on,' he said. 'Sorry, missus. I'm afraid I can't help you. I *am* looking for help, though. If you hear of anyone, let me know.' He insisted on giving Peter his telephone number. 'It's a party line,' he said. 'If I don't pick up, one of my neighbours will. And I do have neighbours here, though it mightn't look like it. Maybe not as close as yours on the coast, but they're here all the same. And if the Hunters were with them, I'd have heard.'

'I didn't make a mistake,' Ilona said, as they drove back to the main road. 'I know I didn't. The man I spoke to at that meeting was quite clear. Numbugga Flats, back of Bogong.'

'I believe you, Ilona. Your hearing's as sharp as anyone's. Perhaps the chap was trying to put you off. Maybe he thought you had links with Welfare.'

'I told him I didn't.' Hot tears of frustration filled her eyes. It was heartbreaking to have come all this way and end up none the wiser.

'There's no reason they should trust the white fellow and every reason why they shouldn't. Anyway, it's quite possible he just made a mistake.' After a pause, Peter added, 'But you can't go on haring all round southern New South Wales. You've done all you can.'

In silence they turned onto the highway. The arid countryside did nothing to cheer her. The desolate plateau with its ringbarked tree stumps was left behind. The paddocks gave way to scrubby bush and soon this metamorphosed into rainforest.

Just before the road commenced its descent of the escarpment, Ilona glanced at Peter. His face was set. This grim expression was due to fatigue, she decided, and they should have accepted Bob Fitzgerald's offer of a *cuppa*. Peter had been driving for hours, ever since they'd left Ferndale that morning, apart from a brief picnic before Bogong and later the stop at Numbugga Flats.

In front of them the road narrowed. Peter swung the car around the first of the many hairpin bends. Where the road bent back on itself, the safety barrier was broken. A piece of tape marked the spot where some poor soul had driven over the edge. There was no trace of a car though and the tyre tracks looked a few days old. Averting her eyes, Ilona focused on the tree ferns crowding down the gully as if desperate to reach the bottom. Above them, the eucalypts struggled upwards, straight and tall. Wisps of cloud trailed around the edge of the mountain side and the next ridge appeared veiled in white lace.

Instead of being soothed by this sight, it made her feel apprehensive. At long last she was able to admit to herself that they wouldn't be able to find the Hunters before the Jervis Bay trip. She wouldn't stop looking though, right up to the day that she and Zidra were to leave. They would somehow meet up with Lorna at Jervis Bay and tell her they'd tried but hadn't succeeded. She sighed. The breeze wafting through the open quarterpane window dropped several degrees. Shivering, she shut the window. The sunlight had vanished, hidden by the low cloud.

Something made her look at Peter again. Although the air was cool, sweat now beaded his brow and his hands were tightly clutching the steering wheel. Too tightly; she could see the white bones of his knuckles.

Surely there wasn't going to be a panic attack, right here on the steepest part of the escarpment. He hadn't had one for nearly a year, not since that time they'd been driving home from Woodlands and a Tiger Moth had flown low overhead. She peered up at the sky. If there was a plane above the low clouds it would be impossible to see but surely she would be able to hear it. Yet there was no noise at all, apart from the motor ticking over and the swish of the tyres on the bitumen, and from time to time the crack of a whipbird.

The road was narrow; too narrow for Peter to stop, she knew. But he'd have to soon, for the sweat was now pouring down his face and his skin was as white as chalk.

'Slow down,' she said. 'Put on your lights.'

'I can't do it, Ilona.'

'You're doing fine. We're not far from the bottom and there's a place to stop there.'

'That's too far,' he said, his words indistinct.

Unexpectedly he braked and the map on her lap shot forward onto the floor. There was no verge at the edge of the road but only the safety barrier, below which the timbered mountain side fell away steeply. The car came to a halt in the middle of their side of the road. Peter opened the driver's door and leapt out, a wartime pilot with vertigo that was not dissipating with the passage of years.

Climbing out more slowly, she heard him panting as he paced up and down the edge of the bitumen. 'You'll have to drive. I'm sorry, Ilona. I just can't do it.'

Though this road was little used on a weekday afternoon, they were parked just beyond a bend. Any vehicle coming up behind mightn't see the parked car before it was too late. 'I'm happy to,' she said, 'but let's keep going.' Quickly she got into the driver's seat and he into the passenger's. Taking out a handkerchief, he wiped his hands and neck, and continued inhaling deeply.

Peering at the rear-vision mirror, she could see that there were no vehicles behind. But she wouldn't look again. What lay ahead was challenging for the inexperienced driver that she was.

Occasionally she caught glimpses of the undulating hills of that fertile band of country far below them. Lying between the coast and the mountain range, these hills were a vivid green. She'd always known them like this, apart from that terrible summer of four years ago when the countryside was bone dry and the bushfires had raged for days. Slowly she steered the car around the hairpin bends and through the dense forest, and eventually around that last sharp turning before the final descent.

When they'd driven up the escarpment earlier today her hopes had been so high, but not anymore. Not even the sudden shaft of sunlight that at this moment broke through the clouds and illuminated the valley below could lift her spirits.

She had tried to find the Hunters, and had failed. She had dragged Peter with her and reawakened his vertigo. It was as well that he was not coming with her to Jervis Bay. Driving didn't agree with him anymore.

And for Lorna it would be a double letdown. Her mother wouldn't be going to Jervis Bay to see her; that would the first disappointment. The second was that they wouldn't even be able to give her any news about her family. All avenues of investigation were now closed. The Hunters could be dead for all anyone knew.

Gazing intently through the front windscreen, Ilona thought again of those words Lorna had written about Gudgiegalah in her letter to Zidra. *IT IS LIKE A PRISON HERE.*

She and Peter each knew what that was like. And they would live with this knowledge for the rest of their lives.

—•—

The truck felt as if it had no springs but he didn't really mind. It was such a relief to have finished picking for the day, and to feel the wind in his hair. The clouds had lifted and he watched the blaze of gold as the sun set behind the jagged mountain range, while the sky faded to a washed-out blue.

It wasn't much further to the turn-off and the pickers' quarters where they were staying. These were quite decent really. No toilet or washing facilities, but at least there was a watertight roof over their heads and somewhere to cook, as well as a tap next to the rainwater tank where they could get good water for drinking and cooking. And while there wasn't enough water in the tank for washing, there was always the creek.

He shifted his position. His back was tired and aching, but he and his missus were fortunate to have the cabin to lean against. Most of the others had nothing to support them. As the truck rattled along they were jostled against one another, not that the kids seemed to mind. They were all laughing and chattering, except for the smaller ones who'd fallen asleep. It had been a twelve-hour day, no wonder they were tired.

He might have missed the car altogether if he hadn't seen the eagle gliding on an updraft not far from the escarpment. His eye followed the bird as it drifted over the valley and then his peripheral vision picked up the grey shape under some trees at the far side of the picnic spot. He craned forward. That car was impossible to mistake. 'Bugger me,' he said, nudging his wife. 'If it isn't Peter Vincent and his missus. Been wonderin' what they've been up to ever since Jack Wheeler said they were lookin' for us.'

Seated at a picnic table not far from the car, the Vincents had their backs to the road and wouldn't have seen the truck if Tommy Hunter hadn't stood up and started bellowing. At the same time he banged the top of the cabin with the flat of his hand. The driver obligingly swerved off the road, skidding slightly on the loose gravel surface of the parking area and at this diversion some of the children started squealing with delight.

———————

Ilona turned at the sound of the vehicle sliding on the gravel and the shrieking voices of the children. 'My goodness, just look at this truck,' she said, her voice breaking. 'I think we've been found!'

'You've got ten minutes, that's all,' called the driver, getting out of the cabin and lighting a cigarette.

Although all the pickers climbed down off the back of the truck, only Tommy and Molly Hunter joined Ilona and Peter.

'I'm so pleased to see you,' Ilona said. She couldn't stop smiling and might have hugged Molly if she hadn't been hiding behind Tommy. 'We've been looking everywhere for you. Where have you been?'

'Pickin' for the last week at that new property opposite Sutherlands,' Tommy said. 'That's where that man drivin' the truck's from. Decent sort of fella. Before that, at Eden, further down the coast.'

'I never thought of going to Eden,' Ilona said. 'And no one ever suggested it.' Jack Wheeler, the man she'd met at the housing meeting in Burford, had been almost right, she thought. The Hunters certainly were here, but at the bottom rather than the top of the escarpment.

'You found us just in time,' Ilona said, smiling at the Hunters. 'Sit down, I've got some news for you.' When they were seated at the picnic table, she told Molly and Tommy about the letter Zidra had received from Lorna, and about the visit of the Gudgiegalah girls to Jervis Bay the following weekend. As Ilona spoke, Molly nodded occasionally and, after a while, she began to weep. Lifting up the hem of her frock, she used it to dab at the fat teardrops coursing down her cheeks. At first she cried quietly, but she soon began to sob.

For four years Molly hadn't seen her daughter, and what that would feel like didn't bear thinking of. Ilona, sitting by Molly's side, put her arm around her. This made her weep the more. After pulling a clean handkerchief from her skirt pocket, Ilona gave it to Molly.

'Gudgiegalah no tellem nothin',' Molly said, blowing her nose loudly. 'Nothin'. Could've bin gone fer all we knew.'

Now Ilona told the Hunters about her planned trip to Jervis Bay, and offered to drive them there.

'No takem kids,' Molly said quite emphatically.

'But why not?'

'Them mob too many,' Molly said. 'Makem too much noise.'

'I suppose they would be hard to conceal. You've got four other children, haven't you?' After Molly nodded, Ilona continued. 'It would certainly be hard to get everyone in the car even with just me driving. And I suppose that many children might *let the cat out of the bag*.'

At this, Molly looked puzzled.

Peter said, 'She means it would make it hard to hide everyone from the people guarding Lorna.'

But even that wasn't quite clear enough, Ilona thought. The truth was that the Aborigines had to be hidden but not the whites. And of course there was always the fear that more of their children might be taken.

It was decided that Tommy and Molly would travel with Ilona and Zidra in the car to Jervis Bay, and that the other children would stay with their aunties at Wallaga Lake Reserve.

The Hunters would go back to Wallaga before the end of the week and Ilona and Zidra would collect Molly and Tommy from there.

'Zidra will be over the moon,' Ilona said when the Hunters had gone off with the others in the truck.

'Even more so now it's clear there'll be space for her too,' Peter said.

Ilona took his arm and rested her head for a moment on his shoulder. 'How happy I am, Peter!'

'I know,' he said, kissing the top of her head. 'So am I. And I'll be even happier if you carry on driving us home to Ferndale.'

PART IV

Sydney and Jingera
1962

CHAPTER 26

Philip rolled over once more. He was awake far too early. It wasn't even six o'clock, but how could you possibly go back to sleep when there was this terrible dread pressing down on you at the thought of being back at Stambroke College in just a few more hours? For several minutes more he lay in bed listening to the sounds drifting up from the street below: a truck collecting garbage, the screaming of an ambulance, some voices raised in anger before trailing off again, and the cooing of the pigeon that landed briefly on the windowsill.

Tiring of this, he got up and began to pace restlessly around the hotel suite. Through the closed door of his parents' bedroom came the noise of his father snoring – or it might even have been his mother, who was getting over a slight cold, but not bad enough to stop her travelling, she'd said last night. In the hallway was their luggage, or most of it. The old girl is travelling light, his father had said. When she'd replied that everything was essential, he'd grinned and said it was lucky they'd be able to leave most of their bags at the Savoy when they ventured into continental Europe, otherwise the porters' fees would be even greater than the cost of their flights.

On the hallstand in the small lobby lay the box of chocolates that Philip had bought his mother in Burford. She must have left them out so she wouldn't forget to take them to the airport today. They had cherry liqueur centres and perhaps that was why she hadn't opened them last night. She would've had to offer him one and they were alcoholic. She'd been awfully pleased when he'd given the box to her though. Never arrive empty-handed, he'd said, quoting her, and she'd laughed and given him an enormous hug. Next to the chocolates were the keys to the hotel suite. His father always made a great fuss of leaving them out, in case the Hotel Australia caught on fire. He had a bit of a thing about fires ever since the Jingera pub had burnt down. That and the fact that he was a reformed smoker.

In the bathroom, Philip washed, not all that quietly, in the hope his parents might wake up and want their breakfast early too, but by the time he'd dressed there was still only the sound of regular breathing from their room. He couldn't bear to hang about any longer waiting for them; he'd have to go out on his own. It was now just after six o'clock. If he walked very fast down to the Quay and back again, maybe he could shed some of this misery. Maybe he'd be distracted by something else apart from his own unhappiness.

Would it have been better if his parents were leaving tomorrow rather than today? Then his return to Stambroke College and their departure wouldn't be so linked. Then they might have had a bit more time for him last night. While his mother had rather reluctantly agreed to play Canasta, she'd let him win. How he hated that, not the winning but that she'd let him. He could tell she'd rather be doing other things. Phoning her friends or fussing about her clothes. She didn't need to worry about the passports and money and tickets, though; those were in Daddy's charge.

Next Philip put on his school blazer. All his other things were packed and the boys were not allowed to wear only part of the school uniform. It was all or nothing and it certainly wasn't going to be nothing. Yet what would the penalty be if he were caught without his cap? He stared at his reflection in the mirror in the hall stand. The cap looked silly and so did the tie. He took them off. That was better; now he seemed normal. Anyway, the worst that could happen if he was caught was expulsion. Imagine how wonderful it would be, never having to go back to Stambroke again. Yet how disappointed his mother would be. Instead of the overseas trip, she'd have to look after him. She wouldn't like that one bit and would start to hate him for it, and he couldn't bear the thought of this; it would be worse even than being back in Barton House. Reluctantly he put on the school tie again, knotting it awkwardly, but that didn't matter, that wasn't an expellable offence. On went the cap as well, this time at a rakish angle. If you were going to look a nong, you might as well go the whole hog.

After this, he removed one of the keys from the hall stand and crept out of the suite, quietly closing the door behind him. He took the lift down to the lobby and strode straight out the front entrance. No one took the slightest notice of him. There weren't too many people in the street, only a few adults who looked like sleepwalkers. He marched down to Circular Quay, following the same route that he'd taken with his father the very first day of the school holidays nearly two months ago. The Valencia Street ferry was just pulling out of the wharf as he arrived. It was a twenty-minute ferry ride at most to his aunt and uncle's place at Hunters Hill. If he'd been five minutes earlier, would he have run away? No, he'd never have the courage, not as long as he had his mother to worry about. It wasn't only that he loved her but also that he was frightened of her anger. An anger that was never savage. There would be no shouting, no raised voices. Just an icy coldness that was far, far worse.

He didn't know how he was going to get through the days, the weeks, the months that lay ahead. The time would never pass. It seemed like forever until the first free weekend even. Then he was to go to his aunt and uncle's place at Hunters Hill, it was all arranged. At least they were kind people. He thought of the Sculthorpe sonatina his aunt had given him, and this led naturally to the Talivaldis pieces. These reminded him of Mrs Vincent and her understanding. At this moment he noticed that the newspaper kiosk in front of the Quay was open. He would buy a postcard for Mrs Vincent and maybe she'd write back. He could do with some letters.

A few days before, he'd posted a letter to himself from Burford. Just so something would arrive for him soon. Sooner than his parents' letters would, although his mother had declared that the airmail post from Europe would take at most a week to get to Sydney. He'd disguised his writing on the envelope. It would be terrible if Keith or one of the other boys discovered he was writing to himself. Inside the envelope were some cuttings from the *Burford Advertiser*, more to fill the envelope than to remind him of life at home.

At the kiosk, he selected a postcard with a picture of the Harbour Bridge for Mrs Vincent and a Violet Crumble bar for himself. You were never so depressed that you couldn't eat a Crumble bar before breakfast. In fact being sad sometimes seemed to make you want to eat more.

The woman behind the counter put the card into an envelope printed with yellow wattle blossom. 'Local stamp?' she asked.

He nodded.

'What's a young man like yourself doing up so early?' she asked. 'Not going off to work yet, are you?'

This was one of the better sort of questions that didn't require an answer. You could get away with just a smile and not have to expose yourself.

Still, once he'd handed over his pennies, he hurried away as fast as possible in case she made further enquiries. He went to the nearest wharf and sat on a bench to eat the Violet Crumble bar. Staring at the green water of the harbour, he thought of that ferry ride two months before with his father. He'd said he should learn to stand up for himself against the other boys. *It's all for your own good . . . You've got to learn to stick up for yourself in life and this is as good a training as any.*

His anxiety at this prospect made him feel sick and staring at the choppy harbour water made the nausea even worse. Dark green water, oily-looking and opaque. What would it be like to dive deep into that water and never come up again? He could put an end to everything in just a few minutes. Or seconds. He stood up. Feeling the pull of the water, as if he were a pin being drawn towards a magnet, he took a few tentative steps towards the edge.

'Hey, you! What do you think you're doing? The ferry's due shortly.'

He felt a firm grip on his shoulder as he was pushed back from the water's edge. The man was old, as old as his father, and he was wearing a cap that made him look official.

'You'd better get well back from the edge,' he said, 'and take that rubbish with you. There's a bin over there. What do you think that's for, eh? Now be off with you.'

Be off with you. That's what everyone thought when they saw him. He wasn't wanted anywhere. He was a nothing and a nobody. Of no value to anyone.

After trudging back to the hotel, he let himself into the suite. His parents were awake now; he could hear them talking to one another in the bedroom. Not the words though, just Mummy's musical voice and Daddy's gruff one, in some contrapuntal duet. They hadn't even noticed he'd gone out.

'Oh, there you are, darling!' his mother said, coming out of the bedroom. She was already dressed in a smart navy suit with white piping round the edges. As she turned her head, he noticed she'd forgotten to check the back of her hair. There was a flattened bit on her crown that someone should tell her about. But not him, not now. Not when tears might come at any minute. The squashed down hair was what moved him, her only physical flaw, and he could have wept for her.

'There you are, son.' Daddy too was dressed, though only in his uniform, those moleskin trousers and blue shirt – he had dozens of them – that he always wore. 'Wondered where you'd got to. Having a spot of breakfast, were you?'

'N-n-no.'

'Good, good. We can all go down together. You do look smart in your school togs. Your mother and I are so proud of you, aren't we, Jude?'

'So proud,' she said, embracing him and he smelled her wonderful scent that he would always remember, that would always invoke his love for her.

Later, when the porter had arrived to take their luggage downstairs, Philip dashed back into his parents' bedroom to collect his cap from where he'd left it on the dressing table. At once he saw the box of chocolates he'd given his mother the day before lying unopened on the bed. She must have forgotten them in the rush to leave. He picked them up and carried them with him.

Only in the lobby, waiting for Jones to arrive with the car, did she notice what he was holding. 'Oh darling, you remembered my chocolates. How terribly sweet of you!' She took them from him and ruffled his hair.

'Here's Jones with the car now,' his father said.

If Philip hadn't shifted his eyes to his mother's lovely face at that point, he wouldn't have seen the wink his parents exchanged. Then he understood that she'd intended to leave the chocolates behind. A gift for the maid. Mummy didn't want his cherry liqueur chocolates. How silly of him to think she'd take them with her on the plane rather than discard them as soon as she decently could.

None of them spoke much on the drive to Vaucluse. Although his mother held Philip's hand very tightly in her own gloved one all the way there, he'd never before felt so alone.

It was either a coincidence or somehow the headmaster had got wind of her arrival and was waiting at Barton House to make a fuss of her. This was witnessed by half-a-dozen boys and their parents but blessedly too early for the busloads of students who'd soon arrive from Central Station.

'Chap wants a donation, no doubt,' his father said as he lifted Philip's suitcase and overnight bag out of the boot. 'On top of the fees.'

'Goodbye, darling!' Philip's mother held out her arms as if to embrace the entire group but only Philip stepped forward. He rested his head for a moment against her soft breast, inhaling her scent. Once again he thought that he might never see her again. She didn't appear to be troubled by such anxieties, although she did whisper to him alone and not to the audience, 'I'll miss you, hugely, dearest boy. Have courage, and don't take any notice of those horrid boys who tease you. Daddy told me all about them.

Be strong, darling, and we'll be back again so soon that you'll barely notice we've gone.'

So she'd known all along, and hadn't said anything to him about it! Although he kissed her, and even managed a smile, inside he was seething.

Next he shook his father's hand and listened to him saying, 'Have a good term and be brave, son.'

Afterwards they climbed into the Bentley and Jones chauffeured them off. It was a relief to have the farewell over and done with. For so long he'd been dreading his parents' departure, but now there was this new information to digest: that his mother had known all along about *those horrid boys who tease you*, and hadn't thought to say a word until just now.

Quickly Philip unpacked in his dormitory, before going outside and heading towards the line of trees beyond the oval. This was out of bounds, but he really didn't care. There was one tree in particular that was easy to climb. It had a flattish branch that you could stretch out on, and from here you could watch the street running up the hill to the main entrance gates to the college. Keith Macready would be one of the last to arrive back, flying in from somewhere near Emerald in Queensland. Until that time at least, he'd be left alone.

———⋄———

Jim, sitting in the coach next to Eric, happened to glance out of the window as they approached the gates to Stambroke College and caught sight of a boy perched in the branches of one of the camphor laurel trees. It was just a fleeting glimpse but the face was unmistakably Philip's. Jim remembered Zidra's words the day they went out in the canoe: *You will look out for him, won't you, at Stambroke?* Perhaps this was why the image stuck in his mind as the boys alighted from the coach and sorted themselves into their respective boarding houses.

Yet perhaps it was also Philip's expression. There was something haunting about it, poignant even, and it struck Jim that the look was almost of desperation. He would have to watch Philip this term, just as he would have to keep an eye on all the juniors in Barton House. This wasn't only because he hated the initiation practices that went on in the first few weeks of the new year, but also because he'd been made a prefect, and so too had Eric. It wasn't a task Jim especially wanted. It was a bit of a standover job and he hated that thought. Pulling together as a team was all very well and it certainly made the boarders easier to control, but he felt that it allowed the development of cultures of bullying as well. You were in a team and one of us, or out of a team and not one of us, and therefore a legitimate target for abuse.

But maybe this was human nature and a boarding school was just a microcosm in which it was easier to observe such behaviour. He would see in the coming term the clever ways that Keith Macready and his acolytes had of making miserable lives of boys like Philip. Boys who were different. Musical or individualistic boys who were not team players. The cleverness of Keith Macready and his ilk lay in presenting their persecutions as practical jokes, and in knowing just when to stop short to avoid expulsion.

Later he would wonder if he should have taken some action then, when he'd seen Philip's expression. Later he'd come to understand what it had meant.

———

Perched in the tree, Philip couldn't stop thinking of his mother. She'd allowed him to return to Stambroke even though she'd known how he was treated. *Have courage . . . Daddy told me . . . Be strong, darling . . . Those horrid boys who tease you.* Her words spun round and round in his head. She'd known, and yet been willing to leave him here.

That was unforgivable.

He was on his own now, with no backup. No support. He could do what he damned well wanted except get out of this place.

He thought again of the attraction he'd felt that morning to the harbour water. Drowning would surely be a good way to die.

He'd heard it was better not to know how to swim if you were going to drown. It was faster. You didn't struggle so much.

CHAPTER 27

The house seemed too quiet, George thought. Andy wasn't home yet and Jim and Eric had left only that morning, so it was just Eileen and George in the kitchen. It still hurt George to think that Jim had gone off in the bus from Burford with scarcely a backward glance or wave. He'd put the two boys on the bus after the usual early start from home. Eric hadn't seemed to mind a bit being ferried to Burford squeezed into the front of the van that had Cadwallader's Quality Meats emblazoned on the side. Indeed, before leaving he'd even taken a photograph of it, with the whole family standing there. Eileen hadn't liked that much, no doubt about it, though she did like Eric. Everyone liked Eric.

'It's not as if we even saw all that much of Jim these past ten days,' Eileen said. 'It's as if he'd already left before Eric came to visit. Not that I'm complaining.'

George knew she was feeling low. But he was too, and perhaps that explained why he flared up when she asked him to feed the chooks. Only she didn't say chooks like everyone else, she said hens.

'No!' he shouted, surprising them both. 'I won't feed the bloody chooks! That Andy's job.'

It didn't take her long to recover though. 'Andy's got to do his homework when he gets back,' she said, leaning on the table the better to hiss at him. 'I wouldn't have thought it was too much of an imposition to ask you to do it.'

'Too much to ask? It's the last bloody straw.'

'Please don't swear at me, George. Not in my own house.'

'It is my bloody house too! Can't you even give a man a bit of peace when he comes home from a day's work? I'm fed up with it all.' Glaring at her, he focused only on the anger he saw on her face, ignoring the hurt that he knew lay behind this.

'Don't shout, George. The neighbours will hear.'

'The neighbours can damned well hear what they like,' he said. How typical of her that she should care more about what other people thought than about what her husband was feeling.

But he was unable to maintain his annoyance. Slowly, his exasperation ebbed away and was replaced by a deep sadness. Sadness or loneliness, it was hard to say which. Shouting at her couldn't disguise the fact that Jim had gone. How tempting was the thought of heading off to the pub for a drink before tea.

'Don't think you can go sidling out the front door, George. I don't know exactly where you go sometimes. Swigging down the beer with that drunkard Hargreaves. I can smell it on you when you get back.'

He chose to ignore this remark. Any response would be construed as deliberately provocative. Eileen was probably feeling pretty much as he was about Jim's return to Stambroke. George pulled out a chair and sat down heavily on it. His gammy leg was hurting; it was doing that more often these days. Maybe he should get a stool to sit on in the shop. Even when there were no customers, he was on his feet all the time.

'I've been alone all day and I'd like to hear a human voice,' she said, sitting down too.

Reconciliation didn't come easy to her. So moved was he by the sorrow in her voice that he said the first thing that came into his head. 'Jim will have a good year.'

'Yes, but it will be his last.'

'He might get a maximum pass.'

'What's that?'

'Getting As in everything and first-class honours in his honours subjects.'

'Do you think so?'

'Yes, probably. And then on to Sydney University.'

'If he gets a scholarship.'

'He will. And a living allowance, besides.'

They sat in a silence that was almost companionable now they'd calmed down a bit. Eventually, he said, 'I'm sorry I shouted at you, Eileen.'

'That's all right. I know you'll miss Jim too.'

'I can't believe they're growing up so quickly.'

'Nor I. It seems like only yesterday when they were babies.'

'You've been a good mother, Eileen.'

'I'm still a good mother, George.'

'Yes.' It was too much to hope that she might ever say that he'd been a good father.

'I'm still not keen on Andy doing an apprenticeship next year,' she said.

George sighed. 'The Army Apprentices' scheme provides more than that. I wish you'd read the stuff that Andy got.'

'Let me finish before you interrupt. That's what I wanted to tell you, I did read it.'

'When?'

'Yesterday.'

'I see.' It had only taken her a month. 'In that case you'll know what it offers. Did you see what they pay?'

'Yes.'

'When I was in the army I knew a number of coves who'd come out of the Balcombe Barracks and moved up the ranks. Of course that was in wartime, but you never know. Anyway, Andy actually wants to run his own joinery business in time. Think of that.'

'Ilona Vincent says there's good money in joinery.'

George winced. When he'd said that very same thing to Eileen some time ago, she hadn't taken a blind bit of notice. 'She'd know,' he said, more rudely than he'd intended.

'No need to be sarcastic, George.'

George refrained from replying. No response was needed. He guessed the discussion was closed, at least for a while, and with a bit of luck Eileen might accept that an apprenticeship could offer opportunities rather than dead ends. It was clearly going to be easier now Ilona had signalled her approval. 'Maybe I'll feed the chooks,' he said. 'It's a nice evening for it.'

Afterwards, George sat down on the chopping block and lit a cigarette. He only smoked outside and he shouldn't even smoke there, he knew. Cigarettes were that expensive these days. If you smoked a few packets it was like burning ten-shilling notes, and he'd resolved to give up next time they put up the cigarette tax.

Through the trees he could see the colour draining from the lagoon as the evening advanced, the water palely reflecting the lightening sky. Against the background roar of the surf he heard birds chittering. Turning, he saw, in the shrubs on the side boundary, a pair of crimson rosellas. They swooped down the garden just as Andy erupted from the passage along the side of the house.

'Have a good day, son?' George said stamping out his cigarette. Didn't do to smoke in front of the boy.

'Yeah. Cricket practice this arvo.'

'Ah, cricket practice.' Really he must take more notice of what Andy was doing. He was growing up so fast, he was taller than George was now. Covertly he inspected his son. All skin and bone but with a handsome open face, and fair skin and hair. George experimented with putting him into an army uniform, like those cut-out paper dolls and their wardrobes that some of the kids used to play with when he was a lad. Andy wouldn't look too bad in a uniform. All the girls would be after him. That larrikin aspect of Andy would appeal to them too. You just wouldn't want there to be another war, though.

Next George removed the uniform and tried putting Andy in a carpenter's apron with pockets full of tools. He wasn't sure where this get-up came from. It certainly wasn't what the carpenters he'd come across wore. Old trousers and shirt more like it. Must have been from that book he used to read to the boys when they were small: *Carl the Carpenter*.

'What are you grinning about, Dad?'

'Was I grinning? Must be because it's going to be a really clear night and I might get the telescope out later.' Although he'd had an early start that morning and was tired, it would be too good an opportunity to let pass. He hadn't looked at the celestial hemisphere for a while. The weather conditions hadn't been right and with Jim home he hadn't really felt like it.

'I wouldn't mind having a look through your telescope again some time, Dad.'

'Sure, son. I'd like that.'

221

'Not tonight though. Too tired. I've got to feed the chooks next.'

'I've already done it.'

'Why? That's my job.'

'Your mother said you had lots of homework.'

'Nah, school's only just started. Anyway, I like feeding them.'

He picked up the pail George had left on the ground and clattered up the back steps. As the fly-screen door banged shut behind him, George heard him shout, 'I'm home, Mum! When's tea?'

Jim would be back at Stambroke now, unpacking and settling in. George got to his feet and slowly climbed the steps to the verandah. Just the three of them for tea tonight and it was going to be cottage pie.

CHAPTER 28

It was way too early on a Saturday morning. Zidra's wretched in-built clock just couldn't cotton on to the fact that it was a weekend and that she should be sleeping in. A few weeks back at school was all it had taken for her body to switch off that lovely *sleeping-in until nine or ten o'clock in the morning* mode. So here she was, as bright as a budgerigar, and it was only seven. She could hear distant clattering of crockery from the kitchen that indicated her mother and Peter were already up.

After climbing out of bed, she flung open all the curtains before collecting from her desk the two letters that arrived yesterday. For a moment she hesitated in front of her favourite view to the west. The early morning sunlight caught the tops of the pine trees and tinted mauve a few strips of cloud above the distant mountain range. Leaning forward, she could see, between the trees, the manager's cottage. It was empty, although not long after their move to Ferndale Mama had arranged for it to be painted pale pink and the window frames white. Only the rusty corrugated iron roof had escaped attention. Maybe she'd shift in there in a few years time . . . but no, she was going to Sydney once she'd passed the Leaving Certificate, and then on to see the world.

Sitting up in bed again, she took up the first of the letters from its slit envelope. This one was from Eric and she'd been surprised to receive it. Surprised but pleased, too, for she loved getting letters.

6th February, 1962

Dear Zid,
Just a quick note to let you know you haven't been forgotten, and I hope you haven't forgotten me either, the Boy from Walgett whom Jim warned you off, I'll bet! Anyway, I enjoyed meeting you and the lovely Sally.

Sometimes when things get tough here – during prep, for instance, when there are insuperable algebraic heights to be scaled that only James Cadwallader seems to find easy, or during prayers – I conjure up the image of Jingera Beach and all that freedom that you enjoy in your beautiful part of the world. Not for me though. To use a cliché (and we all know they're banned by the cliché police who are everywhere at Stambroke College), you can take the boy out of Walgett but you'll never take Walgett out of the boy, and that's why I'm off home again once this last year of school is over.

I know you don't like reading about sport. So I won't bore you with details of our fantastic rowing successes or those on the cricket pitch or the terrific fielding achievements of
Yours truly,
Eric.
P. S. Please give Sally my best wishes and tell her I'm not much of a letter writer, as you will have noticed.

It was quite a good letter, even at this second reading, and she was touched that he'd bothered to write at all. The other letter was from Jim and ran over several pages. This one she'd read three times already. Even at this fourth perusal, she took it slowly, to string out for as long as possible the joy that reading his words gave her. An even greater pleasure lay at the end of the letter, where Jim had substituted a new phrase – *with love from* – in place of what he'd written in all those earlier letters over the past years – *yours sincerely*.

7th February, 1962

Dear Zid,
Thank you for your letter which was such a pleasure to receive as you conjured up so well and so amusingly, what it must be like travelling to Burford on the school bus. But I'm sorry to hear that the Bradley boys continue to give you gip. I would try to sort them out for you, if I were there, although I'm sure you need no help from me. Do remember that there are three of them, not that you can't count, but that three against one can be dangerous. Anyway, warnings aside, I would love to hear more about the school bus and what happens on it.

Life goes on as always here, with each morning beginning with rowing practice. Yes, I know you don't want to read about sport, but this paragraph isn't about sport, it's about how I pass my days and in your last letter, you said you wanted to know about that. So if you're still reading, you now know that we take rowing very seriously. Afterwards we have breakfast; the food is terribly stodgy, but you'd eat anything after exercise. Then we go to chapel, followed by lessons all day, and a bit of training after school followed by dinner and prep. And that's where I'm writing this letter to you.

I'm starting to rev up for some concentrated study. I never worked hard in the past. I never felt I needed to, and anyway I didn't want to be called a swot – pathetic, isn't it? – but I don't want to miss out on a place doing law at Sydney University either. I've finally decided that's what I want to do – unless it's physics! There will be students competing from all over the state.

It's funny how you can miss a place so much but not want to spend the rest of your life there. That's what I feel about Jingera. It's a part of me but soon I won't be living there anymore. I suppose, anyway, that it's been years since I did actually live there. Stambroke College has been my home and it's a bit like a military camp. It's certainly made me tidy which I never was before.

Philip Chapman asks about you from time to time and I'm sure he'd really appreciate a note or a card from you. Your mother has written to him several times and he was very pleased about that. He's mentioned the Talivaldis Variations, which evidently made a profound impression on him, so it seems your actual father was a man to be very proud of, as is Mr Vincent as well of course. Philip practises the piano whenever he can and he's allowed off sport because of this, but that doesn't make him any more popular I'm afraid. He's been acting strangely all term, in ways it's hard to describe. Dissociated, I suppose. Maybe even desperate. He's the sort of boy whom boarding school just doesn't suit. If ever I have a kid like that I wouldn't dream of sending him here. You wouldn't believe the sort of things that go on, or maybe you would. Just think of the Bradley boys.

The weather here continues warm and dry, which makes rowing practice a dream once you get over the shock of rising so early.

Back to the books now.
With love from
Jim

After refolding the letters, she restored them to their respective envelopes. She would write to Jim this weekend, and Philip too. She hated to think of him being unhappy. And maybe a short note to Eric in a few weeks' time. Soon she would get up and have breakfast but first perhaps a little snooze.

CHAPTER 29

'We've got a letter from Jim!' Eileen called to George as he came in after work.

He took off his shoes just inside the front door and trod heavily down the hallway in his argyle socks, the green and red ones that she'd given him for Christmas. He was becoming used to them now. It was just as well. They were good quality and would last forever.

Eileen was sitting at the table in the kitchen shelling peas. Simmering on the stove top was something that might be beef stew, with a bit of luck. Through the open back door, he caught a fleeting glimpse of that pair of crimson rosellas swooping down the hill and settling on the fig tree.

'There's the letter, George. On the dresser.'

As usual, he ostentatiously washed his hands at the tub in the laundry. Although he'd already done this before leaving the shop, he knew that repetition at home gave Eileen reassurance that no trace of Cadwallader's Quality Meats remained on his hands. After drying them on the laundry towel, he picked up the letter and sat down opposite Eileen.

For someone with all those prizes, Jim wasn't much of a letter writer, George decided after he'd read the single page of rather large handwriting. Then he labelled as mean-spirited this slight feeling of disappointment that he often felt after reading his son's letters. The boy was busy in his last year and probably had other letters to write. At least he *did* write regularly, and that was probably more than many kids in similar situations would do.

'Where's Andy?' he said.

'At football practice.'

'It's starting earlier and earlier every year.'

'That's where he said he was,' Eileen said.

George looked at her in surprise. 'If he said that's where he said he was, that's where he is.' He paused. 'What have you been up to today?'

'The usual. And my embroidery.'

'Yes,' he said. 'I noticed it on the lounge this morning before I left for work. It's very splendid, no doubt about that. The two rainbow lorikeets are beautiful. The leaves are too, and that red Christmas bush.'

'That's not Christmas bush, it's grevillea.'

'I could make a hanger for it. It's too beautiful to keep tucked away in a drawer.' He meant it, for it was indeed a lovely thing.

———•———

After tea was over and the dishes had been done, Andy retired to his bedroom where, as usual, he turned on his transistor radio, while George and Eileen sat in the lounge room. With her embroidery on her lap, Eileen perched on the middle of the sofa, under the bright light that made her dark hair shine. In the armchair opposite, George began to read the newspaper. Or to look at it, for his eyes felt tired, and he was starting to think that he might need spectacles; he was having to hold the paper further and further away in order to make out the print.

He squinted at the interesting-looking article about the Parkes' radio telescope.

He was about to get up to fetch the magnifying glass from the kitchen when Eileen said, 'I've been doing some thinking, George. Maybe I could move to Mornington Peninsula, if Andy gets into the Army Apprentices' scheme, that is.'

It took a few moments for the import of her words to sink into George's tired brain. It was her use of the first person that hit him. *I could move*, and not *we could move*. He felt as if he'd received a punch to his chest and only by inhaling deeply was he able to recover enough to speak. 'I don't want to move to Mornington Peninsula,' he said. 'We've got a nice house here and I've got a good business. It is just starting to pick up. There's no way I'm going to throw in the towel and head south to a place where we don't know anyone, and where we'd have to start all over again.'

'That's what I did when I came here, George.'

'You wanted to. Anyway I'd already bought the business when we met. I asked you to come, and you agreed. You could have said no but you didn't.'

'And I'm asking you now.'

'And I'm saying no.'

'I can go though,' she said, smiling, although there was nothing to smile about.

'How could we afford two places? While business is improving, there's only enough to run one establishment.'

'You could sell the shop.'

'Then what?'

'Rent it back.'

George felt a surge of anger the likes of which he'd never experienced before. His heart began to pump so fast it felt as if a wild thing was beating against his rib cage. She was going to use Andy's application to the Balcombe Barracks as a bargaining ploy. *Andy goes, I go. Andy stays, I stay.* She loved him; that was clear. But she didn't love her husband. Maybe she never had.

While he desperately wanted to leave the house and get some time alone to work out the meaning of all that she'd said, he stayed put a little longer. Holding up the paper between himself and his wife, he didn't attempt to decipher the print and after a moment shut his eyes. Deep breaths, in and out, but the palpitations in his chest showed no sign of diminishing, and he thought he might faint. In the meantime, Eileen carried on sewing. He could hear the rasp of thread on fabric and after a while she began to hum. He could stand it no longer. Throwing down the paper, he stumbled to the door and with shaking fingers opened it and shut it behind him. Carefully, slowly; the last thing he needed now was for Eileen to shout, *Don't slam the door, George.*

In the back garden, he sat down on the chopping block. He'd left his cigarettes in the house and couldn't bear to go back inside for them. His heart was still pounding and he wondered if he was about to have a heart attack, although there was no actual pain in his chest, only a mild discomfort that was probably more emotional than physical.

Staring at the bright stars, he tried to concentrate on distinguishing the constellations, but knew that shortly he'd need to try to decipher Eileen's words. He took long, deep breaths, and after some moments found that his heart had settled back into a slower rhythm and he no longer felt faint. Now that he was calmer, he discovered he knew precisely what Eileen meant. She was planning to leave him. Maybe she'd been planning to leave him for a long time, and would do so as soon as the boys grew up.

231

Did he care, or was it simply the shock that had given him palpitations? He loved Eileen and always would. He was the sort of person who didn't change once he'd determined on something, once he had made a commitment. But if she wanted to leave when she decided the time was right, he wouldn't prevent her. There was nothing he could do to stop her anyway.

He was getting ahead of himself though. She was bluffing. Feeling around to see how far she could push him. He mustn't let her see how deeply she'd wounded him. She might exploit it if she knew. Anything could happen over the next year, but he was blowed if he was going to be pushed into thwarting Andy's ambitions in order to keep Eileen in Jingera.

He didn't look around at the sound of the back door being opened, followed by the slamming of the fly-screen door. There was a pause before he heard quick steps cross the verandah and descend the steps to the garden.

'Brought you a cup of tea, Dad.'

Surprised, George turned and took the mug that Andy handed him. Only now did he realise how thirsty he felt. 'Thanks, son,' he said, his voice croaking slightly.

'You've been out here for ages.'

How Andy had noticed him come outside over the blaring of pop music from his bedroom was little short of miraculous, George decided, taking a swig of tea. Andy sat down on the grass next to the chopping block and stretched out his long legs. George covertly inspected him. The moonlight had drained all colour from his hair. It appeared white rather than sandy, and his freckles had become a streak of grey across his nose and cheekbones. Perhaps Eileen had sent him out with the tea, George thought; maybe she'd taken pity on him, although if she had, surely she would have brought the tea out herself, with maybe an apology and an invitation to come inside again.

'I know what Mum said to you before. I heard everything. She'd never do it, you know.'

'Never do what?' George abandoned his fantasy of Eileen apologising and tried to focus on what his son was saying.

'Never move to Mornington Peninsula.'

George felt his heart skip a beat and took a deep breath. The last thing he wanted was to have those palpitations start again. Yet he felt immensely touched by the concern he heard in his son's voice and his heart settled back into its normal rhythm. Perhaps Andy was feeling responsible for what his mother might do, but he shouldn't. She was her own mistress and always would be. 'I know she'd never do it,' he said, although he wasn't at all sure. 'She just says things and doesn't mean them. We all do, at times.' While he knew that Eileen had meant to hurt him, and may even have meant what she'd implied about leaving him, there was no need for Andy to share that burden.

As George sipped the rest of the tea, he became aware of the sounds around them; the surf that was reassuring in its monotony, the eucalyptus trees rustling in the faint breeze, the chirring of a nightjar from somewhere in the bush between the yard and the lagoon.

Eventually Andy said, 'You know the coffee table I gave you and Mum for Christmas?'

'The coffee table, yes.' George was startled by the turn in the conversation. 'Very fine joinery work. Perfect for your mother's embroidery.'

'It was for both of you, Dad,' Andy said, his voice sounding irritated now. 'That's the point. I took a cup of tea into the lounge room for Mum before I came out with yours, and there was nowhere to put it. She's got stuff all over the table. But I made that for both of you.'

'Yes, much appreciated. Thank you,' George said slightly awkwardly. He didn't see quite where the conversation was heading.

There was a long pause before Andy said, his words pouring out in a rush, 'I bet you wish it was Jim at home, and me in Sydney. You've always preferred him to me. Always. For as long as I can remember, I've been second best in your eyes. Whatever I do just isn't good enough. It's not that you ever criticise, it's more that you just don't notice me.'

Shocked at the accusation in Andy's voice, George took a deep breath. First Eileen and now Andy; it seemed he just couldn't make anyone happy. Then the content of his son's words hit him, and the anguish too. Andy was clearly more sensitive than George had ever thought possible and the last thing he wanted now was to say something that might offend him further. And perhaps Andy was right, perhaps George had directed all his ambitions towards Jim and left Andy to his mother, who so clearly favoured him. 'You've never been second best in my eyes,' he said slowly. He hesitated. He found it so hard to articulate affection. It was as if all his life he'd been trained not to exhibit emotions and living with Eileen had reinforced that tendency. Eventually he managed to say, 'I love you, son.' There, it was out and he meant it. 'I'm really proud of you. I'm proud of your sporting abilities, and of the fact that you want to choose what career to follow rather than have it thrust upon you by someone else. And I'm proud of the way you're always so good-natured, and I'm even proud of your sense of humour too. You're a really good bloke, Andy.'

There was a brief pause before Andy said, 'But you didn't

take any notice of the table, Dad. I thought you'd be proud of it. Proud of me for making it.'

The table, it all came back to the table. Smothering a sigh, George decided to be honest with his son. 'I felt left out on Christmas morning, as if I didn't belong in the family,' he said. 'The three of you were sitting on the lounge as cosy as could be and there wasn't any room for me. That's why I didn't say much.'

'You should have said, Dad,' Andy said, the relief evident in his voice. 'We all really love you. You must be blind not to see that.' Andy stood up and turned to his father, still seated on the chopping block. Leaning over, he gave him a big hug that almost toppled him off his perch.

They stayed sitting outside for another half hour or so, not talking much. This new understanding of my son would never have happened, George thought, if Eileen hadn't mentioned Mornington Peninsula. Good can come out of bad. Soon he and Andy would go inside again and Eileen would be in bed asleep. And tomorrow would be another day.

CHAPTER 30

Later that night, George woke up abruptly with Eileen's words about moving to Mornington Peninsula ringing in his head. A few moments after, he heard the grandfather clock in the hall chime four o'clock. Although he felt tired, he just couldn't get back to sleep. For a while he tried counting sheep, but that only made him feel more awake than ever.

Next, to distract himself from what Eileen had said, he began to count his blessings. Far better to do that than count his worries about his wife. Andy and he had become reconciled, and he had another ally in the family. Business was doing well and his sausages had got a bit of a reputation, everyone was asking for the ones with the different sorts of herbs and spices in them. And Eileen, in her sleep, had flung an arm over his chest, a gesture she wouldn't have made when awake. His blessings counted, but his mind still active, George gently removed Eileen's arm. He was starting to feel a bit cramped but tossing and turning wasn't an option when you only had twelve inches of space. She didn't stir when he swung his feet onto the floor. After quietly opening the bedroom door, he tiptoed along the hallway.

From the back verandah he surveyed his territory. He would

never leave here, never, no matter what Eileen might do. This was where he belonged and he'd worked hard to make it a success. The full moon was low in the sky. Deep shadows fingered the garden and between the trees he could glimpse the silvery lagoon. It would be impossible to get back to sleep for a while yet; he felt far too restless. From the laundry he took his old jacket to put on over his pyjamas. After collecting a torch, he slipped on the gardening shoes kept outside the back door. The little book about the constellations of the Southern Hemisphere was where he always left it, in the inside pocket of the jacket, although he wouldn't use it tonight, it wasn't a good night for stargazing and anyway it was too late. Instead he would take his dinghy out onto the lagoon and row upstream. There he would ship the oars and drift back with the flow of the river. He hadn't done that for months.

On the bridge over the lagoon he stood for a while, as he always did, listening to the water slapping against the piers. There was something about that sound against the distant crashing of the surf on the beach that made him feel whole again. The moon was so bright he hardly needed the torch to navigate the narrow track leading to his boathouse. After launching the dinghy, he rowed upstream beyond the point where the lagoon merged into the river, further than he usually went at night. There he shipped the oars and drifted with the current. He thought of more blessings to add to his list. The celestial hemisphere. That he lived in the most beautiful place in the world. That Andy seemed much happier after they'd talked through their misunderstandings. That Jim's brilliant future was assured.

Slowly the current carried George back towards the settlement of Jingera, and only occasionally did he need to use an oar to guide the craft. After drifting back almost to his starting point, he rowed to shore and dragged the dinghy into the boathouse. He'd stayed out for longer than he'd intended and the sky to the east was beginning to lighten and flush with gold. To the west the silvery river mirrored the paler sky, and the lightest of mists softened the layers of hills.

On the footbridge he met two boys of about thirteen or fourteen, each carrying surfboards. They had to be holiday-makers, their faces weren't familiar.

'Morning, grandpa,' one said, his tone friendly rather than offensive.

George returned their greeting. Aware that he looked like a tramp in his red-and-white-striped pyjamas and paint-spattered jacket, he grinned. Eileen wouldn't think much of this get-up, including his feet stuffed into shoes lacking laces, but he didn't care about that anymore. Board surfing for the two lads was probably like stargazing or rowing alone at night was for him. There was more than one way of having a spiritual experience.

As he strolled up the back lane leading to his house, his heart turned with pleasure when he saw Andy walking towards him. A chip off the old block, he thought, Cadwallader and Son wandering the streets of Jingera in their pyjamas.

'Are you okay, Dad? I woke up early and saw you'd gone so I thought I'd try to find you.'

'I was just out rowing.'

'It's going to be a beautiful day.'

'You don't need to worry about me, Andy.'

'I know I don't. But I woke up wanting to walk through Jingera in my pyjamas. Never done it before. By the way, I like your footwear,' Andy said, slapping his father on the shoulder. 'Next craze at Burford Boys' High, eh?'

'That and the pyjamas, I reckon. Only you might sew another button on yours. That's the sort of thing they teach you in the army, you know.'

They both laughed. And that's another blessing, George thought.

CHAPTER 31

The sheets were in a tangle yet Peter lay comatose by Ilona's side. Breathing heavily, he was oblivious to what was going on: the claps of thunder and the flashes of lightning that Ilona could see around the edges of the thick curtains. She'd been conscious even before the storm, managing to wrench herself out of that nightmare that she wouldn't allow herself to think of now she was awake.

The storm moved overhead and the flashes of lightning and rumbles of thunder became simultaneous. As all things did provided one survived them, the storm moved on, and eventually the rain stopped altogether. But sleep was impossible; she felt much too alert. She got up and crept down the hall, avoiding the creaking floorboards. From the walkway, she observed the moon slipping out from behind a cloud. Almost imperceptibly it sliced through the velvety dark sky.

The nightmares would never leave her, she knew. None of the survivors of the war would ever get over the experience. Some of us might find ways of coping with the aftermath, she thought, but we're forever altered. That was another reason, if one were needed, that war and all its crimes should be circumvented if possible. But in *that* war avoidance hadn't been an option.

In the kitchen, she tipped boiling water into the teapot that Cherry Bates had given her before she left for Sydney years ago. It was a rather lovely object, with handle and lid decorated with delicate porcelain gumnuts. Gently Ilona ran her finger over the decorations. She missed Cherry, who'd been her closest friend in Jingera. The teapot was almost too beautiful to use, although years ago Ilona had resolved never to grow too attached to possessions. People and memories mattered, not inanimate things. Now she sat down at the kitchen table, on one end of which was a collection of papers. On top of these was the latest letter from Philip that had arrived a few days ago. She unfolded the page, and read it again.

10th February, 1962
Dear Mrs Vincent,

Thanks for your letter. It made me larf. I am learning one of Beethoven's Piano Sonatas. It's very hard. You told me not to play too much, but there's no chance of that here! At least they let me off sport, so I can practise more and go to the Con once a week for my lessons.

Ilona put down the letter while she poured her tea. Philip might be pushing himself too hard. It was important not to overdo practising difficult passages, in order to allow the muscles of the hand and forearm to strengthen. She hoped his teacher at the Conservatorium wouldn't overwork the boy, but surely he'd know what he was about. Physical damage, mental damage; the latter was much more likely, and would stay with Philip always. Like Lorna Hunter, he might survive, but he would not survive unscathed. It was the next paragraph of his letter that really troubled her though. She picked up the page and reread it.

> *Also I am improving that poem I wrote for Mummy. I need to add more things to it.*
> *Please write agen.*
> *Love from*
> *Philip*

She sighed. *I am improving that poem I wrote for Mummy.* It was easy to guess what that meant, and she couldn't bear the thought of poor Philip being tormented. Though she'd dashed off a quick reply as soon as she'd collected and read his letter outside Jingera post office, tomorrow she'd write again. For some reason, Judy Chapman was unable to supply him with the love that he needed or even to realise, let alone admit, just how dreadful boarding school life might be for him. For a moment she wondered if Jude would ever come to resent the friendship that had developed between her son and the piano teacher. Probably not. Jude was much too egotistical to view her as a potential substitute mother. Next holidays Ilona would invite the boy to spend a few days with them at Ferndale again. Even Zidra, a little resentful to begin with, had enjoyed having him around.

Her tea finished, Ilona put on a raincoat and went outside. Spotless Spot jumped up at once, and followed her as far as the stone steps leading to the beach. When she sat down, he lay at her feet, unmindful of the damp. The stone was cold, and she was glad of the raincoat. Although the storm had moved north-west, the breakers were angrily thumping onto the shore below. Again she thought of Philip's letter: *I am improving that poem I wrote for Mummy.* Anything could be happening to him and his parents wouldn't know. Was it so different to what was happening to Lorna? Although one child was from a very rich background and the other from a very poor family, both were suffering in the institutions to which they'd been assigned, consigned. Philip's persecution was at the hands of a system that permitted bullying, or turned a blind eye to it. Lorna's was at the hands of a paternalistic regime administered by poorly trained and possibly sadistic staff.

She patted Spot, who wagged his tail. While she belonged here at Ferndale, she sometimes yearned for her little cottage at Jingera. It was the verandah that she missed most, with its views of the ocean and the lagoon, and the birds flitting in and out of the shrubbery. There was something about being elevated that appealed to her, that allowed her to put things into perspective and achieve some acceptance. Sitting here soothed her though, and after a time she returned to the house. She tiptoed into the living room, shutting the door behind her. Quietly she began to play the music that Oleksii had composed and that Philip had played so beautifully when he'd visited. The piece that he'd understood so immediately that his exhilaration had been almost palpable.

But it was impossible to perform such music *sotto voce* and soon she stopped. It would never do for Peter to hear her play the Talivaldis music in the dead of night. He would think she'd crept out to communicate with Oleksii through his music and that hadn't been her intention at all. It was its association with Philip that had made her think of playing it now, that was all. Intellectual music was how Peter had described it, yet she suspected it appealed to Philip intuitively. He was too young surely to fully understand its theoretical foundations, musical prodigy though he undoubtedly was.

She lifted the top of the piano seat. After putting the sheets of music inside the compartment, she found a Shostakovich prelude. When she'd finished playing it, she felt more restored than she'd been an hour before. Next she really should try to get some sleep.

As she climbed into bed, Peter stirred.

'Sweet dreams, darling,' she whispered.

'I missed you.'

'You were asleep.'

'Still missed you though.'

'Did you get teased when you were a boarder?'

'No.'

'Did you tease anyone else?'

'Not really. Well, never in the nasty way I think you mean. You've been reading Philip's letter again, haven't you?'

'Yes.'

'I never noticed anything like that at my school.'

He was the sort of man whom everybody liked, in spite of his deep reserve. As a boy he would have been popular too. Average at schoolwork, good at sport, good-looking, kind-hearted and generous. The sort of kid all the others would want to befriend. But if he'd been put into the wrong milieu, what would have happened to him? He would have survived, just as he'd managed to survive the prisoner-of-war camp. He was strong, even allowing for the panic attacks.

Lorna had everything going for her except she was neither black nor white. Half-caste, how Ilona hated those words. What would have happened to Lorna if she'd been sent to an ordinary high school like Zidra, instead of to a training home for domestics that was intent on destroying her identity? 'Is what Philip's going through so different to Lorna's experience?' she said.

At this, Peter sat up and turned on the bedside lamp. For an instant she felt guilty at disturbing his sleep. He looked tired and there were crease marks on his cheek where it had pressed against the pillow. 'They're very different,' he said quietly. 'But I agree with you. Both are forced to be where they don't want to be, so in a sense both are imprisoned. In one case the parents want the child to be there, in the other case they don't.'

Gently he pulled her head onto his shoulder and they sat in silence for several minutes until the hall clock chimed four times. 'Go to sleep now,' he said, switching off the lamp. 'Think of some music. I heard you playing the piano earlier.'

'What was I playing?'

'Shostakovich.'

Thank God he hadn't heard the Talivaldis, she thought. Don't want any jealousy; he doesn't deserve to feel that. Inhaling deeply his scent of warm skin and cotton pyjamas, she at last felt herself drifting to sleep.

CHAPTER 32

Two days before they were to head north to Jervis Bay, Zidra's bag was already packed. Not much, just a couple of changes of clothes and her swimmers. There had to be room in the boot for the sheets and towels they were taking, enough for them and the Hunters who mightn't have any spare linen. Through the tourist information place, Mama had discovered some cabins about half a mile from the boarding house where the Gudgiegalah girls would stay, and she'd booked two. Endlessly popping up and down the stairs to the attic with new instructions, she seemed as nervous as Zidra felt. The most natural way of meeting Lorna, she had decided, was on the beach in front of where the girls would be staying, so they must be prepared to spend quite a few hours on the sand. At this point a beach umbrella was added to her list of things to pack, plus the inevitable zinc cream and sunhats.

The night before they were to leave, Zidra took down from her shelves the book she'd decided to give to Lorna, *The Two Fires,* by Judith Wright. She opened it and flicked through the pages until she found what she was looking for.

Those dark-skinned people who once
named Cooloolah
knew that no land is lost or won by wars,
for earth is spirit: the invader's feet will tangle
in nets there and his blood be thinned by fears.

Earth is spirit: that meant so much to Zidra but what would this poem mean to Lorna? She had no idea and there'd be little chance of finding out over the next few days. Mama had emphasised, again and again, that they could only hope to see Lorna briefly, and that the available time would be for Lorna's mother.

One of Zidra's anxieties was that she wouldn't recognise her old friend. She would have changed, just as Zidra herself had altered. She stood in front of the long wardrobe mirror and inspected her reflection. Was she all that different from four years ago? In appearance, certainly. She was above average height and had breasts and hips and a waist. Her brown hair and eyes were the same, of course, but now her olive skin was inclined to spots that she would squeeze discreetly last thing at night and dab with metho that she'd taken from under the kitchen sink. All sorts of new information – relevant and otherwise – was stuffed into her head, but no one could see that or know her memories and patterns of thinking. Yet she was essentially the same, a flawed bundle of idiosyncrasies that she would never be able to alter, no matter how hard she might want to be someone else. Someone who was less critical, someone who laughed a lot like Sally and made everyone else happy. Someone who was brave and rebellious like Lorna. Narrowing her eyes at her reflection, she visualised Lorna standing by her side. Her dark-skinned friend who had been declared sufficiently light-skinned to become *Australian.*

To become *interned,* as Mama described it. Perhaps she'd still be taller than Zidra but not by much, and those lovely dark curls would be cut short.

How would being interned have changed Lorna? Would she be embittered or defeated? Zidra pulled out of her desk the letter she'd received from Lorna before Christmas and read it again. I'M ALWAYS GETTING INTO TROUBLE – THAT'S NOTHING NEW – AND THEN I GET LOCKED IN THE BOXROOM. THEY DON'T KNOW I CAN GET OUT THE ROOF LIGHT AND SIT ON THE ROOF. HA HA. This was definitely the same girl Zidra had met when she first came to Jingera. The same defiant spirit.

Zidra gazed out of the dormer window that faced east, and saw the moonlight glinting over the ocean. Shortly Lorna would see her mother and that was the point of the expedition.

Zidra and her mother were simply making possible a reunion between Lorna and Mrs Hunter and she mustn't hope for any more than to bring them together again, however briefly. Yet in spite of this her stomach fluttered with anticipation, and it was several hours before she was able to fall asleep.

It seemed only minutes later that her mother's hand was on her shoulder. 'Wake up, Zidra. We've a long drive ahead of us and I promised the Hunters we'd collect them by nine o'clock.'

After rushing Zidra into the car, her mother drove un-characteristically fast along the dirt road to Bermagui, so fast that Zidra had to shut her eyes at several points. Eventually she said, 'Slow down, Ma. We're far too early. We don't want to be hanging around at the Reserve making the Hunters nervous while they finish their packing.'

'What's the time?'

'Just before eight. It says so on the car clock.'

'I always keep my eyes on the road when I drive, not on the clock.'

Or the speedometer, Zidra thought, but kept this to herself. Although they arrived at Wallaga Lake a good fifteen minutes too early, the Hunters were ready. Rather formally attired, they were waiting on the grass just before the settlement, with a group of twenty or so Aborigines and half-a-dozen dogs. Smoke from the chimneys of several of the shacks drifted up through the still morning air, and the lake glimmered palely in the distance. The mountain to the north-west was barely visible, shrouded in mist. On the ground in front of the Hunters was an old over-night bag.

'Thank God they're ready. And travelling light too, Zidra. They don't have much. You could learn from that.'

Zidra laughed. She had a fraction of the luggage that her mother had packed.

Everyone smiled and stared curiously at her mother as she got out of the car. If she hadn't felt so anxious, Zidra might have felt put out at the lack of attention to herself. Probably they were staring because of her mother's act of generosity, although really it had been Zidra's idea, or maybe it was her mother's huge grin as she hugged Mrs Hunter and shook Mr Hunter's hand. She looked as happy as if the journey was over, when they still had hours of driving ahead of them yet.

Eventually the Hunters were settled into the back seat. After they were waved off, Zidra became increasingly absorbed in her own anxieties. She was only dimly aware of the sporadic conversation of her mother and the Hunters as they headed north, and even less aware of the countryside through which they passed. Her nervousness blossomed as the miles passed. What if the Gudgiegalah girls didn't turn up? What if Lorna had got into trouble yesterday and had been banned from making the trip? What if the girls did turn up but Lorna couldn't get away? Anything and everything could go wrong.

<hr>

Ilona watched the Hunters, who were sitting in the shade of one of the Norfolk Island pines. Behind the row of pines was an unkempt stretch of scrub separating the beach at Jervis Bay from the road. Leaning against the rough bark, the Hunters appeared to be settling in for a long wait and trying to make themselves as inconspicuous as possible, although what they were wearing was a little incongruous for the beach. They were dressed as if for a funeral, with Tommy wearing a dark suit and Molly the navy blue long-sleeved dress she'd worn yesterday on the drive from Wallaga Lake to Jervis Bay. Ilona understood their reasoning though. Today was to be an occasion.

Though it had rained the night before, the sky was cloudless and the ground no longer damp. Ilona and Zidra had planted the beach umbrella in the sand opposite the guesthouse and about thirty yards away from where the Hunters were sitting. Perhaps they'd arrived at the beach too early, but they'd all agreed the night before that this was best, in case the Gudgiegalah girls came out for an early morning swim or were taken on a bus expedition. That was what Ilona most feared, that they'd be whisked off for the day to some other spot, leaving the four of them hanging about on the beach and gazing at the holiday-makers and the calm surface of the bay. At another time she might have thought the flat expanse of blue water beautiful, with its waves that were little more than ripples lapping against the white sand. The low headlands at each end of the beach were dense with eucalyptus trees, whose white trunks dappled with grey were contorted into fantastic shapes by weather less clement than today's. Yet the prospect of spending the entire day here without meeting the girls filled her with gloom. Nothing to do but swim and fish and wait, and all of them would become more nervous as the seconds ticked by.

The previous evening, she'd gossiped a bit with the man who ran the fish and chip shop. He'd confirmed that a party of girls was staying at the boarding house. 'Half-caste girls,' he'd reported. 'From somewhere out west. They come here every year for a few days.'

'What do they do?'

He'd looked at her in surprise. 'Play on the beach and swim and go for walks. Do what everyone down here does on holiday.'

'We're doing the same, plus some fishing as well,' she said. 'Though I never can catch anything. That's why I'm ordering fish and chips.'

Tommy Hunter could catch fish of course. That's what he had been doing when Ilona first met him on the jetty in Jingera lagoon. On this trip to Jervis Bay he'd brought his fishing line. It was as good a way as any to justify hanging around by the water for hours, but he hadn't got the line out yet.

Now Ilona, sitting on the sand under the shade of the beach umbrella, felt the muscles in her foot convulse in a cramp and she stood up to ease them. Some ten minutes ago Zidra had grown restless and taken herself for a walk to the far end of the beach. Ilona could see her slender figure striding towards the low sandstone bluff. The Hunters were still sitting immobile under the Norfolk pine. On the other side of the road was the boarding house, a pale green fibro construction with a passageway running along the front and at first floor level a verandah. Curiously there were no windows facing the front and the view, but only doors. The windows must all look out over the bush behind.

'Someone's comin' out,' Tommy said.

He had better sight than she did, although after squinting at the figure she could see it was an old man tipping what seemed to be a bag of kitchen scraps into one of the garbage bins in the front yard. That meant breakfast was over.

At this moment Molly Hunter became agitated. After whispering something to Tommy, she stood up and hurried down the road in the direction of the cabins. This would never do, Lorna would be sure to appear as soon as her mother left. Ilona ran across the sand to where Tommy was sitting.

'Where's she going?'

'Back to the cabins. Call of nature.'

'But she can't go now.'

Tommy shrugged. 'If you've got to go . . .'

Ilona ran after Molly. 'Can't you go behind a bush?' There weren't any lavatory facilities anywhere in sight and it would take Molly a good fifteen minutes to get to the cabins and back.

'No likem.' Molly looked more anxious than ever and her voice quavered slightly.

Ilona rested her hand on Molly's arm for an instant as she said, 'It doesn't matter where you go. There are plenty of bushes. I'll wait for you here and look the other way.'

Afterwards they walked back together to where Tommy was sitting.

'No sign yet but I heard some voices.'

'Don't worry,' Ilona said, although she was as nervous as if she was expecting to see her own daughter after an absence of over four years.

'Hard not to,' Tommy said. 'She'll be punished if they see us.'

'She won't,' Ilona said soothingly. 'The meeting will be a coincidence.' She had been through the same debate in her own mind again and again. Would Lorna suffer more if her part in today's enterprise was found out than if she didn't see her mother? Each time she'd decided that the answer was no. Family was worth everything, every small risk. To have even a short time together, to hold one another, however briefly. She thought of that moment when she'd hugged her own mother for the last time just before the selection. Before she'd been chosen to live and her mother to die in the gas ovens of the concentration camp. Quickly, she brushed away a tear. Her own memories mustn't be allowed to spoil today for the Hunters. She needed to have all her wits about her to navigate through whatever lay ahead of them.

'The girls will come out soon, and no one will notice what happens,' she said. 'It will be a casual meeting. And if someone sees you, I'll create a diversion.' She'd anticipated this, dressing for the occasion in an exuberant orange and pink shift dress, and the lime-green straw sunhat that she'd ordered by mail from David Jones in Sydney, and that was more flamboyant than it had appeared in the catalogue. Your look-at-me hat was how Zidra had described it. The plan was for Ilona to engage whoever accompanied the children in conversation while Zidra joined the girls in whatever they were doing. Lorna was to slip away to see her parents up by the Norfolk pine, although she didn't know this yet.

❖

They were still there, her mother and the Hunters, waiting for something to happen. Zidra kicked so hard at the fine white sand that some of it flew up into her face. Angrily she brushed it away. In the string bag she was carrying was the book for Lorna, though she was beginning to doubt that they would ever find her. Anyway what would she want with a book of silly poems, she'd have no time for those, or maybe it would be confiscated. Irritably Zidra pulled at the strap of the swimming costume that she was wearing under her white shorts and navy blue shirt. Although her swimmers were too small, she was determined to wait until next season to get a replacement. Her mother always made such a fuss about buying anything these days – it had to be just so, anyone would think *she* was the teenager – that even tight swimmers were to be preferred to the alternative.

Today nothing might happen unless they took some action. She started to walk along the sand towards where the beach umbrella was positioned, but shortly afterwards changed her mind and headed towards the road. Soon she crossed it, and strolled across the bitumen yard of the boarding house to the main entrance. There was no one behind the desk, but she could hear voices from the back garden. She sauntered straight through the lobby and out the glazed door on the other side. A group of about eight girls, of varying skin colour and ages, were playing rounders.

Zidra saw Lorna right away in the far corner of the yard and caught her breath.

Probably the oldest girl there, she was certainly the tallest. The girl who was batting thwacked the ball Lorna's way and she ran for it with that same speed and athletic grace that had made her the fastest runner of all the girls at Jingera primary school.

There were no adults around, though you couldn't tell who might be watching from the windows. Zidra stood unnoticed, her back against the fibro wall of the building, under the cantilevered first floor verandah running its width. Two girls aged maybe seven or eight were sitting on the grass at the back of the yard, just in front of the high paling fence. They weren't talking or even watching the game. One was pulling out handfuls of grass and methodically shredding them. The other, staring at the ground with a dazed expression on her face, was rocking backwards and forwards to some inner rhythm.

Lorna was not detached though. Lorna was racing around the yard exhorting the girls who were playing. Despite the shapeless dress of some checked material, she appeared even prettier than Zidra remembered. Surrounded by these other girls who were involved in the game, she was no outcast, not like the two little girls on the sidelines. She was a part of this group, maybe even the leader.

At this thought Zidra began to feel oddly excluded. Now *she* was the outsider, an interloper observing her old friend. Unable to move, she stood so still that an insect settled on her hair. Quickly she flicked it away. This movement must have caught Lorna's attention. Although she didn't wave, she began to jog towards Zidra as naturally as if she was running for a catch.

'Dizzy, you're here, I knew you'd come. It's really good to see you again.' Lorna held out her arms. The girls embraced, so tightly that Zidra could feel Lorna's heart thumping, or perhaps that was her own, and she could smell the faint scent of Sunlight soap and toothpaste. Shortly, Lorna gently pushed her away and held her at arms-length. Her face looked tense as she said, 'Did you bring Mum?'

'Yes, and your stepfather too. They're near the beach with my mother. Can you slip away?' Nervously Zidra looked around. The other girls were carrying on with their game of rounders as if nothing had happened.

'I warned them I might vanish for a little while, and they were to pretend to know nothing and be on their best behaviour. Those two don't need to pretend though. They're so switched off they don't know what's going on, poor kids.' Lorna gestured to the two blank-faced children sitting on the grass at the end of the yard, who seemed oblivious to everything. There was no one else in sight. 'We'll just walk out,' Lorna continued. 'Not through the lobby, though, but along the side passage. I can probably get away for a couple of hours. She flashed her old smile, all those white teeth on show. 'I hoped you'd come today. I got your Christmas card. Knew right away it was from you.'

At the side of the house, Lorna put her hand on Zidra's arm. 'Can't thank you enough for coming today. I knew I could count on you.'

'Those other girls, were they all taken away like you?'

'Yeah. Some of them don't know where they're from; that's the ones who were taken as babies or toddlers. They'll never even know who their families were. They've been told their parents are dead but I don't believe that. That's what they tried to tell me, the liars. At least I've got good memories of my family, unlike some of those kids. You saw those two sitting on their own. They're always like that, completely withdrawn. They were taken as babies.' Almost at the end of the passage, Lorna stopped. 'Shh, someone's coming.'

Zidra peered over her shoulder. A plump middle-aged woman, with tightly permed grey hair and a magazine under her arm, was walking towards the entrance.

'That's the matron. We'll have to stay here till she's inside. I hate her but I never let her see that. She's dangerous. Tells us we're all rubbish. She's cruel too.'

They waited for a few seconds, not saying any more. Zidra's heart was pumping hard again. To be apprehended now would be too much. 'Make a run for it if she sees us,' she whispered to Lorna. 'At least you'll have a few minutes with your parents. They're sitting under one of those pine trees over to the left of here. You can't miss them. I'll hold back that woman.'

'She won't see us. We'll wait a bit longer though. She's got the *Women's Weekly* with her. That should keep her quiet for a bit.'

They heard the entrance door slam shut and nothing more apart from the girls' voices from the back garden and the chittering of birds. Several drops of water landed on Zidra's head, making her start. Grinning, Lorna pointed to the blocked off guttering above them in which a pair of lorikeets was bathing.

'We'll give her another minute,' Lorna whispered. 'The funny thing is that she thinks she's grooming the blackness out of us girls, but she's not. She's grooming it into us. We've got a common bond, you see. Against the staff and her. And against the AWB.'

'The AWB?'

'The Aborigines' Welfare Board.'

'Not against me, I hope.' The words sounded childish to Zidra's ears as soon as she'd said them. They must seem even more infantile to Lorna, who'd changed, Zidra decided. She was grown up now.

'You're family, Dizzy. Do you know I've only got a few months to go before they let me out? They'll send me off to be a servant somewhere. After that I'm going to go home. Or maybe I'll run away.'

'To Wallaga Lake?'

'Yeah. Though maybe they'd come and get me and I'd have to go into hiding. I've heard Wallaga is one of the better reserves. You should hear about the places some of the girls've come from, the ones who can remember, that is. I think Wallaga is the most beautiful spot in the world, that and Mount Gulaga.'

'Mount Gulaga? Do you mean Mount Dromedary?'

'Yeah. That's our name for it. Gulaga.'

'I've got something for you. Here, take this.' Zidra handed Lorna the string bag with the book in it.

'I love presents. Do I get to keep the bag as well as the book?'

The bag was Mama's but Zidra knew she wouldn't mind. She nodded.

'Just joking, Dizzy. Let's make a run for it now, down the boundary and out the front.' Once out of sight of the boarding house, Lorna put an arm around Zidra's shoulders. As they crossed the road, she caught sight of her parents sitting patiently under the pine tree and broke into a run.

Zidra looked away. This reunion was a private affair, but anyway, she couldn't see much; her vision was obscured by tears.

◆

For nearly two hours Ilona and Zidra had been sitting under the umbrella on the beach while Lorna and the Hunters talked. Although Ilona could still see them, they wouldn't be visible from the guesthouse; they'd moved a few hundred yards further away, and were sitting in a spot shielded from the road by a clump of bushes. The plan was that Ilona and Zidra were to watch the guesthouse closely.

'There's someone coming out now,' Zidra said. 'It's that matron woman I saw earlier.'

'Quick, run and warn Lorna,' Ilona said, but there was no one to hear. Zidra was already sprinting down the sand towards the Hunters.

While the matron strolled across the road and onto the beach, Ilona stood up and walked towards her. As she did so, she unfastened her watch strap and slipped it into the pocket of her dress. 'Excuse me! Good morning!' she called, smiling and waving. 'Do you have the time, please?'

'Yes, it's a quarter past twelve.'

'Thank you so much. I forgot my watch. I thought it must be nearly time for lunch though. It's hungry work sitting on the beach and watching the waves.'

'You're not from these parts, are you?' The woman spoke more loudly now, as if she thought that being foreign made you slightly hard of hearing. 'Where are you from?'

'Near Burford. That's down south.'

'I know that. I meant, where are you from originally?'

'I was born in Latvia, but I've been in Australia for many years.'

'You've still got an accent.'

Ilona was used to this comment that sometimes sounded almost like an accusation. 'My accent I will never lose, no matter how hard I try. Where are you from?' While speaking, she discerned, out of *the corner of her eye,* Lorna crossing the road and running towards the guesthouse. It would never do for her to be noticed now. Quickly Ilona waved an arm in the direction of the water. 'Oh, look!' she said, in an exaggerated foreign way. 'How exciting! Isn't that a whale?'

'No, it's much too late for whales, and anyway they wouldn't be in Jervis Bay. I can't see anything though. Of course my sight's not what it was, and I left my glasses inside. If anything, it's more likely to be a boat.'

'Yes, you're right. It's a little rowing boat. How silly of me. Where are you from?'

'Gudgiegalah. That's west of the mountains. Living inland, I really miss the beach. I grew up on the coast near Newcastle, you see.' She sighed. 'Well, I suppose I'd better go back inside again. It's nearly lunchtime and we're on full board here.'

'I see. Are you coming out again later? I'd like to hear more about Gudgiegalah. I never get to travel, you see. Not anymore.'

'I'll be out after lunch with my girls.'

'You have a large family?'

The woman laughed. 'You might say that,' she said. 'You'll see, if you're still here in an hour's time.'

'Oh, I will be. My daughter and I brought our sandwiches with us. We shall eat them here, on the beach. And then later, once we have digested them, we shall swim.'

The matron was true to her word. Within an hour, she and the Gudgiegalah girls were trooping onto the beach. Ilona beckoned the woman over to sit with her. Being foreign gave you a licence for such familiarities, she felt. While the girls ran about on the sand or swam, she and Zidra engaged the woman in conversation, and Lorna sidled off unnoticed, to spend more time with her parents.

The woman was garrulous in response to all the questions Ilona asked, about where they were from and what they were doing and if hers was a hard job.

'They're all half-caste girls, you see. Call me Ada, by the way.' She settled herself comfortably on the extra towel Ilona had spread out for her, under the shade of the umbrella.

'I'm Ilona, and this is my daughter, Zidra.'

'You can call me Deidre, by the way,' Zidra said. 'It's less foreign.'

Ilona narrowed her eyes at her daughter. The last thing she wanted was Ada thinking Zidra was insulting her. Even a fit of the giggles would be preferable at this point.

'You can't believe how difficult it is to get the Abos to adopt white ways of working and responsibility,' Ada said. 'They're a dirty useless lot, unless you train them right and the half-castes are just the same. That's what we're doing at Gudgiegalah, training them right.'

'What about a proper education?' Ilona said. 'The three Rs and all of that.'

'Yes, they get a bit of that but the best they can ever hope for is domestic work. And they certainly won't be able to find work as domestics unless they know how to clean properly. We get them to scrub the floors every day whether they need it or not,' and here Ada laughed. 'Might have to kick the bucket of dirty water over sometimes, if they don't do it right the first time. Practice makes perfect, that's the thing.'

At this point Zidra stood up and walked a few yards closer to the water. Her shoulders were tensed and she began to scuff at the sand with her bare feet.

'Do go on, Ada,' Ilona said.

'Have to lock them up at night, too; they're great wanderers, the Abos, and the half-castes are just as bad. You have to be tough to be kind; that's the thing. We're terribly short-staffed though, and that makes the job even harder. Today I'm on my own, but that's only because I'm really soft-hearted. I gave my assistants a few hours off to go to Huskisson to see their mother. Twins you see; not identical, but twins all the same. Fortunately the girls aren't playing up today. In fact they're better than usual. It must be the sea air.'

Or because they promised Lorna, Ilona thought.

Later, after the girls and Ada had gone inside again, Ilona walked with Molly along the beach in the direction of the cabins, while Tommy stayed sitting under one of the Norfolk Island pines. Zidra waited near him, leaning against another tree trunk. At first Molly seemed confused, as if she didn't know quite where she was, and Ilona didn't wanted to disturb her reverie although she longed to learn how Lorna was surviving at Gudgiegalah. When they were almost at the point where they should turn up the beach to the cabins, Molly abruptly sat down on the sand and put her hands over her eyes. Ilona knelt beside her and gently held her shaking shoulders, and still Molly said nothing.

As the sun sank, Ilona began to feel cool and might have suggested going inside if Molly hadn't at last begun to talk about Lorna. It was hard to understand what she was saying, though. Her voice was soft, and her words muffled by emotion and the handkerchief she was holding to her face, but Ilona managed to piece together a picture of what Lorna's life was like. Incessant cleaning and cooking, with little time for learning. Locked up every night in a long room with many beds and with bars on the windows. Treated harshly, fed poorly. Staff unkind when not being outright cruel, and their goal to make the girls feel worthless. Because of it all, Lorna hadn't remained quite herself. She'd become tougher, or at least that's what Ilona understood Molly to be saying.

'She tough girl. No breakem.'

'Yes, she's strong,' Ilona said. 'And she'll be able to leave Gudgiegalah after her next birthday.'

That evening, once the Hunters had retired to their cabin, Ilona and Zidra compared notes. 'Lorna told me that some of the Gudgiegalah girls don't know who their families are or even where they're from,' Zidra said.

'Can you imagine that? No identity. No sense of belonging. And the cruelty.'

'I'm lucky I've got you, Ma. And Peter.'

That night, Ilona woke from a nightmare with her heart racing. Though she willed herself out of the dream, its content eluded her as soon as she was awake, and for this she was thankful. After rolling onto her stomach, she wept for the Gudgiegalah girls' losses.

CHAPTER 33

T he following day, on the journey south, everyone was quiet. Subdued, Ilona thought, as she drove the car down the Princes Highway. First stop was to be the Wallaga Lake Reserve. After dropping off the Hunters, she would take the turn-off to Bermagui and the dirt road on to Jingera. The visit had gone far better than she'd anticipated. The very worst outcome would have been not to see Lorna at all.

Now the first stage of the return trip was almost over, and they would soon reach the Reserve. Ilona turned the car off the highway onto the road leading to the settlement. Through the tall trees she saw a flock of wild ducks rise from the lake, their harsh cries echoing through the still air.

While Tommy was lifting the Hunters' bag out of the boot, Molly said to Ilona, 'Lorna's gottem new family as well as old. Them Gudgiegalah girls her sisters. She tellem 'bout us and they visitem when they get out. You good missus, Missus.'

'Call me Ilona.' She'd lost count of the number of times she'd suggested this already but she knew it would never happen.

Behind Molly, the dark mountain loomed, the mountain they could see from Ferndale. 'You good missus too,' she said to Zidra. 'Good sister belongem Lorna.'

Zidra grinned but she looked tired, Ilona thought, as the Hunters waved them on their way. Exhausted by emotion. She herself couldn't wait to get home. It was the first occasion since her marriage to Peter that she'd spent more than a day away from him. Two days were far too much. What she wanted more than anything was to hold him in her arms and talk to him about what had happened.

'I'm glad we did this trip, Mama.' Zidra yawned, and a moment later she was asleep.

To keep alert, Ilona began to sing the first thing that came into her head, the opening bars of Mozart's Requiem. You could always tell someone's mood from what they might spontaneously sing or hum. On this trip they'd flouted the regulations of a misguided regime and had made a number of people happier, but this abduction of the children should never be allowed to happen. Mothers losing their children. Children losing their families, their identities, given new names, forbidden to speak their own language, shoved into repressive homes run by people with little or no training. Little ones never even knowing they had a mother or a father.

I am *within cooee* of Ferndale, she thought after some miles. But she lessened the pressure of her foot on the accelerator. There is an old saying in Latvia, she fabricated, that the worst accidents happen when you are almost home.

Zidra woke up just before Ilona pulled the car into the entrance to Ferndale, and was able to unfasten the gates for her. The barking of the dogs as they drove into the home paddock must have alerted Peter, who was standing next to the open garage doors.

'Got the old girl back safely,' he said.

'Do you mean me or the car?' Ilona said, as she quite literally fell into his arms, tripped up by Spotless Spot who seemed almost as pleased to welcome them home as his master.

⎯⎯•═•⎯⎯

The following morning, Zidra woke up early. The night before, she'd left the curtains and windows open, so she could fall asleep soothed by the regular crashing of the breakers. A diagonal of sunlight illuminated her untidy desk as if it were a stage piece, and motes of dust danced in the spotlight. Too tired to get up to close the curtains, she rolled onto her stomach and pulled the pillow over her head. If only she could fall asleep again, perhaps this feeling of depression might dissipate.

It was because of Lorna. No longer did she have that trip to Jervis Bay to look forward to and it might be years before she saw her again.

Yet she knew it was silly to feel disheartened. Everything she'd hoped for had been achieved. Lorna had seen her parents and she'd be getting out of Gudgiegalah soon. It was an unexpected bonus that Zidra and Lorna had been able to speak to one other, though not for as long as Zidra would have liked. She'd had little time to tell Lorna of her own life though there'd been time enough for Lorna to tease her. *You're a country girl now, Dizzy, and not a bloody reffo anymore.*

The sadness pervading Zidra now wasn't because their time at Jervis Bay had been so short. In fact she'd ended up having a much longer conversation with Lorna than she'd dared hope for. It was certainly the case that Lorna seemed far more grown up than Zidra and this seemed to widen the gap between them. Not only was she more adult but she was surrounded by friends who, by her own admission, were united in their loathing for the system. Of course Zidra was glad of this unity. It would give

Lorna more strength. But it also took her further away. Where once Zidra's own connection with Lorna had been close – the reffo and the Abo against the rest – it was now Lorna and all these other girls aligned against the AWB, while Zidra was on the periphery, an outsider to her old friend.

Things didn't stand still. She thought they did because nothing momentous had occurred in her life since the fire and moving to Ferndale. But while nothing much had happened to her, other people weren't so fortunate and they were affected by what they'd lived through. It was true that Lorna still had the same personality, with the same warmth and humour, and the resilience that she'd always had. Best of all, she'd kept alive some of her joyousness in spite of what had happened. But she was also different in a way that Zidra now struggled to define. She'd thought of this alteration as Lorna growing up, but maybe it was more that Lorna was becoming political. *They think they're grooming the blackness out of us,* she'd said. *But they're not. They're grooming it into us. We have a common cause now.*

The sunlight streaming into the room was slowly shifting its focus. Soon it moved onto Zidra's face and she felt its warmth. This new identity was a good thing for Lorna, she decided at length. Her friend wouldn't stay in domestic service long. She'd leave as soon as she could and make her way to better things. She was strong and Zidra should focus on this. The bond between them, although less important that it had once been, need never die.

If Lorna had been white, she and Zidra would have stayed together, probably gone to school together. But she hadn't and would soon be free to follow a different life.

What would she, Zidra, become? If she were unlucky, she would do a secretarial course in Burford and become a receptionist and spend her days travelling to and from Burford by bus, typing dreary letters for the local solicitor or doctor or architect. The Bachelor and Spinster Balls and the picnic races would be the social highlights. In the fullness of time she would marry someone whom she'd meet at one of those balls, some grazier's son or an articled clerk or a businessman who would inevitably be a member of the Burford Club.

She didn't want that though. If she were lucky, she'd go to university. Afterwards, she'd have a brilliant career. Writing well and thinking logically must give you a head start in journalism, that's what Mrs Fox said. Her talents surely made her well suited to that occupation. In spite of her telephone conversation with the social pages editor of the *Sydney Morning Chronicle*, she wasn't going to accept that there might be any bar to her choice.

PART V

Sydney and Jingera
March, 1962

CHAPTER 34

A taxi was to collect Philip for the free weekend in early March that he was to spend at Hunters Hill. He was so pleased at the prospect of getting away for two days that he was waiting outside Barton House ten minutes before the taxi was due to arrive. It was a surprise when Auntie Susan turned up in the Williamsons' car instead. She gave him an enormous hug that was witnessed by half the boarders, but that didn't matter, not with the whole weekend in front of him.

'I couldn't bear to think of you travelling all that way on your own,' she said, 'so here I am.'

She didn't know the distances he'd travelled already, on his own if you didn't count Jones, who had to drive the car just like the taxi driver. Still, he was happier to see her than she could possibly guess.

On the way to Hunters Hill, they took what she described as a small detour to somewhere called Macleay Street. 'Have to drop a little parcel off,' she said, 'for an old friend's birthday tomorrow. I forgot to get it in the post in time and I just can't bear to have a present arrive late, can you? It's never quite the same.'

While she double-parked in the street outside a small block of flats, he raced into the lobby and slid the package into the box of Unit 6. It just fitted through the slot. As he left, he glanced up the street and noticed a tall glass-fronted building looming over the neighbourhood. 'W-w-what's th-that?' he asked his aunt when he was back in the car.

'It's the Royal Albion Hotel. Brand new and much too high. You can imagine the outcry when it was built. All the local residents were up in arms.'

'C-c-c-can . . .?'

'Can you go up? Yes, there's an observation deck there. Would you like to?'

He shook his head. He hated heights. 'Wh-where are w-w-we?'

'Some call this Potts Point,' she said, laughing. 'Others call it Kings Cross. The boundary's a little elastic.'

He didn't remember much about the Williamsons' house at Hunters Hill. He'd been so angry the day he'd visited with his father that he hadn't taken in anything much, apart from the piano and the music that his aunt gave him. Their house was old; older even than Woodlands. It was surrounded by trees through which the flickering harbour water could be seen. After they had afternoon tea – there was a chocolate cake and jam tarts – Philip and Auntie Susan walked around the garden together. His aunt didn't ask questions or seem to mind if he didn't say anything. She pointed out the main landmarks, but when she began to talk about the plants growing in the garden he stopped paying such close attention to her words. Instead he listened to the rise and fall of her voice, and to the occasional hooting of a tugboat, and to the birds, and to the faint rattling of the leathery leaves of what she said were evergreen magnolia trees.

Afterwards, while they waited for Uncle Fred to come home, Auntie Susan asked him if he'd like to play something on the piano for her. He chose the Sculthorpe sonatina that she'd given him, and she was delighted, or at least that's what she said. He would have carried on playing if Uncle Fred hadn't arrived at this point. While he smiled a lot, he didn't talk much; he didn't need to, married to Auntie Susan. Later, he said he liked nothing more than to watch television on a Friday night after a long week at the office. Although watching the box was a rare treat for Philip – there was no reception down south and no television in Stambroke College – he managed to stay awake only through the news and then some more, but fell asleep soon after. He didn't get much continuous sleep at Stambroke. It wasn't only the bullying, but the anticipation of it that made him nervous and on edge. Auntie Susan woke him up when the program was over, and he went to bed in a room that had been one of his cousins'.

The rest of the weekend passed all too quickly, with a walk around Balls Head on Saturday morning, when his aunt pointed out all the sights. In the afternoon, she took him to see a film at Roseville Cinema, *One Hundred and One Dalmations,* which he loved, while Uncle Fred pottered in the garden. On Sunday morning, Philip awoke with the usual dread weighing him down at the prospect of returning to school. Once breakfast was over, he practised the piano. Again and again he played Chopin's Funeral March, stopping only when it was time to head off for lunch at a restaurant near Coogee. Afterwards, they walked along what his aunt called the esplanade towards the southern headland. The apprehension that threatened to overwhelm him seemed to sharpen his hearing. There was no wind, yet the sea made a continuous shushing noise, only occasionally increasing its volume to thump down upon the beach. After reaching the end of the esplanade, they continued a distance along the edge of the low cliff. Here the crash of the surf made him flinch. Sometimes the way a wave broke sounded like the violent tearing of fabric. An unseen bird squealed as if in pain. After a while the sun went behind diffused clouds. The sky became a mottled white-and-grey like the plastic Laminex kitchen benches his aunt and uncle had. They began to retrace their steps.

Soon it would be time to return him to Stambroke College. His depression deepened. He felt intensely alone, although he was walking between his aunt and uncle. The sea was becoming even angrier and occasionally a wave slapped down hard on itself, a warning of what the ocean was capable of, if you didn't take care. Not that he wanted to take care. He wanted to hurl himself over the cliff edge and into the boiling sea, and put an end to his misery.

But not in front of his aunt and uncle. If he was going to do it, he'd have to do it on his own. Maybe a tall building like the Royal Albion Hotel in Kings Cross, or the Harbour Bridge, would better suit his purpose.

Only now did it occur to him that he trusted his aunt and uncle enough to tell them what his life at school was like. He opened his mouth to say something but no words would emerge, just a sort of gurgling sound which neither of them heard over the roar of the ocean and the screaming of the gulls. By the time they arrived back at the car, he was feeling so despondent that he couldn't muster the strength to try again. He knew it was hopeless: there was nothing he could do; nothing they could do.

But he didn't think he could endure the remainder of the term.

Later, when they were standing in front of Barton House, his aunt gave him such a huge hug that his eyes began to water with silly tears that he rubbed off on the front of her dress. Uncle Fred shook his hand and somehow managed to transfer into it what he discovered later was a five-pound note. After picking up his overnight bag, he headed into Barton House. On the verandah he turned. They were still there, standing up straight next to their car like Mr Jones did when he was on duty. Though Philip couldn't raise a smile, he waved. They waved back, and his aunt blew him a kiss. This might be the last time he ever saw them, he thought, and his eyes filled with tears.

As he passed through the doorway into the entrance hall that seemed so dark after the glare outside, he almost bumped into Keith Macready. With a couple of other boys, Macready was blocking the way to the stairs. Dave Lloyd pushed Philip, and Macready put out a foot, so that he stumbled and might have fallen if he hadn't grabbed hold of the post at the bottom of the stairs.

At this point the housemaster came out of his study and said, 'Welcome back, Chapman. The boys will be pleased to see you. They've had a bit of a quiet weekend. Not as lucky as you, eh? Jaunting all over the city, I expect.' He laughed loudly but none of the others joined in.

Only now did Philip realise that Macready was one of the boys who had nowhere to stay in Sydney for the free weekend. This would provide his tormentor with yet another reason to hate him. After picking up his bag from where it had fallen, he raced up the stairs two at a time. 'Run, pretty boy, run!' Macready hissed after him, but the housemaster didn't hear, engaged as he now was in welcoming back the next arrival.

———◆———

From that time on, Keith Macready intensified his campaign against Philip. It began slowly. Often during meals, Philip caught Keith's glance, his eyes as green as the name of the town from which he came, Emerald. He guessed that Keith's hatred of him had now turned into something more. The only word he could think of to describe it was *obsession*. That was the word that his father sometimes used to describe his son's love of music. Love and hatred, that's what Philip felt for his parents, both feelings so muddled up that sometimes he couldn't work out which was which. But he knew that what Macready felt towards him would only be hatred.

Day by day Philip's anxiety grew and he waited each night for something to happen. That it didn't only increased the tension. The Thursday night following the free weekend, after lights were out, he thought there was something afoot. While his own dormitory was quiet, apart from the odd snuffling and snoring noises of the other inmates, from the corridor came sounds of whispering and the odd barely suppressed giggle. He crossed his fingers under the blankets and prayed: *Please God, may it be for someone else*. The sounds stopped and he heard the hall floorboards creaking. After a moment it seemed as if whoever it was out there had moved away in the direction of the bathrooms. Just someone going to the toilet, that was it. Though he began to breathe more easily, he still didn't dare to move. If he kept very quiet, he could direct all his attention to trying to work out what was happening outside the dormitory. Whoever had been out there had gone to the bathroom, but they hadn't come back past the closed door yet and he wouldn't be able to rest until that had happened. He started when one of the boys in the furthest bed called out in his sleep, a distressed sound like a sheep caught in a fence, but the boy didn't wake up. After this, all Philip could hear were the syncopated snores and clicks and whistles of eleven sleeping boys, and the occasional rattling of one of the blinds moving in the faint draft from the open windows.

Still the footsteps hadn't returned from the bathroom. His own bladder began to feel uncomfortable. He would like to have got up to relieve it but that would mean leaving the dormitory and he didn't dare do that, not until whoever had gone to the bathrooms returned. He rolled onto his side but that made him feel the need to take a leak even more urgently, and soon he turned onto his back again.

So quiet was the house now that he began to wonder if he'd imagined he'd heard those noises in the corridor. But a moment later he heard the dormitory door click open. He sat up in bed, his stomach churning and his palms clammy. Three figures crept in. He could see their shapes against the hall light that was kept on at all times. Yes, they were coming towards his bed, and one of them had to be Macready.

'Shut up or we'll kill you.'

He recognised Dave Lloyd's voice. Of course they wouldn't kill him, but there were things almost as bad that they might do. He didn't feel brave enough to shout out though, and anyway, what could the other juniors do? They were as frightened of Keith Macready and his gang as he was. Rigid with fear, he felt rough hands grab hold of his arms and legs and lift him out of bed. Out of the dormitory they carried him, and along the hall towards the bathrooms. 'Pretty boy, pretty boy, arse-licking pretty boy,' they chanted. So frightened was Philip that he lost control of his full bladder, and felt the warm urine trickling through the fabric of his trouser bottoms.

'Yuck, he's wet himself,' Lloyd said.

'Pretty boy has bladder problems, eh?' said Keith, laughing. 'Wouldn't you like to know what we've got in store for you, pretty boy? Going to be something really good. Something you won't forget in a hurry.'

Heart thumping wildly, Philip squeezed his eyelids together. He couldn't bear to look at the expression on Macready's face and see again the cruelty there. He felt the boys swinging him violently as they struggled along with him. When they stopped he would fight them though. He would form his first and middle fingers into a V-shape and aim for their eyes. But then he might break his fingers or his hand, and he had to look after his hands, had to keep them perfect for playing the piano. He felt his gut clenching as if he might be getting the runs.

Dave Lloyd let go of Philip's right arm, and laughed as his body twisted and his elbow hit the floor. 'Watch out for your hands, pretty boy. Got to keep them nice for whatever pansies like you get up to under the sheets after lights out.'

The others sniggered. Philip knew they meant wanking, but they didn't have the brains to guess what he was most worried about. But he was proved wrong when Macready said, 'Now there's an idea. We can give his fingers a bit of a work over. You or me or the piano, eh?'

With one hand Lloyd grabbed hold of Philip's arm again, and with the other hand seized his fingers and bent them right back. It wasn't so much the pain as his fear the bones would snap that made him whimper.

'Did you hear that, Keith? Pretty boy doesn't stammer when he moans. Maybe we've found the cure for stuttering.' Dave Lloyd laughed as he bent Philip's fingers back again.

This time Philip kept his lips tightly together, although tears coursed down his face. After shutting his eyes, he took a deep breath and waited for a bone to snap. To his astonishment, Dave let go of his fingers and a moment later dropped his arm as well. He soon discovered why.

'What do you think you're doing?'

Philip opened his eyes just as Keith and his bully boys dropped him to the floor. In front of them stood Jim, in red and blue checked pyjamas. Though Philip's right hip hurt where he'd landed on it, he hardly noticed now that he'd been rescued.

'Back to bed, the lot of you,' Jim said.

Philip struggled to his feet and stood behind Jim, while the other boys arrayed themselves in front of him. At this point Macready made a move towards Jim, his fists raised.

'You wouldn't dare,' Jim said, his arms hanging loosely by his sides, as relaxed as if he were having an everyday conversation rather than a confrontation.

'Don't you believe it,' Macready jeered. 'You're only a bloody prefect.'

'You punch me and you'll be out of here so fast you won't know what's hit you. So have a go, why don't you? We might all be better off.'

'You won't be better off if I smash your stupid face in,' Macready hissed. His face twisted in anger, and Philip's stomach started to churn again.

'Just you try,' Jim said. His voice was cool although Macready still had his fists raised.

For an instant Philip wondered if he should dash off for help. If he could escape down the corridor behind him, he could run to the housemaster's suite before Jim was bashed up. But before he could make a move Dave Lloyd said, 'Don't do it, Keith. Can't you see he wants you to? Just let it go.'

'Do what your friend says. Let it go.' Philip started in surprise, and so too did Macready. This was Eric Hall's voice, and how he'd crept up behind them without them noticing was anyone's guess.

Jim took a step towards Macready who lowered his fists and

backed away. A second later it was all over, and Macready and the other two boys were swaggering down the hallway to their dormitory at the far end, as if they'd won instead of lost the battle.

'He was about to slug you one, I reckon,' Eric said, 'regardless of the consequences.'

'Can't tell you how glad I was to hear your voice. But if he'd punched me it would have got him expelled all right.'

'Might have spoilt your good looks though, and we can't have that. Anyway a hospital spell would keep you out of the eights and then we'd be sunk for the Regatta. What was up, anyway?'

'They were tormenting young Philip here. Going to give him a cold bath.'

But it would have been more than a cold bath, Philip knew. Sprained fingers, possibly even broken fingers. And no more music, the only thing that made his life bearable. Unfortunately Jim Cadwallader wasn't aware of a fraction of what went on at Stambroke, and Eric was even less clued up. Philip would never be able to explain to them what really happened here.

'I'll have to deal with Macready and his lot tomorrow,' Jim said. 'And now it's back to sleep for all of us, eh? It's been a bit too much excitement for one night.' Though his face was apparently serene, he added, 'It wasn't an experience I'd want to go through again in a hurry, I can tell you. And I wouldn't be surprised if Philip's feeling much the same.'

But there *would* be more encounters like this one, Philip knew. After returning to the dormitory, he changed into dry pyjama trousers that he pulled out of the locker with hands that were still shaking. The soiled ones he hid under the bed. For hours he lay tensed up, willing sleep to come. Never, before tonight, had he been so conscious of odd small noises. The rattling of the blinds, the general creaking of the building, the other boys snoring or tossing in their sleep. Just when he was finally dozing off, one of the boys got up and stumbled out of the dormitory. That gave Philip a terrible start, making him for a second think that Macready was coming back for him, and he got out of bed and hid under it with his stinky pyjama bottoms until the boy returned. Eventually though, just as some noisy bird started calling outside the window, he fell into a light and troubled sleep that seemed to last only a few minutes before it was time to get up again. Time for him to face another day. And after this one was over, there'd be another night to get through, and another and another, and he didn't know how he was going to stand it much longer. He thought again of the raging water below the cliff at Coogee, and wondered how easy it would be to find his way there. Of course there was always Circular Quay. That was easy to find.

The Royal Albion Hotel might be even easier. It was closer too.

——•——

Getting out of bed in the morning with dry mouth and shaking hands, Philip felt overcome with tiredness. The sunlight, streaming into the dormitory between the opened slats of the venetian blinds, made his eyes throb. It didn't help that his head seemed to be full of spongy stuff that made clear thinking impossible.

Enduring the day also proved to be a challenge. His hand hurt slightly from where Dave Lloyd had bent back his fingers, although there was no bruising. So exhausted did he feel in class that his concentration wandered, and this earned the annoyance of the form master, Mr Walsh. At lunch, in the boarders' dining hall, Philip sat next to Charlie Madden. No sooner had he sat down than Keith Macready walked by. He stopped to whisper, 'Hello, pretty boy, we'll get you soon, just see if we don't. The prefects can't be everywhere at once, you'll see! You know what buggery is, don't you? You're going to get a practical lesson in that one of these nights.'

'Keith bothering you again?' said Charlie, after Keith had moved on.

'N-n-n-n-no.' Philip's stutter was worse than ever and his voice quavered. But even if he could have told Charlie, Philip knew there was nothing he could do.

After lessons were over, Philip began his piano practice. He felt too tired to concentrate for long, and anyway his fingers were still sore. Before the period ended he went back to Barton House to put away the sheet music. At the sight of the thick airmail envelope in his pigeonhole, his spirits lifted a little. Carefully he tore open the envelope from his mother and began to read the closely written pages.

12th March, 1962
Dearest Philip,

We are having such a wonderful time in the Loire Valley. We're staying in a delightful town with a walled castle and some quite fabulous tapestries, and I have sent you a postcard of the castle – or chateau in French – by separate post. My schoolgirl French is getting some use, although the French are simply terrible at listening and someone whom I spoke to thought I was Italian, which amused your father very much. He thinks it's all because of the Common Market, the French simply hate the English over this and anyway they can't tell the difference between Australians and British.

The French food is wonderful and I would be getting quite stout if your father wasn't so intent on exercising me by walking through so many delightful little towns and villages. But I will not write to you any more about food. Though I know that Stambroke is a simply marvellous school, the food can't be as good as that provided by Mrs Jones in our dear home at Woodlands.

I have two pieces of news for you, darling. First, I am expecting a baby!

A baby, good heavens! Philip felt quite shocked at this and stopped reading for a few seconds. This news made him feel even more exhausted than before and he wished he could lie down for a while before dinner. Maybe he could skive off to see matron and tell her he was ill; that certainly wasn't far from the truth. But first he had to learn what Mummy's second piece of news was. Slowly he resumed reading.

We found out only yesterday and you can imagine how delighted we were to learn this. (It won't do my figure much good though, and all my gorgeous new dresses will go to waste and be quite out of fashion by the time I'm able to wear them again, but that's the price a woman pays for bringing new life into the world!) The baby's due next September. So then you will have a little brother or sister!

Because of the baby, this will be our last overseas trip for many years. I am over my morning sickness now – it didn't last long, just as it didn't with you – so we've decided to make the most of the opportunity and to extend our holiday – isn't that exciting! I do hope you won't mind, dearest boy. This means

we won't be home until after the next school holidays are over.
You can still go back to Woodlands, of course, if you want to.
Mr and Mrs Jones will have returned from their holiday by
then and they could take care of you. But your father thinks
you shouldn't do this so we'll make some other suitable
arrangements for you. Perhaps a week with the Mellors and
a week with Auntie Susan and Uncle Fred, or even a week
at Ferndale, I shouldn't think that the Vincents would mind
having you. Anyway, I'll make some enquiries and let you
know soon, my darling.

Enjoy the rest of term and don't work too hard. I shall write
to you again very soon.
With gallons of love,
Mummy

Pass the parcel, that's what this was. Quivering with rage, his
exhaustion forgotten, Philip put the two sheets of paper together
and neatly lined up the edges. He tore the pages in half, and after
this into quarters. He carried on ripping the letter until it was in
shreds. That's what his mother thought of him, someone to be
disposed of as easily as this letter. Someone who didn't matter.
Someone who mattered even less now that a new child was
arriving.

There was nothing to stop him now. No longer would he put
up with any of it. What he was going to do next was what he
should have done months ago. He would follow his mother's
advice and would indeed *have courage.*

It seemed easy now that he'd decided what to do.

CHAPTER 35

Friday late afternoon, diagonals of sunlight piercing the trees, the scent of autumn in the air and the whole weekend lying ahead. Enough time, Jim thought as he dashed along the path to Barton House, to see the housemaster about Philip and to check his pigeonhole before dinner. Perhaps pigeonhole first and afterwards the housemaster, there was well over half an hour to spare. The housemaster would ask lots of questions, and then he'd talk to the headmaster, Dr Barker, who'd decide what to do. Maybe Macready and his henchmen would be expelled, or the Chapman parents would be advised to take their son out of school. Jim had been wondering about it on and off all day. If he were headmaster, what would he do? Get rid of the lot of them, that's what. Philip shouldn't be here; he was too sensitive. And he was too different. Too effeminate. And Macready and his ilk were the end; bullies who'd be like that wherever they were. So it was best to isolate them somewhere – preferably near Emerald in Macready's case – rather than put them in a boarding school where they could do irrevocable harm.

Pausing in the entrance hall to Barton House, Jim saw two letters in his pigeonhole. The top one was from Zidra. Though he'd been longing to hear from her, he wanted to delay opening

285

it for as long as possible. Once it was opened there'd be none of this lovely anticipation, and he didn't want to be disappointed, for a short uninvolved letter would almost be worse than no letter at all. He picked up both envelopes. The second was from Andy. Jim balanced them, one in each hand. Zidra's was much heavier than Andy's, and it wouldn't just be due to the different quality notepaper. Her letter wouldn't be short, he could tell that from its weight, and anything she wrote was precious to him. He would delay opening it until after reading Andy's.

His brother hadn't written all term and it was about time a letter came from him. Of course Andy's letter would be a one-pager, not that Jim could complain. His own letters back home were pretty brief too. Only the barest minimum, playing up the sport and homework obligations to excuse the lack of effort on his part, when he knew how keen they were to hear from him.

He ripped open Andy's envelope. There was only one sheet of paper inside, but it was covered on both sides with Andy's scrawl.

22nd March, 1962

Dear Jimmo,

Seems like ages since you went off to Sydney. Sorry not to have written before but the oldies write often enough for three. School's as big a drag as ever, except for woodwork. I got hold of some red gum timber and I thought I'd try my hand at a stool for Dad for the shop. Mr Hargreaves got the red gum for me. Nothing much else has happened, apart from me getting selected for the school footie team. Now how's that for an achievement, eh? The oldies are united in pride, even though she's fretting about the implications for homework. Huh! Dad's going to make a frame for the rainbow lorikeets she's embroidering. I could have done it, but he wanted to. By the way, Sally Hargreaves asked after you yesterday. She's going out with Roger O'Rourke, can you believe. Hope you don't mind. Some girls have no taste.

I wanted to ask you to forget all that stuff I told you last Christmas about Dad taking no notice of me. It's all sorted out now and we've even had a couple of sessions stargazing. You are a hard act to follow but we're all getting used to it now. In fact, I'm bloody proud of you, brov.

Write soon but not about homework. Makes me edgy.

Andy

It was the newsiest letter Jim had ever had from Andy, and the best. Funny how quickly he'd forgotten about Sally Hargreaves though; he didn't care who she went out with now. After reading again his brother's reassuring words, that niggling little doubt that he'd never really articulated dropped right away. A doubt that he could now freely admit to: that Andy resented him. *I'm bloody proud of you, brov.* What could be better than that?

Before opening Zidra's letter, Jim yielded to the temptation to peer into Eric's pigeonhole. It contained an envelope in Zidra's handwriting, written with the Sheaffer fountain pen he'd given her for Christmas. There was no reason why they shouldn't write to one another, yet he felt a stab of jealousy. Although despising himself, at the same time he couldn't resist picking it up.

It was thinner than the one she'd sent him.

At this point he glanced out of the open door and was surprised to see Philip. Wearing his blazer and boater, he was trotting across the lawn. Silly boy, where was he heading? He'd be in trouble with Dr Barker if he were found leaving the school grounds. Everyone knew that meant expulsion.

Before running after him, Jim hurriedly put Eric's letter back into his pigeonhole. He folded his own envelope from Zidra and stuffed it, together with Andy's message, into the back pocket of his trousers. By the time he'd crossed the quadrangle, Philip had disappeared. Cursing, Jim hesitated; it was impossible to guess which way he'd gone. The path to the right led down to the oval at the bottom of the hill. There was an exit down there but hardly anyone ever used it. To the left were the secondary school classrooms, and Philip was unlikely to be going that way. The most probable route was up the broad sandstone steps leading to the main entrance gates.

A movement at the top of the steps caught his eye. It was unmistakably Philip, still sprinting. He'd got up all those steps far more quickly than Jim thought possible. But what was he doing heading that way? Surely he couldn't be running away. He'd have to be stopped and there was no time to lose; already he was out of sight. Mind you, Jim thought as he began to race up the stairs, the boy wouldn't go far. Young Debster had run away last term and been found by the housemaster skulking around in the street just beyond the school gates, unsure of what to do next. As Jim arrived at the top of the steps, the bell rang. Damn it, they'd both be late for dinner, and he hadn't even talked to the housemaster yet.

Now Jim caught sight of Philip standing at the bus stop on the other side of the steady flow of traffic. The Lord only knew how he'd managed to get across so quickly; perhaps the lights at the next junction had only just changed. He called out but Philip didn't hear him, either deliberately or because of the hum of all the cars. And drat it, there was a bus heading towards Philip with *Circular Quay* showing on its indicator. Jim knew he had no alternative but to follow the boy, he couldn't go back to Barton

House now without first finding out where he was heading. He was far too young and naive to be wandering about on his own.

But getting across this continuous stream of vehicles before the bus arrived looked near impossible. Seeing a small gap in the traffic, Jim stepped off the footpath. The car closest to him accelerated, he'd swear. The driver honked his horn and raised a fist and shouted something that Jim couldn't hear. By the time he looked at the bus stop again, the bus was pulling out and Philip had gone. At that moment Jim saw another bus heading towards the stop and this one had *Town Hall* on the front. It might do. He stepped out into the traffic, cars screeched to a halt, and he got to the stop just in time to board the second bus.

He was lucky enough to find a vacant seat right at the front, diagonally behind the driver. He dug into his pockets and pulled out the ten-shilling note left over from the free weekend. Grumbling at the note, the conductor gave Jim a load of small currency coins, and a sixpence fell onto the floor. He heard it rolling away. Yet he couldn't afford to take his eyes off the bus in front. Philip could alight anywhere. The traffic was bad and the cars and buses crawled along. At one stop he thought of jumping off and making a run for it, to see if he could reach the bus in front before it started up again. But it was too risky. He might lose sight of Philip completely. He certainly didn't have enough cash to hop into a taxi.

A van pulled into the lane in front, and Jim swore under his breath. If more cars squeezed in between the two buses he could lose sight of his quarry altogether. Fortunately the van soon turned into a side street. The traffic lights were in Jim's favour. Although on one occasion he thought the first bus might get ahead, the driver went through the changing light regardless. Once into the jumble of Kings Cross, the traffic got even slower.

Now Jim started to relax a bit. Philip would never get off the bus in such a seedy part of town, and he even thought of looking for his missing sixpence.

It was as well he didn't. At the top of the Cross, Philip alighted, the distinctive straw boater making him easy to see. Surprised but ready, Jim leapt off after him. But where could Philip be going? As Jim followed him down a tree-lined street, he saw that the approaching darkness was bringing out the prostitutes and the drunkards, the cruisers and the junkies. Philip seemed to know where he was going though. It was then that Jim observed the map he had in his hand.

'Stop!' Jim cried, but the only person who took any notice was a middle-aged man in a brown suede bomber jacket and blue jeans.

'Like a drink, young man?' he said, smiling as he put a hand on Jim's shoulder. His face was greasy and his nose dotted with blackheads. 'I can make it worth your while.'

Jim evaded his predatory hand and hurried on. A hundred yards further on, Philip turned into a side street, with Jim now no more than twenty yards behind him. Here Jim was stopped again, this time by a blonde woman his mother's age, with the shortest skirt, lowest neckline and biggest tits he'd ever seen.

'Like a nice blow job, love?' she said.

'No thanks,' he said, embarrassed.

'Fancy boy wants a pansy boy, does he?' She laughed, though not unkindly.

Only now did he begin to think of how his own absence from school might be interpreted. He and Philip vanishing together on the same afternoon; it wasn't good, whichever way you looked at it. But it was too late to worry about that now. He would be expelled, of course, and so too would Philip. That this was what Philip wanted, he had no doubt, but it wasn't the future he'd planned for himself. All the while he hurried on, his pulses racing.

Philip was now about a dozen yards ahead of him and oblivious to Jim's shouts. After stepping around some Aborigines sitting on the pavement outside a seedy-looking pub, Philip hesitated before stopping altogether. Taking off his boater, he stuffed it into a garbage bin, and next undid his tie and crammed that in as well. One of the men stood and shuffled across to the bin. He pulled out the boater and crammed it on top of his thick black hair. All his companions laughed and the man began a little jig.

'What are you doing, Philip?' Jim said, catching up at last.

Philip turned. His face was full of despair and he began to run. Unexpectedly he changed direction, and stepped straight off the pavement and onto the road. Only now did Jim see the car that was almost on top of him. He leapt forward and lunged for Philip's legs. There was a screeching of brakes and then a thud. A wave of blackness rolled over Jim as he fell to the ground.

CHAPTER 36

'Can you get the phone, George?' Eileen looked up from her embroidery. 'It won't be for me.'

George heaved a sigh. He was reluctant to get up. It was a quarter past eight on a cool Friday night, he'd had a busy week, and the last thing he wanted to do was talk on the phone. But it would be churlish to grumble. Eileen was busy with her sewing and all he was doing was slouching in his armchair and staring at the flickering red dome of the kerosene heater. As he got up, he glanced at her embroidery: she was putting the finishing touches to the lorikeet's red beak. After limping into the drafty hallway, he shut the door behind him. Although Andy's bedroom door was closed, the blaring of his transistor radio would make conversation impossible, and George banged on the door before picking up the receiver.

'Hello, Cadwallader's Quality Meats,' he said, forgetting he wasn't in the shop.

'Is that Mr Cadwallader?' said a male voice.

At this moment Andy opened his bedroom door a fraction and stuck his head through the gap between the door and the jamb. 'Is it for me?'

'No,' George said, after placing a hand over the mouthpiece.

He waved his son away. 'Yes,' he said into the receiver, 'George Cadwallader speaking.'

'Gilbert Barker here. Head of Stambroke College.'

George's heart sank. A phone call from the headmaster on a Friday night could mean only one thing. There'd been an accident of some sort involving Jim. 'What's up? Is my son all right?'

'No, he's not all right, Mr Cadwallader. That's the thing. He's not all right.'

'What's happened?' George braced himself against the wall.

'He's gone missing. Didn't turn up for dinner and hasn't been seen since about five o'clock this afternoon.'

'He's been missing for three hours and only now you phone me?' George didn't try to keep the anger out of his voice.

'Don't be like that, Mr Cadwallader. People have been searching all over the college and grounds for him. All over. He hasn't called you, has he?'

'No, and my wife's been home all afternoon.'

'That's a shame. I'd really hoped he'd contact you. Philip Chapman is missing too. Do you know young Chapman? From down your way, I believe.'

'Yes.'

'Both of them have gone. None of their things are missing though. Philip was last seen just after lessons were over. It seems a bit odd that they've both vanished.'

It was strange and probably a coincidence. 'You'd better call in the police.'

'Oh, we will, Mr Cadwallader. Don't worry, we're doing that next. Just wanted to warn you though, once I'd checked you'd heard nothing.'

'Warn me of what?'

'That he's missing, of course.' Dr Barker sounded tense and

his vowels strangled. 'And that ten-year-old boys don't persuade sixteen-year-old boys to run away, it's normally the other way around. Big boys lead, little boys follow.'

His voice shaking, George managed to say, 'Jim's a prefect. We won't jump to any conclusions just yet, Dr Barker. It seems to me that, if boys in your care go missing, it's up to you to learn why and to find them.'

'Jim *is* a prefect, Mr Cadwallader, I made him so. And he's a very responsible young man. I daresay they'll both turn up soon, with perfectly reasonable explanations. So don't worry. I didn't mean to upset you. Now let me give you my direct line, so you can phone me right away if you hear anything, and I'll call you too once I hear some news.'

As soon as George had replaced the receiver, Andy turned the volume of his transistor up again and the partition wall began to vibrate with the sounds of *Dream Baby, How Long Must I Dream?*

Jim running away; Jim doing something rash; Jim leading a younger boy into mischief. It was so completely out of character that it had to be a mistake. Much more likely was that the two events were unrelated, the boys each involved in separate accidents.

But George knew that he was kidding himself. Automatically, he thumped on Andy's door before stumping back into the lounge room to tell Eileen the news, or the lack of it. It wasn't a good prospect: Jim was either lost, or about to be expelled, or both.

Later, George went out onto the back verandah. He'd left Eileen and Andy in the lounge room, still talking. Eileen was beside herself with anxiety while Andy was trying to distract her by suggesting over and over again that Jim had gone to the pub, and that of course he wouldn't have taken Philip with him.

George gazed out over the yard. It was the sort of clear night that would be good for stargazing, but he didn't feel in the slightest bit interested in the celestial hemisphere anymore, not even as a distraction.

His nerves were on edge and all he wanted was for the phone to ring.

Chapter 37

When Jim came to, he was sitting on the kerb with his head between his knees. He was okay, but where was Philip?

At the sight of the slender figure lying on the road, Jim's heart turned, and his vision sharpened with the shock. From nowhere, a policeman had appeared: puce-faced, with a body like a rectangular prism. Jim glanced at the people already milling round. Eager, curious, concerned faces. Maybe this accident hadn't happened. Maybe it was just a dream and when Jim chose to look again he would find that Philip was upright yet, and with that awful expression of desolation replaced by happiness. An instant later Jim checked the road but Philip was still lying there. Nothing had changed. The boy was unmoving.

Jim took a deep breath and stood up. Only a few moments could have passed but people were crowding close; there were far too many of them, pushing and shoving and screaming. Shaking too much to hold his ground, Jim was thrust backwards and began to panic. He lost sight of Philip altogether as a couple of large men, reeking of beer, edged in front of him. Forced again to step back, he turned and saw the Aboriginal man wearing Philip's boater disappearing into the pub, and he noticed that the others who'd been sitting on the pavement had vanished. Different people had turned up though, dozens of them. Jim had to find a way round them somehow. He had to get to Philip.

It had been madness to call out when he did. It would have been far better to keep quiet until he was standing right next to Philip, at which point he could have grabbed hold of his arm and asked where he was going. It was the bloody boater that had distracted him. That's what being a prefect did to you, made you focus on trivia like uniforms when all that really mattered was that despair on Philip's face. Perhaps he'd meant to step under the car. Perhaps he'd intended to kill himself, and Jim could have stopped it but hadn't.

On unsteady legs, Jim edged past a man and woman with their arms around one another. They were grinning and laughing, as if the accident had been laid on for their entertainment, and he hated them for that. Elbowing the man rather harder than necessary, Jim wriggled past. 'Watch it, mate,' the man shouted, administering a kick to Jim's shins. 'Look where you're going. We were here first.'

Now at last Jim was standing on the kerb in front of the hefty policeman he'd first seen. Another three had turned up from somewhere and were bending over Philip's body that was lying immobile on the road.

'Stand back, the lot of you,' the hefty policeman bellowed over the racket. 'An ambulance is on its way. Did anyone see what happened?'

Stepping onto the road, Jim said, 'I did.' At that moment Philip seemed to stir but, before Jim could be sure of this, the driver of the car moved towards him and blocked his line of vision.

'The boy stepped straight in front of my car.' Wearing a pinstriped suit, the man was visibly shaking. 'He came out of nowhere. There was nothing I could do. It was his fault.'

'We can get more on that in a minute,' the policeman said.

Jim wiped the back of his hand across his eyes and wondered if he was going to throw up. 'Your car hit him,' he said slowly and carefully to the man in the suit. 'There was a terrible thud.' His anxiety manifested itself in a rush of anger that made him want to punch this man, on whose forehead and upper lip beads of perspiration were starting to form. His own apprehension was now making him feel giddy and it was difficult to think clearly. Philip might be badly injured or even dying. Concussion, broken bones, internal bleeding, who could guess what else at this stage.

'Keep him still,' he could hear one of the policemen saying to the officer kneeling closest to Philip. 'Don't move him, mate.'

'What's the boy's name, you?' The hefty policeman stared hard at Jim.

'Philip Chapman,' he replied, voice shaking.

'What school are you from?'

'Stambroke College.'

'Both of you in uniform in the Cross? That's a bit odd. You don't live around here, do you?'

'No. We're both boarders.' *We were both boarders,* he thought. That period of life was over. Brain damage or even death for one boy. Expulsion for the other.

'Are you brothers?'

'No.'

'Well, you won't be going back to Stambroke yet awhile. Who's his next of kin, do you know?'

Philip's aunt, that's whose name Jim should give. The Chapman parents were still overseas and wouldn't be much use. Philip spoke highly of his aunt and Jim had seen her at the start of the last free weekend, when she'd collected Philip from Barton

298

House. 'Mrs Susan Williamson,' he said. 'They live in Hunters Hill. Philip's uncle's name's Fred.'

After writing this in a notebook, the policeman turned to the driver of the car. Peering around them, Jim saw Philip's unmoving form still surrounded by the three policemen. 'He's opening his eyes,' said one of the officers, a thin man with sharp features. 'No, he's shut them again. He's conscious, but barely.'

'What's that noise he's making?' another policeman said.

'He's groaning.'

'That's a good sign. Keep talking to him. We don't want him losing consciousness.'

Jim moved closer. A trickle of blood was oozing out of Philip's nose and onto the surface of the road. His face was deathly white. At this sight, Jim's stomach churned.

If only the ambulance would come. Too much time was being wasted. What if the rectangular officer was wrong and no one had phoned the hospital? Perhaps he should check, just in case. There was a phone box on the other side of the road and he had plenty of change in his pockets. But after taking two tentative steps in that direction, he found his blazered arm was in the firm grip of the policeman. 'I don't think you're going anywhere yet, son.'

'I thought of using the phone.'

'There'll be time for that in the hospital. You can go in the ambulance with one of my men.'

And here it was at last, its siren wailing and lights flashing. Two of the police officers began to shift back the crowd that was pressing forward once more as the ambulance pulled up. Shortly afterwards, men in white jackets displaced the policemen around Philip's prone body and seconds later he was on a stretcher being loaded into the back of the ambulance.

Jim glanced at the men strapping down the stretcher and fiddling with some tubes, inside the van. Though wanting to look, at the same time he didn't want to see, for he was starting to feel again that he might throw up.

'Get in the back with him,' the hefty policeman said, more kindly now. 'And you get in the front, Martin,' he instructed his sharp-featured colleague.

'A head injury,' said the ambulance man, riding in the back with Jim. 'Could be contusions as well. Subarachnoid haemorrhage maybe. Poor little bugger, what was he doing up in the Cross? Are you his brother?'

'Friend.'

'Keep talking to him, mate. He'll know your voice. Go on, start speaking, we don't want to let him lapse into unconsciousness. What's your name?'

'Jim Cadwallader.'

'Well, Jim, start talking. About anything. Ask him his name. See if there's any confusion.'

Crouched next to Philip, Jim began to speak. 'What's your name? It's Philip, isn't it? What's my name? It's Jim, can you understand me? If you can, you'll know how crazy this is. We're travelling in an ambulance to hospital. We'll soon be there.' But Philip seemed unable to hear and certainly made no attempt to answer, though there was a slight fluttering of his eyelids before they shut tight again.

'Keep it up, Jim,' said the ambulance man at his side.

'Hang in there, Philip. Stay awake. For God's sake, don't let go. You'll never have to go back to Stambroke. Just think of that, it's got to be what you've wanted. Your aunt and uncle are coming to the hospital, and I am too. Wake up, Philip. Don't go to sleep.' Now Jim took Philip's hand, which felt icy cold.

'He's freezing,' he said to the ambulance man.

'There's a pulse though. Here, I'll give him an extra blanket. Keep talking, Jim.'

Jim was only dimly aware of the screaming of the ambulance siren, and perhaps the brakes and the tyres too, as the vehicle hurtled around corners and through traffic lights. He tried not to think that it was his fault the boy had got knocked down. All his energies should be focused on willing him to remain conscious. 'Stay with me, Philip,' he said. 'Think of all the good things. Think of music. Of those pieces you want to play. The Talivaldis Variations, for instance. What's your name? It's Philip, and I'm Jim. Your friend, Jim. Think of Mrs Vincent, and Zidra too. It was Zidra's father who wrote that music. Maybe you'll be a composer too when you grow up. Or a pianist. Well, you're that already. Not a rugby player though, or a test cricketer. Stay with me, Philip. For God's sake open your eyes and look at me. Or squeeze my hand. Just a little bit. Give me a signal. Tell me your name? Squeeze my hand if you can hear me.'

For an instant he thought there might have been the slightest pressure of Philip's fingers on his own. A gentle touch, like a butterfly settling. He put his ear close to Philip's mouth but there was no sound apart from the faintest respiration of air. He'd give anything to hear his stutter once more, anything. Again he felt a light touch on his hand and a surge of hope, before he realised it was just the rocking of the ambulance as it pulled up in front of the Accident and Emergency entrance of St Vincent's Hospital.

'We'll take over now,' said the ambulance man, who'd been riding in the back. Philip and his stretcher were lifted onto a trolley and wheeled off, and Jim was somehow shunted into a chair in the crowded waiting room of accident and emergency, with the thin-faced policemen by his side.

'Time to get a bit more information from you,' the man said, pulling out a notebook and a stub of pencil. 'You're from Stambroke College, I hear. Your headmaster will be turning up soon, a Dr Barker I believe. Now, how come you two were wandering around the Cross on a weekday evening, when you should have been in Vaucluse?'

———

Jim gloomily inspected the shabby cream walls of the waiting area. The policeman had finished with him for the moment, and gone off to find some coffee. Funny how quickly things can go wrong, he thought. When he'd seen Philip running across the lawn just a few hours before, he'd decided that his only option was to go after him. Now he realised all too clearly how wrong that was. He should have informed the housemaster and the principal, and let them make the decisions.

Would Dr Barker believe that Jim had followed Philip rather than plan the escape himself? He had no idea of the answer. Although he'd found Philip, it was too late to stop the accident; he'd maybe even caused the accident. Yet who could say what might have happened to Philip otherwise? Alone in a seedy part of Sydney, a dangerous part of Sydney. Perhaps unsure of what to do next, and unwilling to return to Barton House.

After further contemplation of the cream wall, Jim decided that on balance he'd done the right thing chasing after Philip. It didn't really matter what other people thought. You constructed your own standards of right and wrong – and it might take years – and after that you followed them. Some people accepted society's standards and blindly adhered to these but he wasn't going to be one of those. This wasn't to say that these standards didn't matter. They were crucial, you just had to consider the legal system to see that. It was a society's prejudices that you had to watch out for.

When he'd asked the nursing sister at the desk how Philip was doing, she said it might be hours yet before they knew anything, and he was to sit quietly and wait. 'Probably concussion,' she said. 'Ah, here's the registrar, let's hear it from him. Not that he's looking after your friend. The consultant's been called in for that.'

The registrar looked tired and barely listened to what the nurse asked him. 'Got to go,' he said. 'There's been another emergency.' He paused for a moment to look at Jim. 'Maybe you should go home. A blow to the head's a process, not an event. Things often get worse over the first few days. No point hanging around. Go home for some rest, and come back in the morning.'

'He didn't mean to upset you,' the nurse said after the registrar had gone.

'I have to wait until the relatives get here. And the head-master.'

Jim returned to his seat. Things often got worse over the first few days, that's all the registrar could say. But Jim knew that already from when Meyer got his head smashed in a game of rugby several years ago. Vomiting, confusion, visual disturbances, amnesia. All indicating a rise in intracranial pressure. Meyer had eventually returned to school, but he'd never been quite the same again.

Jim's reason, worn thin by the evening's events, was beginning to desert him. At this moment Philip could be in the operating theatre, or on a mortuary slab, or heaven alone knew where, while all Jim could do was sit and confront the grotesque fantasies filling his head.

Glancing down at his hands, he observed their trembling.

He stood up and tucked them into his trouser pockets before beginning to pace up and down. The room was starting to empty as other visitors to Casualty were attended to, but still there was no news of Philip.

———

'Well, Cadwallader, I thought I could trust you,' said Dr Barker. He'd arrived with the Williamsons, though Jim guessed this was unplanned. Between the Williamsons and Dr Barker there was, if not quite an aura of antipathy, certainly an absence of rapport. Now they were arranged on the uncomfortable seats under harsh fluorescent lighting that drained all colour from everything. Guessing the headmaster needed a focus for his own anxiety, Jim sat up as straight as he could in the rickety chair and braced himself. The Williamsons, facing Dr Barker and Jim, would be an audience for the lecture that Jim knew was to come.

The headmaster continued. 'We all thought we could trust you, Cadwallader. That's why we made you a prefect. But you've let us down terribly. Running off from school with young Chapman; leading him into trouble. What on earth did you take him to the Cross for?'

'He was running away.'

'Running away? His parents are overseas and he's got no family in Kings Cross. If he'd been found heading towards Hunters Hill, where the Williamsons live, I might have believed you. Did he tell you he was running away?'

'No, I just followed. There wasn't time to go back. I thought it'd be dangerous if he was on his own. I hoped I could stop him. He's a bit naive.'

'Innocent,' said Mrs Williamson.

'Vulnerable,' Mr Williamson contributed.

'Carry on,' said Dr Barker.

'He got off the bus at the Cross. That was a bit of a surprise. I'd almost caught up with him but then I called out. He must have thought I'd take him back to school, because as soon as he heard me he stepped onto the road. So I'm to blame for what happened.'

'How can you know that?' said Mrs Williamson. 'It was an accident. These things happen in a split second. Don't blame yourself. We've got enough to be anxious about without that too.'

Jim glanced obliquely at Dr Barker, who was looking his most severe. If Mrs Williamson were not present, Jim knew that the headmaster would be quick to apportion blame. As it was, he contented himself with saying, 'You've let us down terribly, Cadwallader.'

'How can you say that?' said Mrs Williamson. '*You've* let him down, or your school has. Don't make this young man your scapegoat. He was brave enough to show some initiative and follow Philip, and to do the right thing regardless of the consequences. Let's keep the recriminations for later.'

Mr Williamson shifted uneasily in his seat and Jim adjusted his feet. His limbs felt leaden and exhaustion began to wash over him.

'You'd be better off asking Jim *why* Philip ran away,' Mrs Williamson continued. 'In fact, I'll do it for you.'

'Steady on, Susan,' said Mr Williamson.

'Jim, do you know why?'

'Yes, I've got a fair idea.' Jim told them a little of what had happened the night before, with Macready and his band of bullies. It seemed like half a lifetime ago. As he spoke, he heard Mrs Williamson's sharp intake of breath.

'You didn't think of telling me?' Dr Barker said coldly.

'I planned to, after school. Before school I had rowing practice. Then I saw Philip heading out of the school grounds and I followed.'

'If anyone should be blamed,' Mrs Williamson decided, 'it's that bully Macready. Or a school that allows such persecution to occur.'

'Steady on, Susan.'

'I won't *steady on*, Fred. I've got every right to say what I think. Philip's my nephew, after all, and my only brother's son. Jack attended Stambroke when he was a boy, and he thought the world of it. That's why he was so keen that Philip should go. But no school should allow bullying. You can't have sensitive boys sacrificed like this on the altar of mediocrity.'

Dr Barker began to hiss like a simmering kettle and might have boiled over if Mr Williamson hadn't said, 'Perhaps we might have a little stroll now, Susan. To pass the time while we wait.'

After they'd gone, Jim was left sitting with Dr Barker. Without an audience, the headmaster was no longer inclined to talk. 'Go and get us each a cup of tea, Cadwallader,' he said after a while, and shoved a few shillings at Jim. 'White with two sugars please.'

Glad of this distraction, Jim followed the signs to the cafeteria. On his way back, he caught up with Mr and Mrs Williamson. Walking slowly in front of him, they were absorbed in their conversation.

'Poor Philip's probably in the operating theatre now,' Mrs Williamson was saying. 'I don't know how Jack's going to live with this, let alone Judy. It was her silly idea to go overseas and leave the poor boy behind, though she claims it was Jack's. She's going to have this on her conscience forever, if she's got one that is. Which I doubt somehow.'

Jim coughed loudly and they moved aside to allow him to pass. Once she'd seen who he was, Mrs Williamson stopped talking and attempted a smile.

'We'll surely hear soon,' Mr Williamson said. 'So I guess we'd better all get back in there in case we're needed.'

But there was still no news.

After giving Dr Barker one of the cups of tea, Jim sat down next to him. He took a sip from the polystyrene cup. Finding it hard to swallow the stewed liquid, he put it on the table next to him, pushing to one side the out-of-date newspapers and the tattered children's books. Glancing around the room, he saw that there were only two other people left in the waiting room: a middle-aged couple sitting at the far end. The woman was huddled in an overcoat while the man wore a shabby jacket and trousers, and brown-checked carpet slippers. His hand was roughly bandaged in a tea towel. Blood was seeping through the material, adding red blooms to the leaf pattern.

Nervously Jim began to chew at his thumbnail, something he hadn't done for months. The clock on the wall above the reception desk indicated it was nearly eleven o'clock. It had been hours since the ambulance had brought Philip in. Surely there should have been some news, any news, by now.

At that moment a nursing sister appeared at the doorway. 'Mr and Mrs Williamson,' she called. 'Can you come with me? The doctor would like to have a word with you.'

As soon as she'd finished speaking, Philip's aunt and uncle were out of their seats and following her through the swing doors. Jim and Dr Barker were left behind, sitting side-by-side on their uncomfortable chairs. This is it, thought Jim. Shortly would be the moment of reckoning. Having torn off the top of his thumbnail, he began to rub at the rough edges with his fingertips.

The tense silence was broken, after a time, by the squeaking of Dr Barker's chair, as he began to rock backwards and forwards. The noise was almost more than Jim could stand. The two people at the far end of the room were now ushered through the swing doors by another nurse, leaving Jim alone with the headmaster.

Anxiously he looked at his watch. A quarter past eleven. It seemed like hours rather than minutes since the Williamsons had gone. He could bear the inaction no longer and stood up. At this point he saw the doors swing open again. Looking dazed, the Williamsons stood there, while a nurse held back the doors for them. Mrs Williamson's face appeared drawn, and Mr Williamson had an arm around her shoulders. Jim's stomach turned and he broke out in a cold sweat.

But when the Williamsons reached them, Mr Williamson smiled. 'They reckon he's going to be all right,' he said, 'though they're going to have to keep him under observation for a few days.'

'All right?' said Dr Barker.

'Yes. Well, no brain damage, and only a mild concussion, they reckon. He's got a broken nose, though. But there's nothing much more that can be done about that until the swelling goes down. So he'll be in hospital for a few more days. Three at least. Susan and I can go into his ward now and wait for him there. They'll be bringing him back soon.'

It was over at last. The relief that poured over Jim was palpable. It was like emerging from a dumping wave that threatened to swamp you, and finding that there was a smooth swell on the other side, and that the sun was shining. Now Mrs Williamson gave Jim a hug and a kiss, while Mr Williamson shook Dr Barker's hand. Surreptitiously Jim wiped his eyes on his sleeve before shaking hands with Philip's uncle. And afterwards the

Williamsons were swallowed up again in that *no go* area behind the swing doors.

Dr Barker too must have shared some of Jim's euphoria, for he said, rather oddly, 'Glad you turned up safely, Cadwallader, very glad. Now you'd better tell me what else has been going on in Barton House with young Chapman.'

Swiftly Jim sketched out the broad details of what had been taking place. When he'd finished, Dr Barker said, 'We can't expel every boy in the house, Cadwallader, just because of a couple of misfits.'

This wasn't headmasterly talk. It must have been the stress. While Philip was a bit of an oddball, Jim himself was the most normal person he knew. Since his future was not to be at Stambroke College, Jim decided to drop the deference and engage in some straight talking. 'Philip's not a misfit, headmaster,' he said firmly, 'and neither am I.'

'He's a musical prodigy, Cadwallader. That makes him a misfit in a community like ours.'

The *altar of mediocrity*, that's what Mrs Williamson had called it. But she was wrong. Stambroke didn't suit everyone but it did provide opportunities and allowed some to rise above mediocrity. He'd be sorry to leave but he knew it was inevitable. He'd be packing his bags by the morning and heading home.

'You're a bit of a prodigy yourself,' Dr Barker continued, 'although in a different way. But you're also a team player and that's what we like at Stambroke College, team players.' He paused and rubbed his hands together while he prepared his judgement. 'While you didn't follow the team approach this afternoon, Cadwallader, you certainly showed initiative. That's what we also like at Stambroke. We like initiative.'

Jim said, 'What's going to happen to us?'

'I'll speak to Mr Williamson later about Chapman.' Jim noticed that Mrs Williamson had been excluded from this planned conversation. 'You'll appreciate that I'm talking to you now as one of my prefects, man-to-man. You acted with commendable enterprise, so naturally you will return.' He paused, before adding thoughtfully, 'And of course there's the Regatta in two weeks' time. That's a very important event for the school, very important. We'll drive back to the college next, after you've phoned your parents, so that you can be out on the water first thing tomorrow morning. First thing. Can't afford to miss a practice.'

Until now, Jim hadn't given the Regatta a thought. 'Thank you, Dr Barker,' he said quickly. So he wasn't going to be expelled after all. Funny what being good at sport can do for you. It's not what you know but how you row and throw. Now that the uncertainty was over, he could afford to smile at Dr Barker's idiosyncrasies. *Man-to-man, Cadwallader, you're a prodigious misfit, but we sure as hell want you for the team.* Maybe next week he'd talk to Barker about what could be done about bullying in the house. He could use the Regatta advantage to get some action on that.

Dr Barker now said, 'Ring your parents first, though. There's a payphone in the hall. I rang them from Stambroke when you went missing and again after the police told me you'd been found. But they'll be wanting to hear from you.' He pulled a few coins out of his pockets and insisted that Jim take them, in spite of his protestations about having a pocket full of change. 'Talk for as long as you like,' Dr Barker said. 'As long as you like provided it's no more than ten minutes.' He gave his staccato laugh that was more like a bark, and much imitated by the Stambroke boys.

In front of the payphone, Jim delayed dialling for a moment.

Through the window, he could see the cast-iron railings separating the hospital from the street. He'd been reprieved, and so too had Philip, though in a very different way. The future was bright for them both.

Yet he was not unchanged by the episode. He was going back to Stambroke because of the Regatta, it was as simple as that. There was a rule that said you'd be expelled if you left the school grounds. It didn't apply to him yet it was applied to Philip. The *pretty boy* who was a threat, as well as threatened, in the boarding house environment.

In the end things had turned out okay, but for the wrong reasons, and that offended Jim's sense of justice.

Smothering a sigh, he dialled his parents' number in Jingera. His father answered the phone at once. Jim explained what had happened, censoring the bits he deemed unsuitable for parental ears, including the anxieties about expulsion. When he'd finished, his father said, as he always did, 'You've done well, son. I'm proud of you.' Afterwards Jim spoke to his mother. Always reluctant to use the phone, she said little, apart from her relief that he was safe and a desire to get the full story from his father.

Dad would always be proud of him, whatever he did. Maybe that was because he'd never tell him the other bits, the mistakes and the errors of judgement. But no, that wasn't right. Dear old Dad would forgive those too. His love was unconditional.

Jim rested his elbows on the shelf under the phone and covered his eyes with his hands. They stank of the peculiar odour that buses impart, or possibly it was just dirt. Fatigue hit him, together with the realisation that he'd eaten nothing since lunchtime. After straightening up, he found the men's room, and washed his face and hands with soap that reeked of disinfectant. The person staring back at him from the mirror looked exhausted. He'd get at most five hours' sleep tonight before he'd have to get up for rowing practice.

Yet he knew that he was lucky.

PART VI

School Holidays
May, 1962

CHAPTER 38

Irritating man, Ilona thinks. Peter has dropped half the kindling on the floor that she cleaned only this morning. She sits on the sofa to watch him crouching in front of the lovely cast-iron fireplace with the marble surround that his grandparents put in when they built the house. He has a particular way of arranging the bits of wood and the screwed up balls of the *Sydney Morning Chronicle*. While he has once or twice watched her set up the fire in her own special way, it was not without gritted teeth.

Tonight he lights the fire with one match and sits back on his heels, very pleased with himself. The sight of his long back and thick dark hair gives her so much pleasure that she forgets all about the small twigs and the scraps of pine cones littering the floor. Tomorrow she will cut his hair; it has been months since she did it, and that too will give her satisfaction.

Outside, a wind is chasing around the house trying to find ways of getting in. She gets up to turn on the lamps. Before drawing the curtains, she peers out. Though there is no moon, a trace of light is left in the darkening sky, against which the swaying branches of the pines are silhouetted. Cold air blows around the edges of the panes of glass. Shivering, she pulls the heavy velour curtains across the windows. Across the bottom of the door, she places the draft excluder, a sand-filled fabric tube she sewed herself. Shortly afterwards, Zidra arrives and dislodges it.

'Put the sausage back,' Ilona says automatically.

Zidra does so while continuing to reading *Sons and Lovers*. Ilona thinks this unsuitable for her and says so.

Zidra laughs. 'You're a bit of a wowser, Mama.'

Although Ilona doesn't yet know what this means, she smiles. Later she will look it up, and the associated word *wowserdom*, and will seek opportunities to introduce this into her conversation. There will be many in the campaign for Aboriginal housing in Burford.

Sometimes, she thinks that Zidra looks like her real father. This is because, every now and then, her expression is exactly his as it was years ago, before he'd become melancholy, before he'd become bitter.

Thinking of Oleksii reminds her of Philip and the time he came to stay at Ferndale, when he had played the music that Oleksii wrote and which he so perfectly understood. Only now does Ilona notice that she's left sheet music strewn over the top of the piano and on the floor next to the piano stool. After she's tidied it away, Peter tells her to sit down and relax. He pours her a glass of wine and himself a beer, and they sit together on the sofa, holding hands and watching the fire, until he is moved to get up again and make some small adjustments to the wood.

She inspects her family closely: Peter is playing with the fire again and Zidra is still absorbed in her book. Could she ever have predicted, when she and Zidra first came to Jingera, that she might know such happiness as this? No, never could she have guessed.

She'll be right, Peter says sometimes, and so far in their life together it has been so. They have their ups and downs, and at times they each face their own demons, but so far *she's been right* indeed.

———◆———

George Cadwallader, sitting in the lounge room in front of the glowing kerosene heater, is beginning to feel restless. The only sounds are the puttering of the heater and the rustle of thread being drawn through fabric, and of course the distant pounding of the surf. His gammy leg twitches involuntarily, and he shifts position, trying to get comfortable.

Already there are only two of us, he thinks, even though it's the start of the May school holidays. Jim and Andy are out somewhere. Playing table tennis at the O'Rourkes', Eileen says. It won't be long before both boys leave home, one way or the other. After that there will be the two of them, as there are now; sitting in front of the heater, or the log fire at weekends, and growing old together.

That's if he's lucky.

Obliquely he glances at his wife. At his most optimistic, he thinks that anything is possible. Even that he and Eileen will be able to knock along together in reasonable harmony once they've been cast onto their own resources, once the boys leave home. It's even possible that they may grow old *gracefully* together.

Yet at his most pessimistic, he has no doubt that Eileen will one day abandon him. If she leaves him, he'll grow old on his own. Although this thought deeply saddens him, he no longer finds it as frightening as he used to.

Shifting position again, he stretches out his bad leg. Open on his lap is *The Stargazer's Chronicle*, a magazine that Jim brought back from Sydney with him. George will probably take out a mail-order subscription for it, as it is unlikely to be available in Burford. Looking around the room, he sees Eileen's completed piece of embroidery, of the rainbow lorikeets, hanging on the wall. She has already begun a new work. Again it is of birds, for she has a talent for illustrating wildlife. This time they are superb wrens, the male with a vivid blue head and shoulders, and the female more dowdy.

George knows that the night is clear with no moon. When Eileen goes to bed, which he can't help hoping will be soon, he will put on his warm coat and beanie, and go out into the garden. Then he will unlock the shed and wheel out his telescope. Afterwards he will dive into infinite space, in which he can always find peace.

The wind is whistling around Woodlands, rattling the windows and shaking the branches of the trees, which groan and sigh in protest. In the white marble fireplace in the drawing room, a fire has been lit, and three armchairs are pulled up in front of it. Only two are occupied, by Philip's parents. Philip is sitting at the piano, about to play for them Beethoven's Piano Sonata, the one he's now learnt to call the *Sonata Pathétique*.

While he guesses that his father will find the music too much, he's not bothered by this, even though his father has become his hero again since they returned from Europe following the accident. While Philip can recall every detail of the day he ran away from Stambroke, right up to the moment when the car knocked him down, he can remember nothing of the first few hours afterwards. Auntie Susan and Jim have filled in the details though.

Expelling Philip, rather than Macready and his cronies, was something his father would never forgive. Philip heard every word of the telephone conversation in which his father blew up Dr Barker for Stambroke's *omissions of care*, his voice becoming louder and louder, and his face even redder than usual. *A gentle soul, a rising star*, he'd bellowed into the receiver just before hanging up, *who's been badly let down by your school*.

Giving Barker a piece of my mind, he'd explained afterwards. Sending a kid to board at that college costs a fortune, and they should have looked after his son better.

Earlier, Philip had overheard Auntie Susan giving his mother a piece of her mind too. He never let on that he'd listened to what they said though. It had been a coincidence that he'd been passing the door of the study at the time. This was the day after he'd got out of hospital and a few days after his parents had arrived back in Australia, when they were all staying at Hunters Hill. Once he'd heard Auntie Susan's raised voice, he'd frozen. Through the open door he could see his aunt and his mother facing one another. No matter how hard he tried to move, he couldn't.

'I've never understood how you can be so self-centred, Judy,' Auntie Susan was saying. 'You've got a gifted son with a delicate and sensitive soul, and what do you do? You not only connive with Jack to send him to a school which any fool can see is unsuitable, but you actually leave the country.'

'That trip was Jack's present to me for my fortieth, darling. You only turn forty once. How could I possibly have knocked it back?'

'Jack said you suggested it. That he didn't want to go. Really, Jude, you're the most self-absorbed person I've met. Quite frankly, you don't deserve to be a mother.'

Yet his mother had taken this criticism calmly. 'Don't get so het up, Susan. You're right of course, darling. I've been terribly remiss, I know, but really I had no idea what was going on at Stambroke. Absolutely no idea. I'll make it up to Philip, you'll see. And I can't tell you how grateful I am for everything you've done for him.'

His mother was a liar and he'd known that for months. While he couldn't help but love her, he would never again completely trust her.

Now, in the drawing room at Woodlands, he flexes his fingers. His mother has her feet up on a stool and is smiling at him. Of course she will *adore* the performance he is about to give, even though she's tired with her pregnancy. And he certainly wants her to rest now, and to eat well, so that the unborn baby will grow big and strong. Thereby will the future of Woodlands be assured. Though his mother is touched by his concern, she doesn't know his motives. What he wants is for his father to direct to someone else that threat of, *All this will be yours one day, son.*

Yet sometimes he thinks that the little brother or sister might be a joy in its own right. That day he'd spent on the beach below Ferndale with Zidra has stuck in his mind. Having a sister would be company when he needed it. And someone else to love.

Next January Philip will be starting secondary schooling at the Conservatorium of Music High School. After the accident he practised the piano nonstop, and passed the audition with what his teacher described as *flying colours,* playing the Talivaldis Variations as well as pieces by Chopin and Beethoven. The school is next to the Royal Botanic Gardens in Sydney, and a short walk from the Quay. He will attend as a day boy, of course. That's because of his *extreme sensitivity,* Mummy's said, again and again. *And what could be more natural than for him to live at Hunters Hill in term-time and to travel by ferry to the Con?*

As Auntie Susan and Uncle Fred are more than happy with this arrangement, Philip's future is no longer bleak. Next term he will return to stay with them at Hunters Hill and attend the state school on the peninsula. He will come back to Woodlands for the holidays.

Now he begins to play, and soon he is lost in the music.

———◆———

Not exactly nervous but certainly not composed, Jim is standing next to the war memorial. Soon the bus pulls into the square. It circles him before coming to a halt in front of his father's shop. Zidra is waving from the window, just behind the driver, and she leaps out first. In fact, she is the only passenger to alight, although there is a clutch of people waiting to get on the bus that is travelling on to Burford.

Zidra is wearing a thick mauve jumper of some hairy stuff, mohair possibly, and stretch black trousers that show off her long legs, and she is even prettier than he remembers. She comes bounding up to him, and he would like to hug her but feels too shy. Instead they smile and say hello and afterwards there is a slightly awkward silence, if indeed there is ever silence in Jingera, for there is always the sound of the surf breaking on the shore and inevitably some birds calling, even here in the centre of this little township.

'You decided not to ride Star into town,' he says at last, only to break their silence.

'You'd have been waiting half the day if I had,' she says. 'There's nothing like riding a horse to make you appreciate the distance from Ferndale to Jingera.'

'Ever try walking?'

'No, life's too short for that.'

They stroll down the hill to the lagoon. The Talivaldis won't be collecting Zidra from Jingera post office until lunchtime, and so the whole morning lies ahead of them. After crossing the footbridge, they take off their shoes and walk along the beach towards the northern headland. The river is low and only a narrow channel of water escapes to the ocean. At the base of the cliffs, large boulders are scattered from falls over the centuries, long before European settlers arrived. Now these rocks are occasionally obliterated by fountains of white spray. To the east, the deep blue of the sky cannot match the depth of the ocean's blue, while to the south, feathery white clouds litter the paler sky.

'Eric sends you his regards,' Jim says.

She smiles, and thanks him. It looks as if she will say no more, but it doesn't matter, he tells himself. She can write to whoever she wants.

'He's nice,' she says after a little while. 'As you'd expect of any friend of yours. We've written occasionally. Twice, in fact. He writes to Sally too. He probably writes to girls all over New South Wales, and that's why his letters are so short.'

A sea eagle flies overhead towards the headland, where it begins to circle slowly. They walk back again, and conversation is easy for him now. He knows this is because of what she's said about Eric, and is glad. On the footbridge, they pause and gaze upriver, to his father's dilapidated fibro boathouse with its rusting corrugated iron roof, sheltered from sight of the town by a bend in the river and a dense stand of trees. Unseen, a bell miner bird trills its single note.

'Remember when Lorna and I took out your father's dinghy?' Zidra says.

'Yeah.'

'It was my idea and it was fun until we got into difficulties and Lorna fell overboard with one of the oars. Mr Bates rescued me and that gave him a hold over me, or so I thought. Kids think they know it all and they don't know the half of it.'

'We'll never know the half of it no matter how old we are.'

'So speaks Methuselah. Do you remember, Jim, how you said you're not interested in horses and you didn't want me to write about them in my letters?'

'Yes.'

'Well, what about learning to ride instead? You could get the bus to Ferndale one day next week. We could take the horses out, just for a couple of hours at first, because if you rode for any longer you'd be really sore afterwards. There are some terrific routes we could take. Would next Wednesday suit?'

'Sounds good,' he says, and is surprised at the joy that floods through him at this prospect.

Zidra shuts the car door and winds down the window. The car smells faintly of dog. While someone needs to do something about Spotless Spot's blanket in the back, which stinks to high heaven, she'd prefer this not to be her. Now her mother preselects a gear and clicks into it and they begin their stately progress out of Jingera and up North Road. Mama is no speedster today, that's for sure, Zidra thinks. She has plenty of time to observe the bush through which they are cruising, with occasional glimpses of the ocean with its regiments of waves rolling into the shore.

Several miles north of Jingera, Zidra is the first to spot the slender figure trudging along the edge of the road, thumb extended to hitch a ride. As they get closer, her heart stops still. Surely it's not, it cannot be. But it is!

'Goodness, it's Lorna,' her mother now says. At once she slows the car down, and Zidra is out of it before it is stationary.

So tightly does Zidra hug Lorna that her friend says, laughing, 'Stop, Dizzy, I can't breathe. You don't know your own strength!' Yet she is hugging her back too, and there are tears in her eyes.

Now it is her mother's turn to greet Lorna. Only when this is over do they start to question her, Mama first as usual.

'When did you get out?' she says.

'A month ago.'

'You didn't write,' Zidra says.

'Not yet. Been too busy.'

'Where have you been, Lorna dear? And is that a bruise on your face?'

Now Zidra notices the large mark on Lorna's left cheekbone, the side she's kept turned away.

'I was sent to a family near Hay, on a property there. It was hard work all the time, and no days off. The boss's son often hit me; that's how I got this bruise. There's one on my back too. So I've run away and I'm never going back.'

'Good on you,' says Zidra quickly. After putting an arm around Lorna's shoulder again, she glances at her mother. There are tears in her eyes, and for once she is at a loss for words while she fumbles in her pocket for a handkerchief. Now is not the time to ask any more questions about the bruises, Zidra decides. She says, 'How did you get this far?'

'Hitched a lift as far as Jingera and then carried on walking. Not too much traffic on this road.'

'The Princes Highway might have been quicker.'

'Wanted to see my country on the way. Knew someone would come along eventually or I'd get the bus if it ever came. Never thought I'd be picked up by you though!' Lorna says, grinning.

'We'll take you to Wallaga Lake. Zidra and I would like to do that.'

'It's out of your way.'

'Doesn't matter. We were thinking of going to Bermagui anyway,' she fabricates, 'to pick up something from the shops. Wallaga Lake's not that much further.'

On the way north, Lorna tells them how she left Gudgiegalah on her birthday, and how lucky she is compared to some of the other girls. The ones who never knew their family or where they were from originally. The ones who'll never be able to go home because they don't know where or what it is.

As soon as they reach the turn-off to the Aboriginal settlement at Wallaga Lake, Lorna will let them drive her no further. 'I want to walk in alone,' she says.

After Lorna gets out of the car, Zidra and her mother watch her stride down the road. At the bend, she turns to wave, her smile bright. She's going home at last, Zidra thinks. Where she belongs. Like me, she may move on from here. She will be free to choose to move on from here if she wants to. But she should never have been taken in the first place.

At this moment, a flock of yellow-tailed black cockatoos flies overhead, squawking loudly. Though they seem at first to be making for a dead tree down by the lake, they soon veer sharply to the right and head towards Mount Dromedary, or Mount Gulaga as Zidra thinks of it now. She and her mother both gaze up at this splendid sight.

When they look back again, Lorna has gone. Around the bend in the road, hidden by trees. She will be running towards the settlement now, to the old cottage that is the Hunters' home. Shortly she will throw her arms around her mother, and they will laugh with joy, and talk in their language that Zidra doesn't understand.

Then this stage of Lorna's journey will be over at last. But even as she thinks of this, Zidra knows that Lorna's journey, like her own, is really just beginning.

FURTHER READING

Haebich, Anna (2000) *Broken Circles: Fragmenting Indigenous Families 1800-2000*. Fremantle, WA: Fremantle Arts Centre Press.

James, Roberta (1988) 'The Heart of the Matter: The Place of Kinship in the Construction of Contemporary Aboriginal Identity.' Honours Thesis, Department of Prehistory and Anthropology, Australian National University.

McKenna, M (2002) *Looking for Blackfellas' Point: An Australian History of Place*. Sydney: UNSW Press.

Wright, Judith (1955) *The Two Fires*. Sydney: Angus & Robertson.

ACKNOWLEDGEMENTS

Without the enthusiastic encouragement of Karen Colston and Beverley Cousins, this book would not have been written. For their numerous helpful comments on various drafts of the manuscript I thank Karen Colston, Beverley Cousins, Maggie Hamand, Chris Kunz and Lyn Tranter. Thanks also to the wonderful team at Random House Australia, and to Tue Gorgens, Tim Hatton, Sally Humphrey and Justine Small.

Alison Booth was born in Victoria and grew up in Sydney. After over two decades living in the UK, she returned to Australia in 2002 and is now a professor of economics at the Australian National University. She is married with two daughters.

The Indigo Sky is the second volume of the Jingera trilogy.

READING GROUP QUESTIONS

1. Do you think Lorna's experiences at the Gudgiegalah Girls' Home will have the opposite effect on her future to that hoped for by the authorities? If so, why?

2. There are a number of contrasts between the characters of Lorna and Philip. For example, Lorna is a strong and resilient character who will defend herself against institutional cruelty, whereas for a variety of reasons Philip is unable to fight back against bullies, making him an easy target. What are some other differences between these two characters?

3. Ilona and Zidra Vincent connect the stories of Lorna and Philip. How do you think they are altered by their involvement?

4. When Philip is bullied, he tries to tell his family, but he fails because he initially targets the parent without the power. By the time he begins to target the powerful one – his mother – she has made her own plans (though she tries to make out they were his father's) and Philip is too much in awe of her to fight back. What do you think Philip has learnt about his parents and himself by the end of the narrative?

5. Jim Cadwallader and Philip form a bond in spite of the age gap and their different talents. What do you think contributes to this friendship?

6. What is the importance of music in *The Indigo Sky*?

7. Why does the coffee table assume importance in George Cadwallader's relationship with his second son, Andy?

8. The novel is written principally from five different characters' viewpoints. What are the obstacles that each character must overcome and who do you think is most changed by the events in the story?